T0274543

THE QUEEN'S COUNCIL

A Sword in Slumber

SARA RAASCH

Disney · HYPERION
Los Angeles New York

First Edition, September 2024
10 9 8 7 6 5 4 3 2 1
FAC-004510-24192
Printed in the United States of America

This book is set in Bodoni Classic, Wiescher-Design, Lawrence, Fenotype, Yana, Laura, Worthington/Fontspring; Franklin Gothic; Janson/Monotype
Designed by Marci Sanders

Library of Congress Cataloging-in-Publication Data 2024932202
ISBN 978-1-368-09284-5
Reinforced binding
Visit www.DisneyBooks.com

Certified Sourcing
www.forests.org
SFI-01681

Logo Applies to Text Stock Only

No spell needed—you're already enough

PROLOGUE

Three things filled the dawn-drenched glade: the plucked strings of a lute, the fragrant sweetness of picked wildflowers, and the force of the girl's personality.

From where Maleficent perched within the gnarled, shadowed branches of a spruce tree, she had a view of the performance. In truth, other than a few wayward forest creatures, she knew she was the only viewer.

The twelve-year-old girl bounded around the clearing, bare toes tearing at spring-soft grass, her flower crown cockeyed on hair of sunshine gold as she danced and sang.

"O good Sir Knight, O good Sir Knight,
A sword made wild and free;
Thy valor leads from tree to Rhine,
By dream you walk with me."

A boy who played the lute came in with a rolling repetition of "Way, way, way lay lie; way, way, way lay low."

Another girl, this one with dark hair and a dirt-smeared face, popped up from where she had been sitting on a log. In one hand, she brandished a stick fashioned to look like a sword.

"ATTACK!" she shouted, and dove at the first girl, whose song faltered on a giggling shriek.

Briar Rose, the golden-haired one called herself. She continually drew Maleficent's attention, making her helplessly flinch, like at the first light of dawn.

Which was appropriate. Given her true name. A name the girl herself did not know.

Aurora.

"Frieda!" Aurora ducked her friend's attempt at play-fighting as the boy continued with his lute. "We're meant to be *rehearsing*."

"And it was *you* who said we should pretend this rehearsal was at a grand ball," Frieda countered. "And it just so happens that this grand ball is up at the castle here, and the Bavarians are attacking!"

She let loose a battle cry and charged again.

Aurora feinted left before hurling herself at Frieda. Instead of fighting, she hooked her arm with Frieda's and spun them in a circle while she caught the song back up.

"Fortune favored, adventure blessed," Aurora sang. "Refrains of mighty deeds—"

Maleficent's finger tapped on her thigh. In time with the music.

One-two-three.

Counting. Counting.

One-two-three.

Frieda stumbled, dropped her sword. Aurora spun them faster

and added jerking swivels of her hips until Frieda laughed at her own efforts to keep her footing.

"Such gallant turns are sung of you." Aurora's voice was perfectly pitched and lovely. "Though seldom all they seem."

The boy on the lute joined again: "Way, way, way lay lie; way, way, way lay low."

He continued to play as he spoke. "If the castle was attacked, are we to imagine that the two of you are now singing while in the middle of a bloodbath?"

That made Frieda snort laughter.

Aurora stopped her chaotic spinning to give a look of mock affront to the boy. "How outlandish, Benedikt. Certainly not—the moment the attacking army heard our song, they dropped their weapons and joined the dance."

"Ah." Frieda disentangled herself from Aurora and swiped her fake sword from the ground. "So our music will bring peace to the empire, is that right?"

Aurora managed another look of mock affront, though her eyes sparkled. "How could it *not*?"

"Next time you're cross with me, I just need to sing to earn your forgiveness, then?"

Aurora's lips pursed, her eyes narrowing in a way that said she saw what Frieda was doing. "If I say yes, will you actually *sing* and stop trying to stab me?"

"Agreed." Frieda stuck her fake sword through the belt around her dress. "And let me use this blanket forgiveness from you to admit that you didn't lose that shawl your aunt made for you. I dropped cherries on it, and it got a stain, so I hid it under the armoire in your cottage."

Aurora's teasing look plummeted. But not in anger—in confusion. "What shawl?"

Frieda's shoulders were level as though she was prepared to stand her ground in defense, but at Aurora's immediate bewilderment, she relaxed. "Oh. The one that started wide on the end and went narrow for some reason? It was a rather sickly color—I think your aunt tried to dye the yarn herself."

A pause.

Then Aurora burst into laughter, and the last of what barely restrained tension Frieda had vanished.

"*You're* the reason it went missing?" Aurora said through her laughter. "Do you have any idea how relieved I was that it disappeared? Tante Fauna did try her best when she made it, but good Lord, it was hideous."

Frieda cracked a smile. "You're not cross with me, then?"

Behind them, Benedikt laughed. "She's been stressing about it for *months*, Bri. *Months*."

Frieda flushed bright crimson. "Traitor," she shot at Benedikt.

Aurora collected herself, straightening her flower crown. "It's under the armoire, you say?"

"Mm."

"Excellent. I can reuse the yarn and turn it into something that can actually be worn, without hurting Tante's feelings. She dismissed any hope of me ever finding it after, and I quote, *a vile sorceress must have snatched your birthday present*."

From her hiding place, Maleficent's heart beat hard suddenly, a single throbbing jolt.

"Though you should dye it a nicer color," Frieda said. "I may have actually done you a favor with the cherry stain."

Benedikt chuckled but never broke off playing.

Aurora cupped her hand around her ear. "You have been forgiven, and yet I hear no singing."

Frieda rolled her eyes. "You wouldn't have been angry with me at all!"

"That was not our deal. There shall be peace in the realm, but only if you sing."

"You're thinking too simply, Briar. Peace should be harder to come by than that."

Aurora pouted, but stiffness had taken over her posture, like excitement tumbling up against nervousness. "*Please.* Games aside, we finally get to sing at the tavern tonight. I just want us to do well."

Frieda sighed and nodded. "We will."

Aurora raised her eyebrows at Frieda in silent prodding, who sighed again and finally began to sing as Benedikt hit a low note. She belted words that must have been the wrong verse, as Aurora snorted and picked up the right words:

"O good Sir Knight, O good Sir Knight

In dark your eyes do gleam—"

Frieda joined her, her softer voice pushing on Aurora's to uplift it. Soon, the girls twirled around each other, Frieda following Aurora's lead.

It truly was an active choice not to get sucked into Aurora's energy—she emitted a fascinating fervor, helplessly mesmerizing. This was a girl who had found her place, who loved and shared that love and looked out at her future with intoxicating wonder.

Was that a flicker of *guilt* in Maleficent's chest?

Hardly.

What would unfold was necessary. Her hand had been forced. Everything was set, the pieces arranged on the board, the game underway.

All she needed to do now was wait. In a few years, destiny would crystallize.

Or it would shatter.

She smiled, teeth sharp. *One-two-three*, tapping her thigh.

Always three. *One-two-three.*

It haunted her. Stalked her.

"Allow us to walk how we once did," Aurora and Frieda sang. "Upon, upon a dream."

"Way, way, way lay lie," added Benedikt. "Way, way, way lay low."

He finished with a flourish, hitting the strings in an overembellished arch of his arm. He used that flair to swing out, snatch Frieda as she danced past, and spin her into a one-armed dip. She gave a bright shock of laughter, flushed and happy.

Maleficent's eyes, as always, returned to Aurora, who watched her friends with a grin, her dancing slowed to gentle sways of her skirts.

She turned away while Frieda and Benedikt spoke softly.

Did Aurora's eyes meet Maleficent's, where she was hidden in the darkness?

No. Surely not. Dozens of times, Maleficent had come to check on the progress of her plan. Dozens of times, no one had noticed, no one had suspected.

Aurora stared at the tree a moment.

Then turned away, humming the song to herself, effervescent with happiness, with life, with *purpose.*

Purpose she did not yet fully understand.

Maleficent leaned back. Drumming her fingers on her thigh again. *One-two-three.*

It would be her. She knew it would be. She had known all along.

Briar Rose—*Aurora*—would be empress.

For that, she needed Maleficent's help. Would she be grateful? Of course not. But gratitude had nothing to do with it.

One-two-three.

One-two-three.

One-two—

CHAPTER ONE

FOUR YEARS LATER

There was a woman, and she was a stranger.

She ran down an alley in a dress as blue as the sky, her face twisted in horror at what she had seen. Or heard. Or felt, *and that feeling rippled through the air in a tangible fume, the tang of a crowd in upheaval, driven to mania like a startled horse in a stampede. It could not be stopped, that was the worst part—it could not be stopped, this terror, and the girl ran.*

The fear was familiar. It made this girl not a stranger but a mirror.

The scene blackened, changed, and a night sky unfolded, star-speckled and beautiful at first, then rocked by five shooting stars ripping fire and flame across the darkness. A woman looked up in unsuppressed horror, and then she was running, too, running across battlefields strewn with bodies, that same horror resonating on her face.

Again, familiarity bred unity. They were one and the same.

Another woman overtook a new scene, her white-knuckled fingers clasped around a pail of water, a hearth of fire burning before her. She looked down at that fire, beseeching, afraid, confused—her face did not clear as she threw the water onto the fire, snuffing it out.

All of the woman's emotions congealed into expectation—*something was coming. A shadow, a presence, a threat.*

It could not be stopped.

It had happened already, or would happen already, around and around and weaving back in on itself.

"It cannot be stopped, Briar. Aurora." Maleficent's voice was all crooning and cackles. "These girls face the same struggles as you did. As you will. What will you do with yours, hmm? What will you do? What will you—"

• • •

Briar bolted upright, sweat-soaked and gasping, muscles wrenched to fight.

But all that tension quickly shifted inward, to self-hatred.

She'd had those dreams *again.*

The first few nights after breaking free of the sleeping curse, she hadn't been surprised to still see the same images that had haunted those long, restless days. Images of places she had never been, women she had never seen, each dream choked by fear or anxiety or a looming presence she could never find, a shadow waiting, waiting, waiting on the edge. The only solace was in that sense of familiarity she had with the strangers in those dreams; they shared the same emotions, the same terrors, the same obstacles. Were these other women Maleficent had tormented?

It was not enough that the sorceress had knocked her

unconscious—no, she had to plague her with the horrors of others, too.

Now, six weeks out from Phillip defeating Maleficent in her dragon form and rescuing Briar from her sleeping curse, the dreams had lessened but still splintered her sleep most nights.

The curse was broken. She was free.

But one of the cruelest realities that the curse had painted was that being free physically did not equate to being free mentally.

Briar caved forward over her knees, the dense silk bedding too tight, too heavy. That was the problem—these blankets strangled her. And this nightgown, it was too thick; and the room, it was too dark, too quiet, too—too—

Too much. All of it.

Too much, and she couldn't breathe.

Briar froze, bent over, fighting for a single, deep breath. As though breathing would make everything better. But what else could she do?

Her chest ached, lungs trembling, and she had a disconnected, exhausted thought—could she sneak out of the castle? It had been so easy to sneak out of the woodcutter's cottage. But then, she had only had her three aunts to avoid—no, not aunts, were they? Fairies.

Magical fairies, disguised to watch over her.

Briar kicked the blankets off and swung her legs over the side of the bed, fighting for one more breath.

Even if she did manage to get out of the castle, Frieda and Ben didn't want to see her.

Briar stumbled from the bed and crossed the room—such a massive, cold, dark room—and felt her way to a desk by the window. One paper crinkled as she pulled it out, but it was far too dark to read. She knew it by heart, anyway, and she held it in front of her like the words would . . . would do *something.*

Materialize relief.

Bleed comfort from the ink into her arms, down across her chest.

Magic was real. She knew that now. It was real and it had upended her life, so why couldn't it help her, why couldn't it *calm her down?*

The messenger's recorded letter from Ben had his usual tone, as though he had gone off on a stream of thought and only realized near the end that he had meant to be short and curt. From that, Briar knew, at least, that he was well, the tavernkeeper missed the business she brought in, everyone in town thought she'd run off, no one knew she had really been the missing princess *the whole time—*

But you lied to us, Ben had written. *You could have told US. Bri—Aurora—Princess Aurora.*

Don't worry about us. You didn't before.

Frieda hadn't sent any message back at all. Ben hadn't even mentioned her in his letter.

Briar slammed the paper back into her desk and staggered into the middle of the room, hands in her hair. Her braid was in tatters, and she freed it in an angry tear.

She needed to go. To get out. To—to not be in *here,* in this bedroom that wasn't hers, in this castle that wasn't hers, in this *life* that wasn't hers.

Briar found the armoire by kicking it with her toe. She grimaced and yanked open the door, and even though she couldn't see the contents, her grimace deepened.

Of the many revelations that now took up too much room in her head, she knew that *she* was responsible for the fabric shortages that had plagued Hausach and the surrounding villages her whole life. Spinning wheels had been banned since before she could remember, out of fear of a curse claiming the missing princess, which said that she would prick her finger on the spindle of a spinning wheel. *She* was that princess. It was her fault she had felt guilty for outgrowing her old kirtles, her fault the weavers in Hausach had to run their businesses underground, her fault everyone had to use and reuse even the slightest scrap of fabric; her fault. All of it.

And now she had a full armoire of stunning, rich gowns, linens and silks and wool, and shoes by the dozens, and jeweled necklaces, rings, bracelets—more and more each day. Gifts from the king.

No, not the king. He insisted she call him *Father*.

Feeling in the dark, she heaved aside half the princess's wardrobe, still flinching at the thought that her fingers would dirty things so fine—but there, at the back, wedged in despite the protests of her lady's maids, was her old kirtle. Patched and threadbare, but *hers*.

Briar undressed and tugged it on and threw her hair back into a simple braid.

It did help. A little. A familiar weight, the feel of the rough wool.

If she couldn't sneak out and talk to Frieda and Ben, what could she do?

There was only one place that felt even moderately like home in this massive castle. It was where she always ended up. Night after night. For the past six weeks.

Why even fight it?

With a resigned sigh, Briar slipped out of her room.

The halls were empty, and Briar knew now where to duck to avoid the soldiers posted at windows and doors. There were many, even with the villain Maleficent soundly defeated and the kingdom freed from the threat of her evil—but that had not settled the paranoia of the king and queen.

Father and Mother.

Briar, at least, understood their worry. It was over; she had been awoken from the sleeping curse and rescued from the tower; but every sleepless night, every crash of noise, every flash of shadow out of the corner of her eye told her that Maleficent was still here. That she would come back, swooping in with another curse, and this one would hit its mark.

Beyond Maleficent, though, other threats lingered. Austria had a tumultuous relationship with some of its neighbors, Bavaria in particular; it seemed every few years one or the other would initiate a battle that never quite evolved into a full war, squashed quickly by the emperor's involvement. It did not do well for any of the countries that made up the Holy Roman Empire to be at each other's throats, and so Austria and Bavaria would settle like kicked dogs, until their disagreements arose years later, and it started all over again.

As a peasant, Briar had known of this conflict only in that it dragged able-bodied fighters out of Hausach and sent back wounded ones.

Shivering, she pressed on, weaving down stone halls and through silent rooms hung with tapestries showing knights and damsels.

Her first night here, she'd stood in front of those tapestries and stared and stared.

She had never seen anything so grand in her life. She sang stories about places like this, gilded halls of kings and emperors; she didn't *belong* in a place like this. A tavern bard from Hausach who had stolen a princess's life.

Though she supposed she should be grateful for this castle. The queen had been begging the king to leave from the moment the curse lifted. The two of them had made this more provincial stronghold the seat of their household for sixteen years—to be close to Briar, she now knew, something else to feel guilty for, as the queen was open about her dislike of their more rural holdings and how she desperately missed Vienna. The king, though, had delayed and delayed, for *he* had taken to the country life, with hunting aplenty and none of the "pressures of the city," he'd said.

What would life truly be like for Briar, for *Aurora*, when she was hauled far, far away, to Vienna? This was the farthest she had ever even been from her cottage in the woods. Vienna would hardly feel real, and there would be no foothold of familiarity there, nothing to ground herself in. Briar would disappear; only Aurora would remain.

Briar slunk off into the darkness, keeping to the shadows, hugging the walls as she wove down, down through the castle, out a side door, and into the detached kitchen building. It was still early enough that the cooks were not preparing the next day's meals, so the room was lit only by starlight, but Briar knew this space well now. The center held a long, massive table that forever smelled of flour and spelt and yeast, with counters rimming the room, piled with baskets of dried spices and ingredients waiting for tomorrow.

That had first caused her to stop and stare, too.

Ben would be gorging himself endlessly; Frieda would be up in arms at the waste and unnecessary stash; Briar had to fight both of those impulses, because she had found that giving in to either of them only resulted in people staring worryingly at her.

There was *food*, piles and piles of it, waiting here, always. And at every gathering, tables spread with feasts, pastries glistening in honey and fire-roasted vegetables and whole, massive smoked roasts, *meat*, real meat. Briar still could not stop herself from gaping openly at the constant display of food, while everyone else in the castle passed it by as though it was of no more import than the sconces on the walls.

The cook had noticed that Briar came to the kitchen at night, and he now made sure to put out a loaf of bread by the fireplaces at the far end. Food she didn't have to make, food she didn't have to worry about buying, food prepared for her.

It should have felt luxurious. It should have felt indulgent and heavenly and victorious.

But she felt only the long, slow drag of guilt down her spine.

This wasn't for her. This wasn't her life. None of this was *hers.*

Briar trailed her finger along the table, guiding herself forward in the dark.

And stopped.

There was a light at the far end, by the bank of fireplaces, the flicker of a candle.

Unease sprang up from the lingering anxiety of her dream,

and Briar's fingers grasped emptily at the air, searching for a stray kitchen knife, maybe, or a rolling pin—

A shadow next to the fireplace twisted. The light flared brighter, no longer partially blocked by the figure, and in the pulse of yellow and peeling back of darkness, Briar recognized who it was.

Her anxiety turned to effervescent bubbles and floated up, up.

"Phillip," she said on a startled exhalation.

He leaned forward in his chair and smiled at her.

He had been a stranger in the forest. Someone noble, she had guessed—it was etched into his very being—and Briar had been a girl practicing a song in what she'd thought was privacy, and they'd danced and talked and it had been light and playful and so very, very easy.

She had seen the beginnings of a future with him. The same sort that Frieda and Ben had together.

But then Briar had been drawn away from her cottage the very night Phillip had arranged to come meet her and her aunts, and the next time she'd seen him, he'd been kissing her awake in the tower. Maleficent had abducted him and locked him away in an attempt to keep from breaking the sleeping curse, but the fairies had freed him, and he had stood alone facing Maleficent while the whole of the kingdom dropped into a sleeping spell alongside her, thanks to the fairies.

Everything else had broken apart—messy, jagged shards she couldn't even begin to piece back together. She'd lost her home and her family and her friends, her future and her dreams; he'd fought a dragon and waged a whole battle on his own—

But, impossibly, they had not lost each other.

And his smile was a mark of that promise, the same breathlessly grateful shock that came whenever they looked at each other. A hitch of amazement. *How are you still here? How are you real, when everything else was so fake?*

He stood, his taller frame throwing him into gilded silhouette against the candle, the slope of his long neck curving down to wide shoulders.

There was a wooden mug in his hand. Another on a little table by his chair, and a second chair positioned next to where the loaf of bread had been cut, placed out on a tray, set for two.

She closed the distance to the fireplace, lower lip catching between her teeth. "And who could you possibly be meeting here? An errant tryst with a lady's maid?"

His dark eyes flared at her tone. That spark contrasted with the exhaustion on his face, a shadow that slipped away in her presence.

"Ah, I have been caught." He put a hand to his chest in mock hurt. He was in a simple ivory tunic, belted over dark pants and boots. "Do not tell my betrothed. She is prone to flights of jealousy."

"I have heard that about her. They say she's quite unstable."

"Hmm. I have been sending my servants down for sleeping drafts, and every night, they brought the strangest reports. Of that unstable betrothed of mine, lurking in the shadows, stealing our bread and tea. I thought, well, surely they must be mistaken. If she were going to steal anything, it would be cake at least."

Briar's lips cracked into a grin. She took the mug he offered and sipped from it, eyes on him over the rim.

"But I realized . . ." he continued, retaking his seat and claiming his own mug. She sat in the other chair, the candle burning on the low table in front of them. "That if she could steal bread and tea, then I was perfectly capable of doing the same myself."

"Are you? I am shocked, nay, *scandalized* that the prince of Lorraine even knows where the kitchen is."

He gave her a challenging leer. "Is that so surprising?"

"*And* he knows how to use a bread knife."

"Ah, one of those small, swordlike things, you mean?"

"And make tea all by himself! The aristocracy will collapse!" With him, it was a joke; he had proven to be far more capable than most in the castle. But truth clung to it. Too much truth.

Phillip chuckled. His short brown hair was a little mussed, like he had been wrestling with sleep too, and the mundanity, that he'd come to meet her and hadn't worried about the decorum of it, was enchanting.

He leaned forward. She thought he might take her hand, or reach out for her—he had the intent in his dark eyes, in his smile going limp.

But he only held on to the edge of his chair, and in the proceeding silence, her skin warmed, and her smile went limp, too.

"Hello," he whispered.

They would be married in one week. Briar thought for a moment—one week *exactly*, from this very morning.

And they had hardly seen each other these past weeks, what with wedding preparations, and Briar being swept into a new life—nobility to meet and lessons on propriety that her peasant upbringing had not prepared her for. Meanwhile, Phillip was the center of everyone's fixation, dragged to meet this or that lord or duke or king who had come to fawn over the prince who had slayed a dragon.

They had seen each other at meals, at celebratory balls, where they had danced and would talk in earshot of others.

But for the first time since the tower, since the forest, even, they were alone.

"Hello to you," she whispered back. And then, because the candlelight created a halo of dreamlike fog, and she had not slept, not truly, in weeks, she said, "I've missed you."

Phillip's smile could have lit the room. It vanished quickly and he dragged a hand over his mouth, righting himself, but Briar latched on to it with a vicious smirk.

"Don't be too pleased with yourself," she said. "I miss many people at the moment. I am practically giving away my affection."

The candlelight was indescribably dangerous, this hazy atmosphere they were creating. She would say more she shouldn't. She would, even worse, *do* things she shouldn't.

But things *Briar* shouldn't, or things *Aurora* shouldn't?

With him, though, she was neither, and she was both, and that was dangerous, too.

"How are you?" he asked. His brow pinched in the earnestness of his question. "My servants truly did say you've been down here most nights."

"How are *you*, if you have to send servants down here most nights, too?"

His eyes dropped from hers. He worked the mug in his hand, rolling it between his palms, before he set it on the table.

Briar stared down at it. "You are not enjoying your well-deserved adoration?"

But she knew already. When she had seen him throughout the castle, he was being quickly ushered to the next meeting—and his movements had been stiff, overly formal. His face had been smooth with practiced cordiality. Nothing about him had been the man she knew from the forest. The prince she had watched get hauled around the castle these past weeks was the same ghost she had become to get through her duties as Aurora. Hollow and performative.

Phillip leaned his elbows on his knees. And said only, "No."

Her eyes flared up to his. But he was looking away now, and the muscles in the sharp edge of his jaw were bunched.

She sank back in her chair. "Aren't we a pair. You saved me from a sleeping curse only for neither of us to be able to sleep at all. Maybe that was the real curse."

One corner of his lips lifted, not so much a smile as an acknowledgment. "If only."

"If only?"

He scrubbed his hands over his face. "Oh, don't mind me. My father says I'm far too morose these days. I could be a bard, belting out melancholy songs to— What's funny?"

She was trying to hide her laugh, she really was, but he looked at her and she couldn't help it.

"You've not met many bards, have you?"

Phillip cocked his head, not seeing what she was getting at. "No, I suppose not."

"We're hardly *morose* and *melancholy.* What good would only gloomy songs be for rousing a tavern to drink and joy?"

A look of interest fixed on Phillip, a hunter setting a mark. *"We?"*

Briar's cheeks heated. She had not spoken about her life *before* since coming here. Only to ask for messengers to go down into Hausach, and even that had taken days of fighting with the king and qu—with her mother and father. During the short time she had spent with Phillip in the forest, neither had told the other who they truly were, or any identifying things about themselves.

She picked up a slice of bread. As she chewed, she kept her eyes anywhere but on him, the telling of this suddenly making her feel raw.

She wasn't a bard anymore, with dreams of traveling the Holy Roman Empire, singing and learning new ballads.

She was a princess, and she was bound to Austria.

"I was part of a troupe. In Hausach." Her chest ached. *Say it quickly; say it and be done with it.* "My . . . companions and I. We would sing, bring in coin that way. My aunts were loving, but downright shortsighted when it came to actually providing for us. Which I see now was due to their overreliance on magic up until our departure from the castle." She made herself dust the bread-crumbs from her hands and not lick the remains, and grabbed another piece. "But once I was old enough, I began singing to help us pay our way."

"How are you not wealthier than the king?" Phillip asked. "I remember how talented you are."

She finished the second slice, reached for a third. He hadn't touched a single one—there was *food*, sitting here, and he did not eat? Insanity. Utterly. And it was *good* food, too.

"Ah, yes, villagers are known to throw their spare coinage at performers, rather than, say, providing for their families."

Phillip winced. "That came out wrong. I meant—when I first heard you, in the forest, I thought, *That voice is too beautiful to be real.* I cannot imagine anyone else hearing you and not immediately wanting to swear their souls to you."

Heaven help her, but he talked really, really well.

"Oh, I am rich in souls, did I not tell you that? Coin, no, alas, but souls I have aplenty."

He smirked. "That, I do believe. Singing was your fairy gift, was it not?"

She frowned. "My what?"

"Your fairy gift? You've heard the story."

Yes. She had heard, before, when the story was of a distant, faceless princess, not her. Of how Maleficent had arrived at the princess's christening after Flora and Fauna had bestowed blessings on her; of how Maleficent's blessing was the curse that would come to destroy her life. And how Merryweather had tried her best to undo the worst of it, changing the curse to one of sleeping, not death.

Flora's gift to her had been beauty. Fauna's gift had been song. The former Briar had immediately detested, and she had to fight hard not to be upset with her aunts. Beauty she could have come by naturally. Had her parents not been insulted, that Flora had assumed their daughter might otherwise be *ugly*?

But until this moment, Briar had not realized that singing, too, was something else that had been manufactured in her life, something that was not truly hers. She was not a singer; she had been created to be a singer, created by the same magical forces that had manipulated everything else.

It cracked into her chest like a thunderclap on a clear night, and she sat in that chair, eyes drifting into the middle space, all her inner thoughts gone to reeling chaos.

Now Phillip did take her hand.

She cast a startled look up at him and he immediately released her.

"Forgive me—"

She snatched his hand back.

An instinctive reaction, that.

She had wanted him to touch her for . . . well, since the forest, since they had danced to no music, and all through the balls here, and when she had her hand on his arm at presentative events, and when he put his fingers on the small of her back to guide her through a door.

She wanted him and she was going to marry him and all of this was enormously terrifying, but the persistent spark that flickered and squirmed in the base of her stomach when she saw him was, in its own way, an anchor. *He* was an anchor.

Saying all that, though, was not simple, and so she sat there with her hand clasped around his in midair, her eyes locked on him, her lips parted.

So much easier to sing these sorts of feelings. But the idea of breaking into spontaneous song was too absurd, even for her.

Hellfire and damnation, she was pathetic, and at least *that* had not changed.

"I did not mean to upset you," Phillip said. His shoulders were hard planes of tension, his hand extended, caught in hers but in a way that said he feared moving would make her let him go. "Your fairy gifts were a . . . blessing."

"Were they?" Slowly, she brought their hands down, between them. She turned his hand palm up, and in the unsteady light of the candle, she was able to do unsteady things, like look at his hand, his calluses from wielding a sword, and trace the lines across his palms with her fingertips. "Did you have fairy blessings?"

He shuddered. It rippled up from her touch.

"Yes," he whispered. "I— Strength was one. Honor. Bravery."

Still more things that could have been come by naturally.

What good were fairy gifts, truly? Better to have gifts like *You can poison anyone at will* or *All who look upon you with ill intent will vomit frogs for a month straight.*

But her aunts had explained it to her after everything. Their magic was in goodness, joy, happiness, and so on. They could not give such aggressive gifts to anyone—Flora had been scandalized that she would even ask. Fauna had laughed in her uncomfortable, trying-to-keep-the-peace way. Merryweather had grumbled about how Briar was right, they *should* be able to make people vomit frogs, that would certainly bring *her* joy.

Briar kept Phillip's palm resting in hers, her fingers moving back and forth over the lines, and her breath came in tight, quick pulls as she became aware of the heat of his skin, the contrast between the soft texture at the base of his wrist and the rough pads of his thumb.

"Do you ever think about who we might have been if our lives had been uninfluenced?" She poured the question down into his open hand. "If we had been allowed to . . . to *be*?"

"Yes," he said instantly. She felt the corresponding brush of air and looked up, realizing he had shifted to the edge of his chair. "But I know one thing that would not have changed, magic or no."

Briar's eyebrows lifted. She found her throat incapable of functioning to ask what he meant.

He was very, very close to her.

And he smelled of the floral tea and a richness like mint soap and some unnameable musk that did exceptionally unfair things to her ability to breathe.

"I still would have met you," Phillip said, eyes flashing gold in the candlelight. "That was always real."

Now it was her turn to smile like the sun.

"Sir Knight, you need not woo me; I am yours already," she managed.

His head tipped, a flash of interest. "Sir Knight?"

Oh. She smiled again in self-deprecation and shook her head. "It was, uh, how I referred to you in my head. After the forest. *Sir Knight.* It's from a song."

"Sir Knight," he echoed again, as if trying it on. His smile pulsed. "I like it. It's steps down from 'prince,' so it sounds like a vacation. Far less responsibility."

"Oh, I wouldn't say that. Knights tend to have to actually *work.*"

He bellowed a laugh and jerked on their tangled hands, yanking them both to their feet, and she went, giggling, feigning wrestling away, until the position put her right against his broad chest, their hands clasped against his shirt.

His words were still thick on the air, in her head: *That was always real.*

She kept her eyes firmly on his collarbone—which was not the best place to stare in an attempt to regain control of herself, because it was a rather nice collarbone—and remembered, remembered a brush of satin on her lips. A shock of fear, then a wave of confusion when she had opened her eyes and seen him, someone she recognized, but his face had been in such a scowl of terror that she wondered, often, if he even *had* kissed her awake. No one could look like that after a kiss. Like they were on the edge of a nightmare.

His hands clamped around hers, and she realized it was in an effort to hide how he was shivering.

"I would like to hear you sing that song," he said. It came out in a rush.

Song? What song? Any song. She would sing anything he asked.

"Actually . . ." He whipped his head toward the kitchen windows, where the night still hung dark and impenetrable. "Come with me."

Briar blinked up at him. "All right. Where?"

He looked at her with a roguish grin. Such an enticing, teasing, *mischievous* grin that it struck her speechless.

"It's not yet midnight," he said. "No self-respecting tavern would be closed."

"You—you want to go to a tavern?"

"I want *us* to go to a tavern. Your tavern. Hausach is a twenty-minute ride away. Well, maybe longer, with both of us on Samson."

Something broke loose in Briar's chest. It dropped, and in its descent it sprouted wings and took flight, fluttering feverishly against her ribs.

"Yes," she said, knowing it sounded overeager and desperate, but she was, and she couldn't hide it. "Yes." And then, "Can we? Won't we be stopped? The guards—"

Phillip put his hand on her chin. Just the barest brush of his thumb there, and it rattled through her with enough force to break stone.

"You want to go to your old tavern?" he clarified.

She nodded helplessly.

"Then it will be done." He adjusted his hold on her to encase one of her hands in his, and before she could find any words, any at all, to thank him, he was grabbing the last of the bread, handing it to her, and hauling her out of the kitchen, making fast for the stables.

CHAPTER TWO

The night was cool and Briar was *free.*

She closed her eyes as Phillip worked Samson down the road at a steady walk so as not to risk him rolling his ankle in the dark. The moonless sky showed stars at least, gave the trees on either side of the road casts of blue and onyx, and the air smelled of early summer greenery, tilled earth, and damp leaves.

That alone would have been enough to send Briar reeling out into the radiant ether, just being *out of the castle.* But Phillip sat behind her, his whole body encasing her as they rode, his arms resting on the curve of her hips, his face bent over her shoulder—

Perhaps it had been a blessing they had not seen each other often these past weeks. It was distressingly hard to think of much other than *him* when he was around.

Briar remembered how inseparable Frieda and Ben had been once they had admitted their feelings for one another. How their trio would often dissolve into Briar finding reasons to excuse herself before the pressure between the other two snapped right in front of her; how Frieda and Ben would come to performances looking a little more disheveled than usual, and Briar had tried hard—well, maybe not *that* hard—not to mercilessly torment them.

She completely understood now.

It was actually annoying, this feeling. She had things to *do*, didn't her heart realize? She was on her way to Hausach for the first time in months and she should be thinking of what she would say to Frieda and Ben—

That did sober her. Aggressively.

She went rigid against Phillip, and he noted it with the way he shifted closer, his arms tightening until one draped across her waist.

Which only served to reignite those blasted *feelings* again, and that was how she spent the trip, jerked back and forth between worry about the impending arrival and the excruciating nearness of this man at her back.

Fully exhausting to have feelings.

Infinitely easier to merely sing about them.

Do not break into song, she begged herself, and Samson trotted down the main street of Hausach.

All the buildings save for one were dark, the windows of the tavern glowing softly from the fireplace within. Bodies moved against the windows, laughter and conversation peppered the night, and there was a gentle melody within, a lute being played, a voice ringing out in song.

Briar recognized that lute, that voice, immediately.

Ben.

Phillip halted Samson at a hitching post. He started to slide down first. Briar heaved her leg over and dropped, and Phillip made a shocked noise and leapt down after her, but she was in a panic.

Ben was in there, and that meant Frieda was, too, and Briar's focus narrowed to those two points.

"Briar?" Phillip quickly tied off Samson, but she was walking already, twisting back to give him a powerless look and then she was off, dragged toward the tavern, her tavern, as if in a dream.

"Briar!"

She hurried up the steps and pushed inside.

Nothing had changed.

If she stood on the threshold and held perfectly still, it had not been several weeks, and *nothing had changed.*

The same dented, ancient tables were stained by ale and food. The same massive stone fireplace scented the air with woodsmoke and ash. The same crowd of the same farmers, craftsmen, soldiers even, and servers packed the space, the latter expertly scurrying through the room with steins of beer and bowls of whatever goulash the keeper's wife had made that day.

And there was Ben, in his usual place back by the bar, strumming on his lute and swaying around the room as he sang, eyes sparkling, smile wide on his pale face. His dark hair was held back by a piece of twine, his lean frame making for easy movement.

Briar stood frozen, watching him, and a weight sank in her stomach.

To the room, he would look joyful, and they were clearly buying it; their energy was effusive.

But she knew him. And she knew that smile was stiff, those eyes sunken.

Briar looked down, at the spot where Frieda sat—

It was empty.

Well. Ben first, then.

Briar felt a hand on her back. She twisted to look up at Phillip, thanking the stars above that they didn't look out of place—him in his simple linen shirt and pants, her in her old kirtle. No one would suspect who she was, who she had become—and no one would suspect him, either.

A cry rang out. "Briar Rose!"

She couldn't help but smile. It cut across her face so large it ached, sparking tears in her eyes as she saw Rolf, the tavernkeeper, a massive, burly man who had once been a blacksmith and a soldier and still had the frame to prove both.

Ben's head snapped toward the cry. Briar was yanked out of her excitement by the way his eyes went from Rolf to . . . her.

Mid-song, Ben didn't falter. But his face went wide momentarily, the look of a man seeing a ghoul.

He turned his back to her, singing to the other side of the room.

Rolf rounded the bar and wove through the crowd, limping slightly, an injury earned from a brief spurt of conflict between Austria and Bavaria more than a decade ago.

Briar forced her smile back on as Rolf neared her, arms open, and she pushed herself up on her toes to hug him.

"Where in heaven and hell have you been off to, lass?"

She sank back to her feet. "I—" Oh, what lie would even make *sense*? She had not planned for this. She'd had dozens of pretend conversations with Frieda and Ben, but none with Rolf or anyone else.

Phillip came up alongside her and extended his hand to Rolf. "Hallo, I'm—"

Rolf grabbed Phillip's hand and assertively clapped his shoulder, nearly throwing him off his feet, all the while giving Briar a look of impish realization. "You went and got yourself *married*, Briar Rose?"

Her mouth went dry. Well, it wasn't far off from the truth. She shrugged and smiled, and the room was warm, but she blushed. "It often happens, I'm told."

Around them, the crowd was still besotted by Ben's song, voices overlapping to sing along.

Phillip extricated himself from Rolf and, rubbing his arm, he gave her a bemused smirk.

Rolf bellowed a laugh and clapped Phillip on the shoulder, again, and he staggered, *again*, and it was nothing short of hilarious to see Phillip's solid frame soundly manhandled by Rolf.

"I don't suppose you've come back to resume your place here?" Rolf asked, having to nearly shout over the rise in the chorus. "Benedikt could surely use your skill."

"Unfortunately, no. This is a passing visit. I—"

Rolf had said *Benedikt could surely use your skill.*

No mention of Frieda.

A strange tightening pulled in Briar's gut. "Do you know where Frieda is? I was hoping to talk to her."

Rolf scratched his shorn black hair and gave a frustrated sigh. "She left not long after you did. Thought she'd joined up with you, honestly. Left poor Benedikt to wrangle this crowd on his own."

Briar stared at Rolf. Willing his words to coalesce.

Frieda had left, too?

Because . . . because of Briar?

No. She would not have left Ben. They were going to get married. Even without Briar, Frieda had a life here, she had a life and a future—she would not have left.

But Briar once had a life and a future here. And she had left.

"Well, take a seat." Rolf jerked his head at the room. "I'll bring you food, eh? And beer?"

He left without waiting for confirmation.

There were a few open booths, and Briar walked stiffly to one and sat so she could see the room. And Ben.

Phillip eased in across from her. His eyes were on her face, studying, and even through the din of the crowd, she heard him ask, "Who is Frieda?"

Who was Frieda?

Briar slumped on the bench.

Frieda was the first person she'd met in Hausach. The two of them had run wild as children, united in orphanhood—Briar with her aunts, Frieda as a ward who stayed with a tumble of children under the care of the church—and in their birthdays, a week apart. The forest was their sanctuary, where they would play out all sorts of games of fairy tale and fantasy, reenacting the stories they heard sung in the tavern. And as they grew, they began singing, making up their own songs, often terribly, and laughing at awful rhymes until they couldn't breathe. Frieda was the one Briar snuck out to cry to when her aunts tried to cook but only succeeded in burning the spelt Briar had worked hard to buy; Frieda was the one Briar went to when she needed to talk about the world beyond Hausach, how one day, she would leave, and see the empire, and do *more.*

Frieda never talked like that, about the future. Until Briar realized the brewer's son could play the lute, and she'd dragged him into their forest song rehearsals, and suddenly, they were a trio. But not a trio—they were Briar, then Ben and Frieda.

But they had been Briar and Frieda first.

"She was my sister" was all Briar could think to say.

Phillip's brows bent inward. "Where would she have gone?"

Briar shook her head. "I don't know. She— He's done. Wait here."

And she was up, barely hearing Phillip's startled "Briar—" before she threw herself into the crowd.

Ben was making fast for the door at the rear of the tavern. He didn't want to see her.

Well, that was really too bad for him.

A tangled knot of concern and anger drove her forward. She missed him, and Frieda, and she understood why they would be upset with her—but she needed them. Her friends. She was drowning in this new life and she *needed them.*

Briar shoved past a drunk patron and managed to grab Ben's elbow right in the doorway.

He went rigid. Lute under one arm.

"Please," Briar said. "I'll buy you supper."

He didn't move.

"And ale, of course—that should have been a given."

She watched him suck his teeth.

Finally, he gave her a tired, flat look.

"You're in luck," he said. "I haven't eaten yet."

They made their way back to the booth, Briar having to glance over her shoulder every few seconds to make sure Ben hadn't changed his mind. But he was there. Then he was here, sliding into the empty bench, so Briar took a seat across from him, hip-to-hip with Phillip.

Ben laid his lute beside him, folded his hands on the table, and stared off into the tavern. Business was winding down, but groups remained, and in moments, Rolf returned with bowls of goulash and steins. Only two, though, not knowing Ben would be here; but Briar pushed hers to Ben.

"Keep it coming," she said to Rolf. She had money to spare now, didn't she? She had thought of sending bags of it down to Frieda and Ben, not flinching at stooping to buying their forgiveness; but she hadn't wanted to insult them, or make them feel as though she was parading it before them.

Though, she didn't actually have any of that money on her *now*, and she cut a look at Phillip, who motioned to the coin purse on his waist.

She would never stop being grateful for him.

Briar faced Ben, who was shoveling goulash into his mouth, his eyes already waiting to latch on to hers.

"To what do I owe the presence of our fair princess in this lowly place?" Ben asked around a mouthful of food.

Briar winced and cut a gaze around. No one was within earshot. "I wanted to see you."

"Hmm." Ben swallowed. "Well, you've seen me. So. Goodbye?"

"Ben." She wanted to explain. Again. She had said in her letter to them that her aunts had forced her to the castle the day of her sixteenth birthday. Maleficent's curse had taken hold that very night. And by the time she awoke, and the kingdom was free, she was a princess, she was under near constant watch, and she had no idea how to undo what had happened.

She'd explained everything in the letter she'd sent with the messenger. He knew it, so what would saying it again change?

There was only one other thing she could even think of to say. And it gutted her.

"Where is Frieda?"

Ben's jaw worked. He dropped the spoon into the now-empty bowl and picked up his lute. "Been great seeing you, Bri, really—"

She leaned across the table and grabbed his arm. "Please. Sit. Please, Ben. What happened?"

"What *happened*?" he snapped, and Briar had never heard him this way, derisive and hurt. He was the sun, he was buoyancy and joy and jokes, always eager to do something foolish with her while Frieda chastised them for being reckless. "What happened is that I lost the two of you in the same week. What *happened* is that you two *left me*, without so much as a farewell."

When Ben and Frieda had first admitted their feelings to one another, Briar had been insufferable. They had all been about twelve—well, Ben was older—but, looking back, Briar knew she had been an awful pain. She'd picked fights with Frieda, intentionally let secrets slip to embarrass the two of them. She'd been an utter nuisance, and she'd only realized why after about two months of that behavior while Ben and Frieda blushed at each other.

She was jealous.

Not of Ben—she loved Frieda, and she knew of women in Hausach who preferred other women to men, but she had never seen her friend in that way; and not of Frieda—she loved Ben, too, but she imagined being with him would be like trying to put out a fire with a lit torch, flame on flame, until they both burned out.

No, she was jealous of what Ben and Frieda had. Love. Such easy, natural love.

She'd admitted her jealousy to Frieda, finally, after Frieda had exploded at her over another petty slight. At the end of Briar's childish explanation, Frieda had slapped her upside the head.

You'll find it one day, too, you nitwit, she'd said with assumed confidence, as though Briar had been afraid the forest would run out of trees.

Frieda and Ben's relationship shifted from being something Briar envied to being a beacon of what she would one day have.

And now she had it. She had Phillip, and he was every bit as made for her as Ben was for Frieda.

So seeing Ben alone, broken, ripped a jagged, messy hole in Briar's heart, because she could not, in any reality, imagine what force would compel her to leave Phillip in the same way. So why had Frieda gone? She wouldn't have. She . . . she *wouldn't* have left. It made no sense.

"Frieda wouldn't have left you," Briar said, for lack of any explanation. "She wouldn't have—"

"Well, she did. And you did, too. So again I say, *goodbye*."

He was halfway to standing when he seemed to notice Phillip for the first time.

The tension around Ben vanished, his anger snapping into astonished recognition so roughly that he made a little wheezing noise.

Slowly, he sat back down. "You," he said, eyes wide, face slack.

Phillip shifted on the bench. His chin dipped, as if he were bracing himself, as worry raced across his face, worry that this evening would be another onslaught of fawning over his deeds. And while Briar didn't understand why he was so resistant to praise he had earned, she grabbed Phillip's hand under the table.

"You're—" Ben's jaw wobbled. "You're the Pain from Lorraine."

That snapped Phillip's head up. "What?"

Briar's mind faltered. "What did you call—"

She looked at Phillip. Who did not seem at all confused by the name. In fact, he was smiling, a relieved, true smile.

Unexpected pieces connected from months past, and Briar rounded on Ben in an almost hysterical rush.

"*He* is the *Pain from Lorraine*?" she squeaked. Then, to Phillip: "*You* are the *Pain from Lorraine*?"

Phillip's cheeks reddened. "I did not choose that name."

Ben folded himself back onto the bench, gawking between her and Phillip. "How—how do you know him?" To Phillip: "Why are you here? *How* are you here? Not that you can't be here. You can be anywhere. But in Hausach? With *Briar*?"

Briar laughed, a sharp burst that was as surprising as this whole situation.

She had thought she had uncovered all the areas in which Phillip's and her lives had overlapped, a gentle braid of fate bringing them together even before they'd known who they were to each other. But this was another piece she could add: that Ben had been raving, fawning, and otherwise *gushing* over the jousting champion known as the Pain from Lorraine for the past year and a half.

All those times she and Frieda had shared eye rolls during Ben's seemingly endless, incredibly dull jousting stories, he'd been talking about *Phillip*.

"I saw you," Ben spluttered, color rising to his cheeks. "I saw you joust, I mean. In Tübingen, last year."

Phillip's eyebrows lifted. "You did? That was a good one."

"No, it was a *great* one. You unseated Leon the Lion in *one lance*."

"Rumors said he'd been drinking, so the win wasn't entirely—"

"Oh, spare me the humility; you didn't just win that tournament, you made the reigning champion heel, sit, and beg at your feet."

Phillip laughed. "I suppose I did."

"Suppose?" Ben shook his head. "No. No. There's no supposing anything. You waltzed into that tournament and trounced a jouster *twice your age*. And the one before that, in Stuttgart?"

"You were at that one, too?"

"Well, no, I wasn't there, but I heard how you stole the win from the Gelderland Giant—two lances on both sides, the crowd losing their *minds*, thinking the Giant would take it, and he was a right awful bastard, everyone hated him—and then *bam*! The final lance, it was poetic the way you dodged his blow and lanced him right in the head. This man is a hero!" he shouted to the tavern. No one reacted. "You're all in the presence of a god, you uncultured louts!"

Someone mumbled drunkenly, and Ben batted it away dismissively.

"Toads, the lot of them." He swung back toward Phillip. "Not a single soul in Hausach even knows what a list is."

"I believe that," Phillip said. "There are not many I meet even at the castle here who care much for jousting. It isn't as popular in Austria as it is in Lorraine and farther out."

"The bane of my every waking moment. Because when we all heard about Prince Phillip's mighty deeds—yeah, impressive, with the dragon, and so on, great of you and all—*that* made people care about you. But when I was going on about your streak of wins across the Swabian regionals last summer, *did anyone listen?*"

"No," Briar said with a laugh. Because she had been on the receiving end of Ben's near-delirious rants about the different types of wood used for lances and how the Pain from Lorraine had the best lance heads and she had not cared, not even a little.

But she cared now, about the way Phillip was grinning, and how the tension had gone out of his shoulders, and the fact that he looked more like the man she knew. The man she had danced with in the forest. Carefree and settled and happy.

Ben gestured wildly at Briar. "No! Listen to that derision. *No.* You have no idea who you're sitting next to, do you, Bri? The youngest jouster to ever crack a dozen unseated competitors in a single season. Why is he even roughing it with you? Do you have any idea what this man has done in the list? What he's *accomplished?*"

She was all-out beaming now. This was the Ben she remembered, too. And if a shared interest in jousting was what it took to bring both these men back to her in some way, then she'd bear it.

"Oh, I have some idea of his accomplishments, outside the list, at least," she said. "He's my betrothed."

Ben stared at her. Stared like she'd said she could conjure diamonds from thin air.

"You are engaged," he stated awestruck. "To the Pain from Lorraine."

"Which part of that is surprising?"

"Both. Equally. You could have come in with the emperor himself and it'd be less unexpected. *Strike me down*, Bri—*he* is why you left? In that whole letter you had that messenger read, you never once thought to mention that you absconded with *him*?"

"I thought you would have heard who the princess was engaged to. Or had been engaged to, her whole life, apparently. And I didn't realize until now that he was your jousting idol."

Ben's face froze in an expression of realization.

Then he cupped his hands over his mouth and rubbed his face, hard.

"I did. I knew who you were engaged to. Everyone knew. But I didn't—It was *you*. Of course it was." He smacked a hand to his forehead. "It didn't connect that his betrothed was *you* now. None of it . . . none of it felt like you."

"I know," she said, her voice softer. "You have no idea."

His eyes lifted to hers. He looked at Phillip again, back at her, and splayed his hands flat on the table.

"It is possible," he started, eyes down, "that I have been too quick to judge your new life, Bri."

She fought a smile. "Oh?"

"Yeah. Terrible business, all that, um, nonsense about accusing you of lying and—I forgive you."

"Do you?"

"Having a remarkable change of heart, suddenly."

"I can't help but feel this is coming from a place of wanting access to my future husband." She waited until Ben looked up at her. "But I am glad to be forgiven, selfish reasons or no. Though"—she licked her lips, all her anxiety about coming here rearing up again—"I do not know how I can make you realize how sorry I am. I never would have chosen to leave like that. I never would have chosen to leave *at all*. And as for Frieda, I don't . . ."

Ben shook his head. His levity dipped, and silence stretched between them, as he looked at Phillip in discomfort.

"I don't want to talk about Frieda."

Phillip coughed into his fist. "I can give you two a moment, if you need."

"No!" Ben jolted and rocked the table. "No. It's fine. You don't have to, um— It's fine. We're done. We're all right now, aren't we, Bri?"

Hardly. Mostly. Her chest still ached, but alongside that ache, she felt like herself again in a way she had not managed to find in months.

She reached out and took Ben's hand. He squeezed her fingers and released her to take the new bowls of goulash a server brought, tearing into the food without pretense.

But he peeked up at her, his brow furrowing. "You'll head back to the castle, I imagine?"

Briar took a bite from her own bowl of goulash now. It was tasteless, and not because of Rolf's wife's cooking, but because yes, she would have to go back. When could she get down here again?

She nodded. And they ate in silence for a long moment, until Briar felt Phillip's eyes on her.

She looked up at him, and he was studying her, then Ben.

"Ben," he said. "How would you like to be a squire?"

Ben's whole body went stiff, arched over his goulash, his eyes going to saucers.

Those wide eyes slid up to Briar. "Is he joking?"

Briar grinned at Phillip. "I don't think so."

"It is an honest offer." Phillip smiled. "I am well within my right to train up a squire, I just have never found anyone of interest. But, if you'd be willing, you'd make a fine one. Perhaps even a knight someday—"

Ben dropped his spoon with a clatter and cupped one hand over his mouth, elbow on the table, looking at Phillip the way someone might try to look at the sun, squinting and in pain.

"It is exceptionally cruel of you gentry to tease us lowly folks in such a way."

"This is no joke." Phillip picked up his stein of ale. "Think on it. Come to the castle if you're interested. I'll have space made in the barracks for you, and we can begin."

Ben was fully sputtering. Coughing, clearing his throat, taking a drink of ale only to cough again, and he only barely managed to pull himself together enough to nod at the table.

"All right," he said, head twitching. "Yes. Of course. All right, I'll . . . think on it."

Phillip nodded. "I hope you do."

He set down his stein and faced Briar, and she couldn't contain her smile, hating that they were in public, that she could not throw her arms around him.

If she could not come back to Hausach, Phillip had found a way to bring Hausach to her. Because Ben would agree—he had older brothers who were set to take on their family's brewing, and he was a talented musician, but his dreams had always laid in what Phillip had offered.

Did Phillip realize what an immense thing he had done for her friend?

Phillip smiled at her and winked, and Briar's whole body went to liquid.

Ben grabbed his lute. "This calls for a celebration."

Briar looked around the room. Only three people remained, two dead drunk, slumped over tables, the third nearly there.

"For what audience?"

Ben strummed a chord. "For *us.* For you, the prodigal daughter returning. For the Pain from Lorraine, for merely existing."

Briar laughed. She laughed and she felt weightless, and then Phillip leaned in, his shoulder brushing hers.

"I did want to hear you sing," he whispered to her. "That song, what was it—'Sir Knight'?"

A blush arched down across her chest. "I would rather one day sing a song about the Pain from Lorraine."

He groaned and his head slumped, resting on her shoulder for a beat, before he rolled away. "I don't suppose there's anything I can do to make you forget that rather absurd nickname?"

"Absolutely not."

"Damn."

Ben stood from the booth, fingers moving steadily over the strings.

Briar relented and stood with him, and to the nearly empty tavern, they sang "O Good Sir Knight."

No crowd to feed off.

No Frieda, her clear, gentle voice backing up Briar's.

But it was renewing to sing here again. To have Ben egging her on. Quickly they were dancing around the room, and Phillip was beaming watching them, clapping along, and Rolf and his wife came out to see. She sang a song about a great knight and his glorious gallantry, and here she was now, engaged to such a man, living such a gallant life.

It was not a life she had ever asked for, though. She sang tales of these deeds; she had never wanted to *live* them. Because it wasn't merely glory that came with great deeds, it was responsibility, too, and as she and Phillip took their leave, she remembered the armoire of expensive dresses she had, and the box of gold and jewels, and how Rolf had been saving up to fix the roof, and one of Ben's brothers was prone to coughing fits—

Briar leaned into Phillip before they left the booth. "Can you leave your money purse? I will refill it when we return to the castle."

Phillip's eyebrows went up. "Of course. With Rolf, or . . . ?"

She took the money from him—handfuls of gold that he had just *had on his belt*, like it was nothing, when it was enough to pay for the roof repair three times over—and split it into two piles.

She snuck one behind the bar, where Rolf would find it.

The rest she kept in the bag and forced into Ben's hand, closing his fist around it as he turned for the door.

"Come to the castle," she told him. Begged him.

He settled the lute on his back and kept his hand around the money, eyes going momentarily starry at the feel of how much coin she'd given him.

"This is all-out bribery now, Bri."

"You are not above it. Neither am I." Frieda was. Frieda had been their moral compass, their voice of reason, the clear line between right and wrong.

"Ah, *Briar Rose* is not. But what of Princess Aurora?" Ben smirked.

Briar's heart twisted. The shadow of Princess Aurora lurked around her, like at any moment, that girl would launch out of the darkness and take her over and Briar Rose would be well and truly disintegrated.

"I'm still me," she said. To him, to that lurking shadow, to any other forces that sought to snuff her out.

Ben nodded. He pocketed the money and stood there for a moment before he rolled his eyes and held his arms out.

She dove into him, a crashing, tight hug, and he gripped her just as strongly.

He peeled back and looked sheepishly at Phillip, who leaned against the doorframe, arms folded.

"Prince," he said in farewell.

Phillip smirked. "Phillip."

Ben looked liable to start babbling again, but he nodded. "Phillip." A slow whistle, and he pushed out the door with a parting "This was not how I saw my night unfolding."

Then he was gone, though Briar hoped not for long.

Phillip fell into step with her as they left the tavern, too.

"I can't tell you what you have done in offering Ben a position with you," she said to him. Concern grabbed her. "You did not have to, though, if you'd rather not have a squire—"

Phillip waved it off. "I would not have offered out of pity. I like him; I do think he has potential. He has a certain levity to him. He reminds me of you."

"Are you saying you want to make me your squire?"

"Well, I was trying to ask it delicately."

She laughed. It sobered, though, and heat in her chest built.

"I will pay you back for the money you left as well," she promised again.

"Briar, truly. What I did tonight is not piling into a debt. Is that not our duty, to provide for these people?"

It cut into her. "Yes. It is, isn't it? And I have done nothing these two months."

"No, you have merely been recovering from a curse, from your life being overturned, from everything you thought to be true actually being a lie. But, yes, that is nothing."

Briar gave him a sardonic grin that did not hold long. "What I meant was that I have everything I need for the first time in my life—I haven't been hungry in weeks, I don't have to think about *money* anymore. And what have I done to spread that relief? Meanwhile, the king lavishes ever more expensive gifts on me."

They reached Samson, the quiet of the sleeping village wrapping around them in a protective shield much like the candlelight had in the kitchen, a haven in which anything could happen or be said and it would stay safe.

"He feels guilty," Phillip said. "Your father. That's why he's showering you with things."

"He should feel guilty." It came out of her on a snap.

The king wasn't to blame for what had happened to her.

Maleficent was.

But she could not help but hate the king a little, too. For sending her away, then expecting her to come back rejoicing as though she had any ties to him or the queen beyond the fact that they were her rulers, as though he hadn't ripped her away from a life he'd let her create in ignorance.

Phillip's words hooked her, though, and Briar frowned at him as he worked Samson's reins free.

"Is that what tonight was about?" she asked, lungs tightening. "You feel guilty as well?"

The light was heavily dim, stars only, but dawn was beginning to toy with the horizon. She could see him in a haze of rising navy blue as he shifted to face her, and she was fixated on the way his throat worked, the muscles contracting.

"It is now my sole task to make you happy." His voice was a whisper. "We have not had a moment to speak about our wedding, and I— You should know. I need you to know that what happens between us next week is not a simple thing for me."

"Phillip—"

"Wait. Please. If I don't say this all at once, it will choke me."

She pinched her mouth shut. They were a hand's width apart. And in that drop of silence, she felt every inch of that space, the air between them vanishing.

"I fell in love with you," he started, and her heart hammered,

hammered in her chest. "Not Aurora, not even Briar—but *you*, your joy and your dreams and your laughter in the woods. The fact that you ended up being Aurora anyway solidified that this is fate. You and me. If it is magic manipulating us yet again, then this is one coercion I accept with open arms. I know everything you've been through, everything you've lost and been given anew, but I want you to know that I am going into this marriage fully and clearly. I am yours, *yours*, whoever you choose to be, Briar or Aurora or someone new. There is no iteration of you that I will not fall in love with, and I hope you can see me as something solid to lean on when all else is in question."

She stood there, staring up at him, her skin too constricted, too sensitive, that heart of hers inexhaustible.

A dozen ballads came to mind. Lyrics about unrestrained love that would put words to the tumult of things she was feeling, slippery, dancing feelings that surged and twisted and shook through her body. But nothing was good enough, nothing was expansive enough to explain to him how much that meant. How, yes, he was the one thing that had remained constant. How she had fallen in love with him, too, every version of him, Sir Knight and prince and kind, honorable, virtuous man.

She stepped into him, and his breath hitched, his eyes all gone to pupil with the darkness and the way she reached up with shaking fingers. She took his jaw in her palms and brought him down to her, and he bent willingly, in amazement, it seemed, the dream state bleeding into their veins so they could have been asleep, they could have been many things, but they were here, and that was a collision.

His lips parted, and hers did, too.

For a moment, she held her mouth under his. His exhalation tasted of ale and spices and warmth.

That memory reared, a satin awakening, and he was trembling now like he'd been then, but this time, his hands came down around her waist and molded her hips to his, and it steadied them both.

He held her, mouth opening a little wider, making his posture a question, letting her take what she wanted, an offering and a surrender.

She arched up against his chest and kissed him.

It wasn't gentle.

She didn't want gentle.

She wanted to make up for the weeks of not touching him, and so she locked her fingers around the base of his neck and drove into him hard and ravening and breathless, tongue and teeth and an embarrassing noise of need.

The force of her seemed to briefly stun him, a half-strangled mewl in his throat, but then he met her there and rode the motion and returned it.

He kissed her like he could kiss the past out of her, or maybe the present; he kissed her like he was trying to create something new.

And Briar created it with him, that foundation she had been looking for, the solid ground amid the rubble that had taken over both their lives.

Home. That was the foundation. That was him. *Home.*

Chapter Three

The days leading up to the wedding were unchanged from the previous weeks, endless rounds of meetings and lessons and preparations for which Aurora was needed, but Briar had no purpose.

But the hours were made bearable by the now nightly meetings she had with Phillip in the kitchen, where they would huddle by the bank of fireplaces and eat and talk—or at least she made sure they talked, against the insistency of her heart wanting to reenact their kiss in Hausach. The strain of that kiss hung like a taut thread between their every move, even when they were in the castle with dozens of people between them. So to be in that kitchen, alone, was nearly unbearable.

Luckily, Ben joined their midnight meetings as a much-needed buffer shortly after, having accepted Phillip's offer and moved into the castle's barracks and become his squire. Which meant that Briar went from feeling like she had wholly stolen someone else's life to the barest beginnings of something that was *hers* again, laughter and stories and camaraderie.

She used their time together to ask Ben about Hausach and any surrounding area news, and she tried to send what allowance she could to the village. The king and queen were scandalized that she would even ask to do such a thing. Her *responsibilities* lay in preparing to be married, they told her; she should focus on finalizing the details of her wedding, on memorizing the names of the nobility, on perfecting her waltz.

Absurdity.

All of it.

And that absurdity, on top of the late-night get-togethers, where she was certain a soldier would storm in and chastise them for the noise they were making well past midnight, left Briar with the itch of absence. How Frieda was not there with them.

Ben didn't have the mind for justice and responsibility that Frieda did, and Phillip was ever eager to put whatever plan Briar hatched into action. But Frieda would have been the one to calculate the best use of Briar's funds, to know where to send the money so that the greatest needs were met. She would have known what to say to the king and queen to get them to understand the imbalance of wealth in the kingdom, whereas all Briar could do was distract them with charm and wit so they didn't know that Phillip had Ben deliver money and resources down to Hausach without their approval.

Briar's life was healing, slowly, but there remained a gaping wound where Frieda should be. She knew Ben felt it, too, for he refused to speak of her still.

And then, two days out from the wedding, while her aunts and mother were aflutter over her final gown fitting, Briar realized she had been an absolute fool. There was a huge resource at her disposal that she had not used, not even *thought* of using, and she hated herself for her shortsightedness.

In her bedchamber, as Flora levitated the gown before a trio of mirrors and Fauna beat her wings to lift up, inspecting the roses she had enchanted into the neckline, Briar tucked her dressing gown around her and sidled up next to Merryweather.

"I was wondering if you could do something for me," she said, trying not to make it sound like she was whispering.

Merryweather was bent over a table, bespelling tea to boil in a pot next to a tray of buttery springerle cookies with mere flicks of her wand.

The queen, at the table, took a cookie, nibbled a bite, and even in her decorum, she made a quick face of distaste and demurely set it down.

"Of course, dear," Merryweather said to Briar, half watching the queen's reaction. "Anything. Oh, Fauna made these cookies, didn't she?"

Flora and Fauna, in an argument over lace, paused long enough for Fauna to give an excited grin. "I did! I daresay my baking skills are so improving! Aren't they scrumptious?"

"Quite," the queen said with a full lack of emotion.

Merryweather gave a deep sigh. "What is it you needed, dear?" she asked Briar.

"I—" Briar's eyes went to the queen. Now she did whisper. "I was hoping you could look in on Frieda for me."

Merryweather went stiff. She twisted her back to the queen, Flora and Fauna again in dispute.

But she smiled, and Briar's tension alleviated.

"You did not ask them, did you?" the fairy whispered with a nod at her sisters.

"Ask Flora to check in on Frieda? You know she always hated her." It was an understatement. Flora had hated that Briar had left the cottage *ever*, let alone that she had made friends. If she'd had her way, Briar would have grown up in utter solitude but for her three aunts, *for her safety.*

But what Flora did not see was that they *had* protected Aurora. They had protected her so well that she had ceased to exist.

Merryweather's plump face blossomed into a mischievous grin. "I saw Benedikt in the training yard. You are glad to have him here?"

"Very."

"And Frieda did not want to come?"

Briar winced. "I do not know where she is. She left after I did, apparently."

"Ah." Merryweather's face softened in sympathy. She scratched at her linen headdress that arched over the back of her hair; she was forever adjusting it and fighting with it. "Perhaps she does not want to be found, hmm?"

"It's not that I want to find her"—a lie—"it's that I want to make sure she's safe. For my peace of mind. For Ben, too."

Merryweather patted Briar's cheek. "Oh, you know I can never resist you. Give me a moment. Oi!" she shouted at her sisters. "These cookies are utter dust! I'm to the kitchen for once."

Fauna chirped in offense. "They are not *dust*! I followed the recipe exactly!"

"Bespell cookies with your wand, Merryweather," Flora said. "No need to traipse all the way to the kitchen."

Briar swallowed a tang of frustration. Her aunts had been capable of creating food with ease *all along* and had let them all suffer in hunger and worry for sixteen years rather than reveal the truth to her. Their magic was incapable of letting them create enough food to sustain all of Hausach, they had told her recently; but still, they could have staved off the worst of their own hunger. They could have alleviated Briar's burden as a child to provide for the four of them.

"I do not *want* magically created cookies," Merryweather said. "I *want* freshly made, and I was a fool to believe Fauna could provide such. You still have taken no actual baking lessons from the cooks, have you?"

Fauna pouted. "I follow the *recipe books*—"

"And they are useless if you do not understand the steps. I am off, back with edible treats."

Flora gave a flinch of distrust. "*Now*? But Aurora's gown—"

"If the three of you are incapable of getting one gown on one girl, then I will certainly add nothing to what will be a comedy of disaster. Cookies!" And she left with a wink at Briar.

The queen stood, setting her teacup on the table. Every motion from her was a reminder of what Briar was expected to become—dripping grace. Collected, intentional, controlled movements, nothing out of place, not a stray smile or even a flick of her eyes that was not polished.

But it looked nothing short of painful, to be so constrained by propriety like that, and Briar had yet to have a single conversation with the queen that felt anything like motherly. They had not talked about the past sixteen years, about what Briar had done with her life. They had not talked about how King Stefan and Queen Leah had endured. They had not talked about *anything.* They had gone about their days as though this was a happy ending.

It was an ending, certainly.

But it was not happy.

"Let us see it, Aurora," the queen said, gesturing to the dais before the mirrors.

Briar's jaw set. *Briar. Briar. Not Aurora.*

She obeyed, stepping up, letting her dressing gown drop so she stood in a thin wool shift.

Flora and Fauna clothed her through a combination of magic and tugging. On went a boned underdress, then a laced kirtle, the two snugly fitting to the curve of her hips so she could scarcely take a breath, but Flora exclaimed that was the point. The gown was next, a massive heave of silk that draped over Briar's body and immediately staggered her, the bodice woven with jewels and small flowers.

The king had insisted on no expense spared. Which meant this single garment was worth more than all the money Briar had ever made in her life multiplied thrice over.

The deep maroon silk gave a pink flush to her skin, her golden hair complemented by and glowing against the ruby shade. The jewels sparkled and glinted in the light, the sleeves dropping off so her shoulders were bare, the skirt full and trailing.

It really was extraordinary.

And so, so *much.*

Flora fluttered about and quickly styled Briar's hair, not the elaborate weave it would be in two days, but enough to get an idea; and then Fauna set a crown upon her head.

Briar went fully immobile, staring at herself in the mirror.

No. Not *herself.*

This was Princess Aurora. This was the girl who would one day, likely soon, take over Briar and smother all memory of her old life. This was the girl she could have been, should have been, if fate had not intervened.

Briar was the interloper here. Not Aurora.

The queen came up alongside her in the mirror. They looked quite similar now. The same striking hair, the same kind eyes, the same stature, even, with Briar motionless.

"You are exquisite," the queen said.

"Thank you," Briar managed.

"Phillip will be unable to take his eyes off of you."

That earned a twittering giggle from Fauna. "Oh, it's so *romantic*!" she squealed, hands folded beneath her cheek.

Flora huffed. "Do not start this again—"

"How can I not? The prince and the princess, married! Austria and Lorraine, united! Oh, I mustn't."

Fauna was crying. As she often did these days. It had been a taxing sixteen years for them, to keep her safe, to keep her secret, and they had very nearly failed to stave off Maleficent's curse.

Briar reached out, and Fauna put a hand in hers. She squeezed. "You need not weep now, Tante. It is over."

"I know, I know!" Fauna dabbed at her eyes. "These are happy tears only! You so deserve this, Aurora. All this happiness."

Briar forced a smile to accept the well-wishes graciously.

The door opened with a bang and Merryweather toddled in, a tray of cookies spinning on magic in front of her.

She stopped behind Briar and gave the gown ensemble a judgmental flick of her eyes.

"It should have been blue," she muttered.

Flora held her wand poised, a threat. "Bespell this gown, and spend the rest of your life as a flea."

Merryweather gave Flora a horrified stare. "I am *evolved* now. Unlike *some* of us, throwing about such vile threats in front of the *queen.* Try these cookies—I am undecided. The tea is cold! Why is no one feasting? Her gown fits, doesn't it? Away with you. I'll get her out of it!"

She made quick work of ushering Flora, Fauna, and the queen to the little table, and while they set about arranging the tea, Merryweather swept over to Briar in moderate privacy.

At the flick of Merryweather's wand, the gown began to lift, and as it sank back onto the dressing mannequin, Merryweather cut a look up at Briar.

"Your friend is fine," she said.

Briar's heart lurched. With relief? Why did it not feel like a weight was lifted? "You're sure? Is she—"

Merryweather pocketed her wand and worked the laces of the kirtle with her fingers. "She was laughing at a banquet table, somewhere fine and grand. She's moved up in the world as well, it seems."

Briar blinked down at her aunt. "A banquet table? Where?"

"My magic did not see. Or could not, rather. I do have limitations, unfortunately."

Briar had hoped to find sense in this, a reason why Frieda had left. But why, *how*, would she have come to be somewhere *fine and grand*? She had talent too, like Briar; perhaps she was there on her skill? Performing for some grand lord?

Just as Briar had always dreamed. Traveling, singing in far-off places. Briar was the dreamer. Frieda was the practical one. Frieda had never wanted that. She had wanted Ben, and Hausach, and a steady, reliable life.

Briar caught sight of herself in the mirror, looking miserable.

"She is safe," Merryweather reiterated. "And happy. Rest on that."

Briar gripped her aunt's hand and squeezed. "Thank you."

Dressing gown back on, she sat at the table with the queen and her aunts, and they all idly talked of the wedding, and of the gown, and of nothing at all of consequence, and Briar felt the mirror at her back. The image of Princess Aurora in that wedding gown, watching, waiting, ever ready to overcome her.

• • •

Ben was in the sword ring, getting soundly annihilated by Phillip.

Briar leaned on the wooden posts, her terra-cotta kirtle brushing the sand under her thin shoes, both of which would earn her stern chastisement for getting dirty. But her watchers were occupied with some issue regarding flowers, and so she had slipped, no, *vaulted* away.

Ben toppled backward, practice sword skittering away, and unleashed a torrent of curses so foul that even the seasoned soldiers near the barracks gave him looks of horror.

"New boy!" one snapped. "Princess about! Straighten up!"

Ben looked upside down to where the man pointed at Briar.

"I beg your pardon, fair lady," he said. "I would not dream of sullying your delicate ears so profusely."

Briar had taught him at least two of those curses.

"Off with his head, I think, Prince Phillip," she ordered. "You did try to make something of this one, but he's a lost cause, I'm afraid."

Phillip grabbed Ben's arm and hauled him up. "Oh, I don't know about that. He very nearly disarmed me moments ago."

"I *did*?" piped Ben.

"No."

Ben's gaze went dull. "That was cold."

Phillip walked to where Briar stood, the fence between them. His linen shirt was stuck to his skin with sweat, showing none-too-subtly the contours of muscles across his arms and chest, and his face shone, eyes bright with physical exertion.

She really should watch him train more often.

"What brings you here?" Phillip asked with a half grin, no doubt noting her eyes on him, the flush on her cheeks. "Not that I dislike the interruption. Would that it happened more, in fact."

"It might," Briar said, and a deluge of self-hatred surged over her at how high and squeaky her voice had gotten.

Burn these feelings right to ashes, honestly.

Did he have to be so impossibly good-looking?

She had never had a chance of composure, honestly.

"I need to speak to Ben," she said quickly, against Phillip's too-pleased-with-himself smirk.

"Ah. Of course. No other reason for being down here?"

"None. It is a grotesque place. Nothing at all of interest to look at."

"I mistook your repulsion for gawking, then."

"Yes, you did. I am a princess, sir; I do not *gawk*."

"Not today, no. Come back when it is hotter. We fight shirtless then, and perhaps we'll find you something to truly gawk at."

Oh, *unfair*.

She knew the look her face took on. Or she could imagine, at least, based on the way Phillip broke his teasing with a victorious, gleaming smile.

Heat lit her cheeks. She bit her lip to stifle her exasperated grin and lurched to the side, to see Ben putting his practice sword away across the ring. "Benedikt! Your lord is debauched. Come save me."

Phillip laughed and walked away, heading for a trough of water.

He took a full bucket of it and dumped it over his head, shirt as good as gone, showing how very, very many muscles were in his back, and Briar's whole mind went to a white-hot flash.

He dropped the bucket casually, looked over his shoulder even more confidently.

And winked at her.

Oh, burn *him* to ashes, too.

This would be the game, then?

She gave him an unamused grimace, and he grinned and hopped the fence of the training ring in one graceful arc, which, given his current clothing situation and the sheer agility in his movements, was the final weight on the teetering scale of her self-control. Not that she could *do* anything about it here, though, *princess* and all.

She would marry that man in two days.

There would have to be a way she could torment him equally before then. Or on that day, even, all throughout the ceremony. She'd think on it. Unlikely a bucket of water could be involved.

Ben came up to her and grinned. "I do believe," he said, "that you are infatuated with your betrothed, Bri."

"Hardly. We detest each other, isn't it obvious? Can barely stand to be in the same room."

"Oh, I've been in the same room as you two far too often now, and the only thing detestable about it is how badly you both clearly want to rip off each other's clothes."

Briar chirped, but they were more or less alone, the nearest soldiers back by the barracks. And so she laughed. "Consider it payback for all those times you and Frieda—"

Her words fell short.

Ben's teasing dimmed, too. He sniffed and ran the back of his hand across his nose.

"What did you need?" he asked, stonier.

Briar kicked at the dirt. "I had one of my aunts check in on her," she said. "Using magic."

Ben's hands knotted at his sides. He said nothing.

"She's safe." Briar made herself look up at him. "She's in a castle, somewhere."

She didn't say that Frieda had been laughing, *happy*. It had gutted Briar to know that; it would destroy Ben that Frieda was off without him, and not only okay with it but joyful.

Ben sniffed again and looked at the sky over Briar's head. "Well. Good. Is that all?"

"Ben—"

"I should get back to training."

He jogged off across the ring, and left Briar wilted by the fence.

She started to follow him around the fence, when an uproar near the front gate of the castle stopped her.

Shouting. A chaos of voices, all pinched in worry, and in a flash, she took off, skirts in one hand. Soldiers left the barracks after her, some calling out for her to stop—but she was already around the corner as they gained on her.

By the castle's grand front entrance, around the fountain of gray stone, a messenger stood in the stirrups of his horse's saddle. He held a scroll, and he was trying to read it, but the overlap of shouting concern from the castle staff and nobility around him drowned out everything.

Finally, a trumpet sound hit the air, silencing the crowd.

The messenger flinched at it but nodded his thanks.

"An announcement from the seat of the empire," he began.

Briar felt a presence on her right. Without looking, she leaned into him, feeling Phillip's solidity against her arm. His hand rested on her hip, and she did glance then to see that he had changed into a dry tunic, although his face was still flushed and his hair damp.

"I bring news from Frankfurt," the messenger continued, drawing her back. "One week ago, the emperor of our most glorious Holy Roman Empire journeyed into the arms of heaven."

The crowd gasped as one, and voices began in earnest again, but softer at least, hung with shocked sorrow.

"In one month's time, the council of Prince Electors will begin the process of selecting our new esteemed emperor," the messenger shouted. "Candidates are to put themselves forth to Frankfurt before such time."

He sank back into the saddle and wheeled his horse around, and the crowd broke, shouting again, panic and speculation and wails of grief.

Briar waited for reaction in her chest. A wash of feeling. But she had been an Austrian peasant, no more attached to the emperor than she was to her own king. The Holy Roman Empire was composed of dozens of territories, duchies to kingdoms to bishoprics and more, and though the emperor controlled the overarching territory, the individual rulers were far more present in the lives of the peasantry. Even so, Briar had not known what King Stefan looked like until she saw him after she awoke from her curse. She had not known the emperor, or cared at all for him—why would she feel anything for his death?

But a bridge built out before her, connecting this moment to the next.

Candidates.

The process of selecting our new esteemed emperor.

"Briar, we should go," said Phillip, angling them toward the castle. "Our fathers will be in discussion."

She gaped up at him. "They wouldn't put themselves up for emperor, would they?"

But she knew, in the set of his fear, that was precisely what he thought.

CHAPTER FOUR

King Stefan's throne room was where Briar had been reunited with her parents.

She and Phillip had descended the stairs from the tower, him bloodied and beaten and exhausted from the fight with Maleficent, her shocked and reeling from the upheaval of all she had known. But she had clung to his arm, clung with everything she had, because he was the sole thing in this castle that she knew.

It was that way again, Briar clinging to Phillip's arm, the two of them standing off to the side while Stefan paced before his throne. Leah sat on hers, hands demurely in her lap, unreactive. Phillip's father, Hubert, the king of Lorraine, was on a padded bench, his face gaunt and sweaty from an ailment that had been working him for weeks.

"And when did the emperor die?" Stefan clarified with one of his councilors.

"A week past, Your Majesty."

Stefan paced. "Candidates? What do we know yet of others?"

"Nothing, sire."

"That will not do. Send messengers out, to Frankfurt first—inquire who has put themselves up. What think you, Hubert? Who will step forward?"

Hubert's jowls swayed as his face went severe in revulsion. "Matilda of Bavaria, surely."

"She can try," Stefan scoffed, "but she is hated too strongly. They never did prove that she did not kill her late husband, but all know she did. And the whole of the empire has seen her constant attempts to invade Austria. She is a warlord, and she will win no favors with the Electors."

All knew the process for choosing an emperor: The position was not hereditary, and each one was chosen after a three-week process of candidates putting themselves forward to a committee of Prince Electors, who then cast votes and selected the next emperor. Thinking of Electors siding with Matilda of Bavaria was unpleasant, but it wasn't necessarily what now made Briar frown; in her experience, from what she had heard in Hausach, Austria instigated as many fights with Bavaria as Bavaria did with Austria. Bavaria was known to be far more aggressive when provoked, though, razing villages on the border without mercy or hesitation.

Frieda had known more about the war goings-on than Briar did. She had a mind for it, loved games of strategy, discussing where troops should go and what weaknesses were on either side. More than once Rolf had commented that Frieda should run off to join the front.

But they saw the aftermath of Bavaria's aggression, even in sleepy Hausach. Soldiers returned wounded, limbs missing, eyes ghostly. It sickened Briar every time Frieda spoke of battle strategy. The war had hurt the people of their village, of their country. How dare she talk about it like it was a clever game?

Frieda, though, had been as offended by Briar's offense. *War is inevitable*, she had argued. *And pretending otherwise is a fantasy that will only get more people hurt. But learning the strategy of it, accepting the game and conquering it? That is what will save lives.*

As though either of them had ever truly thought their opinions would matter.

Now here Briar was, in a throne room with two kings.

"Bavaria is the second-largest territory in the Holy Roman Empire after Austria, Stefan," Hubert said. "Their heft and wealth may be enough to make the Electors forget."

"Then they will be reminded repeatedly. No, no, who will be candidates of *merit*—"

And they began to toss out names Briar did not know, kings and princes and queens and more, all who might put themselves forth in Frankfurt in a month.

Briar glanced at Phillip, who had not moved. The room had been cleared of all but the essential few, and Briar knew the fairies were up on a balcony above, watching, listening.

Finally, Stefan stopped his pacing and looked down at Hubert. "We would make a strong play, then," he said definitively.

Hubert gave a hearty laugh. "*You* would make a strong play, my friend. A gout-riddled old codger like me would be laughed out of the election! No, do not try to argue. I am not too proud to admit when I am best set aside. After the wedding, Lorraine will fully support your play, Stefan. The unity of our kingdoms behind your leadership and reputation? There will be no candidate who could compare."

The breath left Briar's lungs in a rush.

Phillip put his hand over hers on his arm and squeezed.

"Thank you, Hubert," Stefan said. "You honor me."

Emperor. Her father would become *emperor.* The Holy Roman Empire operated as a bundle of principalities, city-states, kingdoms like Austria, and more, with one emperor at the top, keeping the illusion of control over the chaotic lot of them.

She had scarcely begun figuring out how to be a princess of Austria. And now. Now—

The queen stood from her throne and fell into a deep curtsy. "My king," she said, and it set off the vassals bowing, until Briar and Phillip alone remained upright.

Phillip tipped at the waist, tugging Briar's arm to follow suit.

Briar remained standing until Stefan faced her. To his credit, he noted her discomfort immediately, and his face went soft.

"Aurora, my dawn," he said, hands opening to her, but not in an offer of a hug, merely an expression of kindness. "Do not fear. This will not interrupt your wedding plans."

Her . . . her *wedding* plans?

That was what he thought she feared? Not the immense responsibility he had chosen to put on her in declaring his candidacy?

Phillip nudged her gently, and she descended into a curtsy, holding herself there, holding, until Stefan left the room, trailed by his vassals, the queen, and Hubert leaning on his valet.

Briefly, the room was empty of all but Phillip and Briar, until the doors would be opened for the normal courtly functions to resume. The fairies might have been lingering, too, but Briar didn't care. She used that pause to take Phillip's hand. With no one else around, he scooped her up immediately. No question or need to speak. He clasped her to him and she grabbed his shoulders and let him take her weight.

"Emperor," she whispered.

"It does not pass hereditarily," Phillip assured her. "It will not pass to you. You remain Austria's, and soon Lorraine's."

"A waterfall traded for rapids. And how will his responsibilities not fall upon us? We will be the weight behind his throne. Any conflicts he enters will first go to us. And while he is ruling the empire, will we be expected to immediately become king and queen here?"

She was spiraling, thoughts racing too fast to catch, breath not far behind, air going in, getting trapped, not coming out.

Phillip hugged her tighter, almost bruising, and it grounded her, the rigidity, the force of him. "Breathe. I'm here, Briar, and I'm not going anywhere. We're in this together, you and I."

Together. The word was a crack in curtains, light streaming into darkness.

"Together," she echoed, feeling it on her tongue, and she pressed her face to the incline of his shoulder.

He made a rumble of assent. "Our duties combined are to our kingdoms, but my individual duty first is to you. Your happiness, remember? That is my sole focus."

She pulled back to look up at him. The doors were opening,

people beginning to reenter, but she wasn't done with him, not by a long way.

Eyes watery, she touched his cheek. "Mine too. I am yours as much as you are mine, Phillip, and I desire your happiness. I want to be your pillar as well. Do not let my fears prevent you from voicing your own to me."

The spasm that fled quickly across his face told her that he was doing precisely that.

She had been so selfish. Stupidly, foolishly, she had let her problems grow too large and suffocate the fact that he was worried, too.

The room filled around them with nobles who whispered and gawked, but Briar cared nothing for them, for any of them; all she cared for, would ever care for this much, was the man whose jaw she took in her hands.

"Together?" she repeated, a question.

He dropped his forehead to hers. "Together," he answered, a promise.

• • •

The night before the wedding, the dreams came upon her tenfold.

The woman in the blue dress, standing on a dais, watching a kneeling man being crowned. Nothing terrifying about that, at least, but it came over and over, that crown lowering, rising again, lowering, rising—

The woman who had watched the five shooting stars, standing in a massive hall, and words ringing around her, "marriage" and "proposal," and the image of a snarling, cruel man.

The woman who had snuffed the fire was now seated at a long table, a handful of disapproving faces turned her way, eyes sharp and cunning, as though they knew she would falter, they knew she would fail, and they hungered for it.

Through every dream, Maleficent's laughter curled, the cackle that had led Briar up the stone steps to the spindle. Laughing, laughing.

"What will you do with it, Briar, Aurora? What will you do?"

• • •

Briar had thought she was becoming moderately accustomed to opulence, what with all the magnificent things she had seen these past weeks—but none of it had prepared her for the throne room's decorations the day of her wedding.

The morning had been a whirlwind from the moment she arose—makeup and hairstyling, dressing and primping and pinning—so as she found herself standing alone outside the wide open doors of the castle's grandest room, her aunts rushing off to join the front of the audience, Briar came into her body as if waking up just then. She gasped in a serrated breath, *knowing* she was awake, but the view of the throne room was too spectacular to be anything but a dream.

No cathedral had been good enough for the wedding, Stefan had declared, and so they had gotten the blessing of the priest to host the ceremony here. The queen, in a rare act of actual personality, had said that cathedrals in *Vienna* would have been good enough, but luckily for Briar, Stefan still did not seem at all inclined to leave.

Briar could not imagine any cathedral grander than the transformation of this throne room.

The gray stone walls and floor were a muted backdrop for catastrophic rainbows of color. Flowers in every hue climbed the high, high walls, draped along balconies with ripples of white-and-blue fabric. Pennants showing the symbols of Austria and Lorraine hung from the ceiling while finely woven carpets covered the floor, glinting with hints of jewels and threads of gold. Everywhere the guests stood was a riot of fine gowns and vests and hats and headdresses—silk and satin, rubies and diamonds, gold and silver. Each corner was a new onslaught of wealth and beauty.

She was almost grateful for the garishness; it let her forget, for a moment, the nerves that had plagued her all morning.

Briar stood staring at the room in taut numbness, trying to orient herself.

The only place *to* orient herself was at the end of the long, long aisle. Distantly, she could make out Phillip, and near the head of the crowd to her right was Ben.

Not Frieda.

Frieda had been planning her own wedding. She and Ben had been saving and saving. It would be small, at the church where Frieda had grown up, and Briar knew she'd hated that, all the memories there of her loneliness and hunger. So Briar had been working with Ben to arrange to have the wedding in the forest, under the light through the trees, in the clearing where they'd practiced their songs.

This was so very different. In too many ways. But not different enough in others, and Briar's chest ached.

An uproar of trumpets had her jerking out of her thoughts, making her heart ricochet, bringing her back to awareness. She was alone at the end of this long aisle on her wedding day.

Her wedding day.

Nerves flickered again, agitated butterfly wings, and Briar braced herself and walked, a peasant bard in the lavish maroon silk gown, now fitted to her body precisely. She was surrounded on either side by lords and ladies and other fine, highborn people. She did not think about how in that moment she looked like Princess Aurora, not Briar Rose.

The doors shut behind her and music began to strain the air. Oh, she hated whatever composition this was. Briar had tried to explain how she'd loved music in Hausach, and the queen had promptly hummed *That's lovely, dear*, and chosen this tune without consulting her.

She'd made it halfway down the aisle when the weight of her gown and the heat of the room with all its bodies became too much, too overwhelming, and she had to stop.

Movement at the edge of the crowd yanked her gaze. And there was Ben, with a smile, and the moment she looked at him, he pulled a ridiculous face that had her tension cracking.

How could he do that still? Wasn't he thinking about his own abandoned wedding with Frieda?

Thank you, she mouthed to him.

He inclined his head. *Keep walking, you fool*, he mouthed back, with a nod at the aisle.

She took another step, and realized the simplicity in that moment. She needn't think of everything that awaited her all at once; in this moment, she only needed to do one thing. Walk.

She could see Phillip clearly now.

If her gown was the epitome of wedding fashion—as she had

been repeatedly told by Flora, who did not think Briar was sufficiently grateful for it—then Phillip's outfit was its equal. A tunic of maroon velvet set off by hems of gold, glistening black boots, a sweeping cape of deepest hunter green. His hair was neatly styled, catching light from the windows and the chandeliers so streaks of red showed in his brown locks. He had a sword at his side, one for ceremony—but Briar looked twice, and no, it was the Sword of Truth. The one Flora had created for him, the one that had defeated Maleficent.

She could not imagine he had chosen to wear that, with how uncomfortable any mention of that day made him. Indeed, he was not touching it at all, holding his arm stiff so it did not rest on the hilt.

Briar's pace increased. Both because she wanted to end their discomfort as soon as possible, let this performance be over, and because she wanted to be married to him.

She wanted to be married to him quite extraordinarily.

Suddenly, little else mattered.

The king and queen sat off to the side, where their thrones had been repositioned to make space on the dais for Briar, Phillip, and the priest. Hubert had his own throne next to theirs, and the fairies stood beside him. Fauna wept openly with joy. Flora eyed her sister with distaste. Merryweather's nose was scrunched in a grin.

Briar stopped, curtsied at them all, her blond hair dipping down across her shoulder.

She ascended the dais and stood next to Phillip.

He took her hand.

She jolted, surprised—he wasn't supposed to touch her yet. But she smiled up at him, and as the priest's voice boomed through the throne room, a speech about the holiness of marriage, Briar twined her fingers with Phillip's.

He leaned close to her, his nose brushing her ear. "You are beautiful," he whispered.

The room was hot in early summer, and this gown was thick and heavy, but still her body flushed with even more heat. "Wooing me still, Sir Knight, though we are at our marriage altar? If I didn't know better, I'd say you were quite taken with me."

He pulled her hand to his chest. "Fully taken. Enraptured, even."

"It's this gown, isn't it?"

His eyes flashed. She had been joking, but ah, she was not wrong.

Her grin went a little wicked. "Let us hope it is not merely the gown after all, for getting out of it is one of my top priorities after we're married."

She watched his face redden, and she beamed—her own victory. She had not even needed a bucket of water after all.

The priest guided them through the ceremony, reciting vows that they repeated, grinning more and more like fools. Not that it was ridiculous, but that it was so very much *not* ridiculous, and though they were in a room filled with people, Briar's whole focus narrowed to Phillip's crooked grin.

A valet presented a ring, and Phillip slid the thin gold band onto Briar's finger.

The priest, arms spread out over their heads, projected his voice to the room. "Peace and blessings be upon this couple. Let them kiss, and they are wed."

The word "kiss" had hardly left the priest's mouth before Phillip had tugged Briar to him, hand catching the back of her head and lips connecting with hers. She laughed against him, and he laughed, too, a disordered interlocking of smiles, as music began again, and the crowd cheered.

Briar looped her arms around his neck and kissed him properly, his hands strong against her, and it fell over her like a torrent of rain. He was her husband now. *Her* husband. Her own, and whatever came next for her, he would be there, too, and she likewise for him.

Her laughter balled in the base of her gut and she rested her head against his temple, holding there as he stroked her hair behind her ear.

"Together," he whispered, a moment before she could say the same thing.

She bit her lip, unable to speak beneath the winding of love for him, wondering if it was possible for a body to implode from that strain, knowing she wouldn't mind, wouldn't fight it.

On the edge of her happiness, poking through the crowd's applause and the watching eyes of the king and queen, came a sudden, percussive thud, the doors that Briar had entered through slamming open.

"Oh my. Am I late?"

Terror charged from Briar's head to her toes, but that voice was not Maleficent's. It was a shadow of it, though, wicked and conniving as she had been, and it grabbed the attention of the room in a painful listing from celebratory to confused and leery.

Briar shifted, still in Phillip's arms; he, though, stayed facing her, breathing shallowly into the space against her neck.

She did not recognize the figure standing at the end of the room. A woman in full plate armor, the breastplate showing blue-and-white diamond shapes, to display a thin gold band on her head, a mimic of a crown. She was alone, which was all the more odd, given the air of menace that palpitated off of her.

"Not Maleficent," Briar whispered to Phillip. He still had not moved. "Not— It isn't her. Phillip?"

Finally, he jerked upright, pupils contracting, but he did not let her go. He looked down the aisle, and his face twitched with confusion.

"Matilda of Bavaria," he said absently.

Briar's body went cold.

No one from Bavaria had been invited to their wedding.

Immediately, the mood of the room transformed further. What Austrian guards had been positioned at the edges of the room moved forward as best they could, but the packed crowd of guests kept them mostly at the outskirts, the guards' weapons now drawn. It was only Matilda who stood in the open doorway, though in armor, and her mere presence was threat enough.

Stefan was up, in the center of the aisle before Briar and Phillip. "You were not invited," he boomed. "Leave peaceably; this is our joyous day."

Matilda laughed. It was so like Maleficent's cackle that Briar unconsciously stepped forward, out of Phillip's arms, wanting to face it, to face *her,* because last time she had been confronted by such a person, she had been defenseless and bound by magic and unable to fight back.

Whatever was happening now, she would *not* be helpless. Not again.

"I missed the wedding, did I?" Matilda looked beyond Stefan, to Briar and Phillip, and clicked her tongue. "They are married? That does change things. Blame this course of action, then, on the resiliency of your soldiers outside, and how they delayed my interruption."

There was further noise. Boots marching, armor clanking, and in the entryway behind Matilda, soldiers appeared, all in the same blue-and-white diamond markings.

Briar trapped a breath in her lungs, fingers clenching and unclenching. She had never held a weapon in her life, yet right now, she twitched for a sword, though what good could she do with one?

The Austrian guards reacted as well, moving with purpose not for the doors, but toward Stefan, Briar, those clustered by the dais—but what of the guests? Who would protect them? A few cried out in alarm, realizing that they were quickly becoming an obstacle between two rallying armies, and ripples of unease sent bodies jostling into one another as reality broke in slow fragments.

This was an attack.

Bavaria was here to *attack*.

Music was no longer playing. Had it been playing the whole ceremony?

Someone screamed as the guests shoved each other harder, harder, until hysterical scrambling began, people trying to escape through the doors at the sides of the room. The Austrian guards were still too far from the dais, and the sudden intensity of the crowd hindered them further, ever more frantic guests heaving into them, panic rising in a sharp, cresting onslaught.

The rattle of noise set Briar's heart racing even more, but what could she do? *What could she do?* She was helpless, again. She was at another's mercy, *again*, and she felt that invasion over every part of her body, the prickle on her skin and the tension in her shoulders and the shiver through her muscles.

She could speak. She could say something, beg Matilda to—to *stop*. It was a mistake for her to be here. Only more bloodshed would come, because Austria would retaliate, and then Bavaria would fight back, and on it would go, it had to *stop*—

Stefan's hands bunched against his long robes. "You would *dare* invade my kingdom outright? This is foolishness, Matilda, even for you!"

Matilda took a step forward. "What is foolishness is you believing I would allow Austria to absorb Lorraine without a fight. And now you will position yourself as emperor? You must see how that will not do, Stefan."

They shouted at each other over the clear aisle, the center parting for them as both sides of the crowd fought to exit.

"To arms!" Stefan bellowed. "To arms!"

"Since I am too late to stop Austria from merging with Lorraine," Matilda declared, "then I will simply have to prevent you from becoming emperor."

She lifted her hand and brought it down.

A signal, Briar realized, a beat before the room shifted, color and light and rainbow flowers, then stone at her back.

Phillip had grabbed her, slammed her to the floor behind the dais, using it as partial cover.

Briar drew a shaking breath, fixed her eyes on him—and the room erupted.

The terrified screams went feral, agonized shrieks, chaos, and bodies running and soldiers pouring in, enemy or ally, weapons clashing. It was all noise, noise and the crash of a battle slamming into this finely appointed throne room, gold-embossed terror.

Ben was at Phillip's side, his face gaunt. "What do we— Oh no."

His eyes were over the dais.

Briar whirled, pushed herself up to see, Phillip's hands on her hips.

The room was bedlam, too many people scrambling for cover and escape, the flash of swords. The fairies flew up to the corner, doing their best to throw magic to help innocents get away. As Briar watched, many of those innocents simply . . . collapsed.

At first, she thought, *Are the fairies magicking them to sleep? Why?*

But then she realized. Disjointedly, slowly: *No. They have been struck down.*

There, a sword bloodied; there, an ax being swung; there, a burst of blood in the air, like a scatter of dust caught in the wind, droplets raining on frantic wedding guests who cried, struggled—none of these people were fighters.

Briar spotted Hubert and the queen being hauled from the room, Leah's lips parted in a wail that was such a contrast to her usual decorum that Briar stared at her, locked on that oddity.

She followed the queen's gaze.

And she saw.

The panic of the room congealed.

The king lay on the floor, fallen precisely where he had stood in the aisle, an arrow through his neck. A puddle of blood, perfectly circular, soaked his head, an echo of the golden crown still firmly on his dark hair.

More soldiers charged in, those in Lorraine's colors now, three mighty kingdoms warring in this confined space. The Bavarian contingent was still mostly by the door; they were not fighting to advance, and indeed, seemed to be in retreat, death in their wake. And no wonder: They had come to stop the wedding, and if not to do that, then to stop Stefan from becoming emperor.

Sweat broke across Briar's skin, her eyes flashing around the room as a swell of horrified mania overcame her. This invasion was not Maleficent, but it was the same, a power exerted over Briar's life with its own will, imposing itself on her by force. And not just on her, but on these people, the guests of *her* wedding, and the soldiers sworn to protect *her*. Bavaria had chosen to harm them.

She would not be helpless again.

She did not know what she would do, but she started to rise, a small, subconscious part of her pushing herself up to cross over the dais.

Phillip made a choked sound of alarm and ripped her back down next to him. "Briar—"

"Release me, Phillip!"

"No." She had never heard him speak like that. Panic and utter,

desperate fear, his eyes wide pools. "No. Briar. You can't—you can't go—"

Briar sank down next to him, her fingers going to his face as her determination abruptly shifted its focus, broad to narrow, the battle to her husband. "Phillip?"

He was breathing hard. Harder. Quick, insufficient sips, and Briar glanced over him to lock eyes with Ben, who shook his head, fear turning his own face white.

"I won't," Briar tried, rubbing Phillip's jaw with her thumb, trying to get him to look at her. He was, though; he just wasn't *seeing* her, and that distance grabbed her lungs with relentless hands and twisted, wrenching the air from her body.

"You can't go," he said again, a prayer. "You can't. Please—"

"It's all right," she told him. "I'm here. I'm here, and I won't leave."

The noise of the room was settling. Fewer weapons clashing and piercing screams; instead there was sobbing, voices barking orders.

The Bavarians had been pushed out.

Or they had left willingly. They were the victors, after all.

Briar pulled Phillip to her, and after a moment, his muscles gave, and he yanked her into his chest and held her in a tangled twist behind the dais. His tension fled in violent shudders that she tried to counter by clinging to him, pressure and relief, and he began taking deeper breaths.

"Shh," she whispered. "It's all right. I'm here. I won't leave. It's all right."

He only stayed like that for a moment—just one beat too long for Briar not to worry—and then he shifted back, face flushed.

He said nothing. Wouldn't look at her now, his cheeks no longer drained and pale but a brilliant red as he swallowed hard.

"Phillip—"

But he didn't look at her, still, and instead peered over the dais, at the throne room.

Despair descended on him in a thick cloud, and it tore Briar in half—she needed him to be all right, but what had happened here needed her, too.

"Phillip," she tried again.

"I'm fine," he said, but it came out strangled as he stood quickly and helped her to her feet.

Ben rose too, silent and severe behind them, and he shared a look with Briar of concern, of unspoken, uncappable shock.

"Your father," Phillip said numbly. His eyes slammed shut.

Briar did not look down at the body again. Some of the court were around the king, weeping; others knelt over different fallen victims throughout the room.

The high walls and ceiling were still in order, flowers and decorations and banners untouched, as though nothing had happened. If she kept her eyes up, just up, the day had gone as intended.

She looked down, though, and reality was too surreal. Everything had unraveled so quickly that Briar was still struggling to make sense of that initial sound of the door opening—that thud of it against the wall—and Matilda—and an ax swinging—an arrow flying—whom had it struck?

The room's fine, jeweled carpet was now a resting place for mutilated guests and soldiers—and a king.

Tart bile rose in Briar's throat. She thought she was shaking, but when she looked, her hands were oddly still, her whole body motionless, numb.

One of the high-ranking vassals saw Briar rise. She was on the dais, so it made him look up at her.

Immediately, he dropped to one knee before her, and others followed suit, until those in the room who were able all bowed low.

Dread knotted in Briar's gut.

"The king is dead," one of the vassals declared, voice echoing. "Long live the queen."

CHAPTER FIVE

Stefan's council room was in tatters.

No, Briar's council room now, wasn't it?

She had not been crowned yet, though. Queen in name only.

Queen of Austria.

The Bavarian contingent had been small, swift, and effective. No grand army; they had come for the sole purpose of either stopping the wedding to prevent the unity of Austria and Lorraine, or stopping Stefan from making an attempt at becoming emperor with both Austria and Lorraine at his back.

They had succeeded in one goal, and then fled.

Briar sat at the head of a long table, staring down at the surface covered in maps of the Holy Roman Empire, some of Bavaria specifically, others of Austria, and willed herself to feel something.

All she could conjure was rancid terror over Phillip. Who sat at her right, his eyes on her face, his own concern for her pinching his features. How he could worry about *her* after his state in the throne room, she didn't know. Or, no, she *did* know, because this was *him*, honor and loyalty above all, and she loved him and all his dedication to her, but in this moment she wanted him to damn his honor and let her help him.

Even if he would, though, she was unable to.

The room held Stefan's five closest vassals. And the fairies, at the side of the room, silent and mourning. Ben was behind Phillip's chair, hands folded, eyes on the floor.

Queen Leah was in hysterics, apparently unable to be calmed; she had been sequestered to her rooms.

Hubert was similarly distraught and had been moved to his chamber as well, for his health.

One vassal turned to Briar. Lord Lehmann, who oversaw the troops in the castle. "This act cannot go unaddressed. I can have an army mobilized within the day, Your Majesty."

"You would attack Bavaria?" The words were ash in Briar's mouth.

Not *you.*

We.

Her.

Her first act as queen would be death?

"What other course is there?" Lehmann asked.

"There is subtlety!" another vassal countered. Lord Köning, who dealt in communications and diplomatic relations. "There are ways to react that do not bring more loss of life and all-out war!"

Yes, she thought. *Yes, that, whatever it is.*

Lehmann purpled, enraged—the vassals were all enraged—and Briar shoved to her feet.

"I will not condone a war," she said. That, at least, she could be sure of.

Did no one else hear how absurd this was, coming from her lips? As though she had any experience in these matters. As though she knew *anything*.

But she did know. She knew the families of the soldiers in Hausach. She knew them and their spouses and children. She knew the guests who had been at her wedding—she knew *of* them, at least. She knew the aftermath, how many of them were still soaking blood into her throne room floor. They'd had no choice. Those who lived under the powerful rarely did.

Briar would not, would *never*, condone endangering anyone.

Köning nodded, grim. "Then we move to declare another candidacy."

Briar blinked at him. "What do you mean?"

"Bavaria sought to prevent Austria from gaining even more power. But we are not without options for continuing the king's plans to bring the seat of the empire to Austria." His eyes fell on Phillip. "Prince Phillip would make a fine replacement."

Briar went stone stiff.

"His heroics would make him a candidate to be rivaled," Lehmann admitted. "Defeating the dragon, ridding Austria of the tyrant Maleficent, rescuing the king's daughter and breaking her curse—he has proven his valor beyond denial, to such glorious extent even Bavaria would have difficulty smearing his name."

Smearing his name? But Briar could not linger on that, for when she looked down at Phillip, his face was paling, whiter with each word Lehmann spoke. Strain in his jaw wrenched tighter and his chest fluttered with those too-short breaths again.

Defensive panic tugged hard on Briar's stomach, and she slammed her hand on the table to drag attention to her. "This is an Austrian matter. We should leave him out of this."

The room eyed her.

Uncomfortable, Köning tried, "He is Austrian now—"

"Why would we need to make a grasp for emperor still?" Briar asked honestly. "Why is that a goal we should have?"

Another awkward shift. Had she asked an obvious question? Possibly.

"To back down would be to let Bavaria's acts today be victorious."

It was not a vassal who had spoken but Flora.

Briar flipped a startled look at her. So did the vassals. But they deferred to Flora, respect evident in their softening postures.

She floated to the table, wings carrying her aloft as she gripped her wand like another attack was imminent.

"Stefan's candidacy would have been the only one strong enough to dissuade Matilda of Bavaria from becoming empress," Flora said.

Briar thought back. "When he spoke of it, he made it seem as though she would be dismissed."

Köning made a grunt of disagreement. "It was a possibility. Her reputation walks the line between fierce and warmongering. Depending on the Prince Electors, if they are the battle-loving sort, it would not be difficult for her to sway them."

A weight was slowly collecting in Briar's gut. "So she will be empress now?"

"The woman who invaded your country," Flora said, and her

voice was all sympathy, but none of it reached Briar. "The woman who killed your father."

The woman who had killed her king, Flora meant. For that was all that had happened today. The king had been murdered, and Briar reacted to it as she had the news of the emperor's death: a twinge of sorrow, then moving on.

What did sit with her, a welling iron tang, was the ease with which Matilda of Bavaria had invaded, assassinated the king, murdered wedding guests—and set that look in Phillip's eyes. It was foolish, perhaps, but *that* was the crux of Briar's growing foundation of action, that she wanted revenge not for her father's death but for Phillip's fear. For the terror wreaked on this castle and its people. For the disgust that yet another being had exacted its invasive will on her life, on her future, on innocents around her.

She had been helpless again. Matilda so easily could have murdered her, too. Or worse.

And the guests? Those who had been killed? *They* had been truly helpless. Briar, for all her station now, for all her power now, had done *nothing* to help those she was meant to safeguard.

If Bavaria came to have control of the Holy Roman Empire, then there would no longer be a third party to mediate its long-standing feud with Austria. The only thing that had ever kept the battles between Austria and Bavaria from growing to full wars had been the emperor's decisive intervention; now, Bavaria would have all the resources, all the strength. They would consume Austria—and Lorraine, too—without question or obstacle.

Austria would be laid waste, to blood and ruin. Everyone who lived here, everyone Briar knew and loved and was now destined to protect, would be thrown into helpless, indefinite turmoil.

Briar's hands curled into fists. Something new took root in her, and it was strong enough that it overpowered the corresponding kick of shock that she was capable of feeling this emotion.

Fury.

She was furious.

She had been terrified and hurt and scared and *weak*, ever since Maleficent's curse. She had been confused and lost and in pieces.

But she had not been angry.

Now she was.

"What about me?" she heard a version of herself say. Not Aurora. Not Briar Rose. This was new, and it was a wild part of her that spoke calmly and clearly.

Her eyes were on the table. But she felt Phillip look at her. Heard his intake of breath.

"What about you, Your Majesty?" Köning pressed.

"What about me for empress?"

The room went silent.

And it was Flora, still nearby, who released a sigh of hope. "Yes! Oh, *yes.* Think of the position! The exiled princess, recently reunited, only to lose her father in a brutal attack on her very wedding day. The sympathy alone will sway the Prince Electors."

"But not mere sympathy," Fauna added, hovering next to her sister. "Aurora grew up among the people. She has their knowledge, their heart. She brings experience beyond that of any other candidate."

"And with Stefan's resources . . ." Köning said, thinking aloud, and the room shifted from hesitant to considering.

Her chest bucked.

She did not want them to agree.

She did want them to agree.

She was split, split again, and she had been in pieces already, so what was she now? Shards, sharp, wicked shards, and her hands were bleeding on them.

Lehmann rose. The others at the table followed him, until all were standing, save for Phillip, who was stiff with shock.

The vassals bowed to her. "We will press forward with your coronation and alert Frankfurt to your candidacy," Köning said.

Briar nodded. She should thank them. They were her vassals now, her supporters.

"Thank you," she managed.

Her eyes met Ben's. He was a ghost, fully pale, but her eyes held on his and he gave a weak smile and he felt very, very far away.

She left the room in a rush.

Got paces down the hall.

And vomited in an alcove.

A hand touched her shoulder. It was not Phillip.

Merryweather.

Briar wiped her mouth on the sleeve of her wedding gown. "I am fine."

"Are you?"

She turned to her aunt, unsure of what expression she was showing. "I'm to be empress, so how could I not be? Princess to queen to empress. Next I shall make a play for God, I think."

She tried to laugh.

It came out croaking and wretched.

Merryweather magicked up a floating goblet and urged Briar to take it. She sipped minty water, cool and clean, and it washed away the sour tang in her mouth.

The goblet vanished as quick as it had come, and Merryweather gathered Briar into a hug, soft and warm and, for a moment, familiar.

"If it gives you comfort," Merryweather started, "you did the right thing."

Briar peeled back. "*How?* What part of this could be right?"

Gentle hands on her cheeks. Motherly, grounding, when Briar had never had much of either. "You limit yourself, Briar. You always have. Yes, much has happened that is unfair to you—but you are meant for so much more than you realize. Great things will come from you, I promise. Have faith in yourself."

Great things? She did not want great things. She wanted to sing in taverns and laugh with her friends and she wanted—

The door to the council room opened, and Phillip rushed out, sighting her immediately down the hall.

Merryweather released her without another word, and Briar ran to him. He met her and caught her in his arms.

But she pulled back almost instantly and looked up at him, studying him in the hall's low light. "Are you all right? Are you—"

"Am *I* all right?" He laughed, empty. "Briar, you did not have to do that. If you did it for me, to avoid my candidacy, you did not have to."

"It was only partly for you," she whispered. "I did it because I'm tired of not being in control of my own life. And this way, the move I make is my own."

She was so tired. Exhausted, inside and out, from her head to her soul. But she had spent too much time sleeping as it was; it was time for her to wake up, to reclaim her life, whatever that would look like now.

Phillip was tired, too. He swayed on his feet, his cheeks still a pallid gray. She put her hand to his jaw, but Köning and the other vassals had already flooded the hall, seen her, and moved in.

"Your Majesty, wait but a moment—plans must be made."

"The caravan to travel to Frankfurt will be arranged. But who should be with you?"

"The coronation can begin as soon as possible. When would you have it?"

Her head rang. Rang and rang and Briar closed her eyes, knotting her fingers with Phillip's. She pressed that tangle to her lips.

Then she turned to face the choice she had made—the first she had ever made for herself.

• • •

The next weeks passed in a dream. Which was, Briar thought, rather cruel, given that her dreams—nightmares—were coming upon her more and more in what infrequent sleep she managed.

They were always of the women she had seen while she'd been asleep under the curse. Women she did not know, only she did, for how often had she seen them in various states of fear or worry or strain? They were in positions of power, as she was; she saw them surrounded by advisers and supporters, but even with that help, they were tormented, as she was. Were they others Maleficent had cursed over the centuries? Whoever they were, they were surely meant to torture her, fragmented ghosts of her fate, and so she would not take them on, for she had plenty in her waking life that tortured her just fine.

Most horribly, she had been denied a wedding night with Phillip.

She should probably not have listed that as the *most horrible* thing that was happening to her, but she was greatly annoyed by its interruption and subsequent delays. Even their nightly meetings in the kitchen had taken a pause, first due to preparations for her coronation, and then due to the endless hours of chaos that came from becoming queen of a kingdom fractured by a regicide. Guards trailed her every move, fearful of another attack. And, when those duties did not keep her up until well past midnight, the electoral embassy that would escort her to Frankfurt was being planned, and preparations were being made for her campaign to become empress.

Seven Prince Electors would cast votes to name the new emperor of the Holy Roman Empire. The whole process would stretch over three weeks, during which time the Electors would meet with each candidate to get to know them, pose whatever questions they had, and judge their worth. Throughout those three weeks, there would be structured events—jousts and games, banquets and balls, all the typical pomp of the upper classes—but Briar had been warned that these events would be positioned to reveal the candidates' strengths and weaknesses. Games would be designed to reveal cunning and mental prowess; banquets would be designed to reveal social standing and command of attention; jousts to show the strength of one's soldiers; and so on.

Stefan's vassals—no, Briar's; damn, but she still had trouble believing the claim was hers now—had been coaching her in the ways of campaigning, how best to present herself and her strengths. When first they had sat down with her to go over such things, she had laughed, because weren't her strengths the very things they had told her already? That she would win sympathy for her father being murdered so soon after she'd reunited with him, and that she had intimate knowledge of life *among the people.* How would she *present* those things except by simply entering a room?

So it stunned Briar silent when Köning handed her a list that had been decided on by all the vassals, debated over in a prior meeting and compiled so they agreed on her best qualities:

Self-assured

Thoughtful

Passionate

Envisions a peaceful future for the empire

And the one that set her mind spinning, dazed:

Fearless

She looked up at the vassals. "Truly?"

Köning, already shuffling through a stack of parchment for his next set of notes, half looked at her. "Which one, Your Majesty?"

All of them.

They saw her this way?

They barely knew her. They had only seen her in passing these few weeks, had only interacted with her on the periphery. So were these attributes truly hers, or were they things her vassals *hoped* she could emulate?

Fauna, who hovered just behind Briar's chair, placed a hand on her shoulder. "You have displayed all these traits in your time here,

Rose," she whispered softly. "They honor you by recognizing what you are."

She used the name that Briar's aunts had called her by. That *only* Briar's aunts had called her by. Briar Rose had been her full name, but Frieda had thought Briar sounded more interesting, thorny and sharp, and so Briar had acquiesced to being Briar because she had been about six and had wanted so desperately to be *interesting.*

But she realized, hearing Fauna say *Rose* now, that the split of who she was had happened even earlier than she had realized. As a child, she had been *Briar* to some and *Rose* to her aunts and *Briar Rose* to even more—

Had there ever been a time in her life when she had simply *existed*?

Briar sat down the paper with her *best qualities*, eyes blurring as she read it over, and over.

Were these the traits of Briar?

Or of Aurora?

Which would best win empress?

She looked up at her vassals, who had fallen silent, watching her, waiting for her reaction.

Köning leaned forward, sincerity in his dark eyes. "This list is not of things you should force yourself to display. They are qualities we have noted you display innately, and so we will work to enhance what is already natural to you."

"Far easier to do so," Lehmann added, "than to choose qualities you do not have and force you to play a part. The Prince Electors will see through any act."

Briar nodded absently. *Self-assured. Thoughtful. Passionate. Envisions a peaceful future for the empire.*

Fearless.

"Thank you," she said. "I shall strive to continue displaying these traits to the fullest of my abilities. For Austria."

She smiled and they returned it with gracious bows.

Briar felt, in that moment, that no matter who she would need to be in the future, maybe these weren't just Stefan's vassals after all.

Maybe they really were hers, too.

• • •

Campaign preparations aside, as queen, she did begin pressing to understand how she could extend Austria's resources to counter the inequities she knew of in Hausach. She would not wait to stanch the helplessness she knew people suffered under now, and no one could dismiss her requests for such things anymore, though her vassals seemed confused about why she would ask for reports about the poorest areas of Austria as compared to the wealthiest, advice on the ways they could address those imbalances, and a list of the most common complaints made by village leaders. That was her only solace, that she was at least *trying* to improve life for the people she knew and loved.

She had power now. The *most* power in Austria. And she would use that power to help the powerless.

After a quick, private coronation—now husband and wife *and* king and queen, with no time to celebrate either—Phillip left to escort his father home to Lorraine, and so he was not even under the same roof as her for days that stretched to weeks. Soldiers accompanied him, no chances taken now, though Briar doubted Bavaria would strike again; they had been successful, and even if they heard of her candidacy for emperor, would they truly fear her? Ben went with Phillip, squire that he was, and *that* was a strange, irksome blow, that he was now more tied to Phillip than to her. Briar tried not to be too annoyed at feeling abandoned, but she had been, and she was bristling and anxious and so very, very alone.

She had her aunts. She had the Queen Mother now, who had not spoken a word since Stefan's death, clothed in mourning black and utterly unresponsive.

But she was alone, and she was terrified, and the date of her departure for Frankfurt loomed.

She almost asked Merryweather to check in again on Frieda. To reassure her that her friend was still well. To see if, maybe, Frieda was as alone as Briar, and then she would have reason to seek her out—

But she did not ask. Could not allow herself to.

Peasant to princess to queen to empress.

To spring from the first to the second was an act of God. To leap all four in a single year—it was *impossible.*

And yet here she was, living her impossible life, Briar Rose the peasant bard, Aurora the princess, some new furious woman the queen.

What version of her would rise up once she became empress?

How many different versions of one person could she hold within her body until she broke from the strain?

• • •

Her electoral embassy left the castle in an unintentional parade. That was the natural pomp that came with being queen, Briar had found; where she went, finery followed, and her dozens of carriages, mounted soldiers, attendants, and carts were beset with well-wishers who lined the road all the way past Hausach.

She watched out the window of her carriage as the procession made its way through the village, noting faces she recognized in the crowd. Rolf and his wife, a few from Ben's family. People she had grown up alongside and loved, and now she watched them through a gilded window frame.

Whatever she met in Frankfurt, whatever challenges arose in this campaign, *this* was what she was fighting for, that there might not be such a disparity between her position and theirs. That it might not be such an impossible thing for a peasant girl to be a leader. That a little girl might not be shocked to see real meat on her table, as though it was some rare, special thing.

She left silent promises on the road as they passed, and off her impressive retinue went—bound to meet up with Phillip's caravan when they were outside Heidelberg, one day from Frankfurt.

Briar knew the decorum that was expected of her. She had the Queen Mother's fixed grace implanted in her mind, and she had sat through dozens of lessons on propriety.

So it was entirely intentional when her entourage stopped to wait for Phillip's caravan and she took off at a dead sprint as he rode up.

"Your Majesty!" Flora cried in horror.

Briar hefted her blue skirts to free her legs, feet pounding on the summer-dry dirt road, racing past her carriages, laden with her vassals and luggage and household excesses, so much *stuff* for her, for who she was now.

Phillip saw her coming, of course he did, and gave her a wide, gleaming grin. He vaulted from Samson, landing with that soldier's grace, and tore up the road toward her. He was dressed in lighter travel wear, a brown tunic and boots caked in dust, his face sweat-slicked—and those were the only details that registered, because he was here and he was safe and he was *hers*.

She threw herself into him, and he caught her, and the stress of the past weeks, of simply not being near him, evaporated as he held her forcefully against him.

Then she remembered she was angry with him, and she swatted the back of his head.

"You abandoned me," she grumbled into his shoulder.

He tried to put her down, no doubt to look at her to plead his case; she clung tighter, not ready to let him go yet.

She heard a satisfied moan in his throat and his grip on her went almost painfully tight.

He smelled of travel and horses and that heady musk that was *him*, and he was as solid as ever.

Home, part of her sighed. *Home.*

"I did," he admitted. "There was far too much business piled up to leave it all to my father. But I know, I am now—"

"'—so fully in my debt that you will never be out of it,'" she parroted. They'd had had this conversation already, in letters, but it bore repeating.

"I sign my life away to you entirely," said Phillip. "If I remember correctly, you collect souls? Consider mine best among your stock."

"*Best?* You certainly think favorably of your soul's quality, Sir Knight."

He laughed, and now she did pull back to see his face, the way the laughter lit his eyes and broadened his smile.

His eyes were still sunken with sleeplessness. She knew hers matched his—she and Phillip were ever the rather haunted pairing—and as his smile faded, a weight settled in her gut.

"You are well?" she asked. They were surrounded by dozens of members of her court. He would not answer the way she wanted.

"Are you?" he pushed back.

She gave him an incredulous look. "One day, you will answer that question."

"I say the same to you." His face collapsed, but before she could question it, he pressed his lips to her temple, holding there a moment. Something went out of his shoulders, of his arms, tension she had not noticed. "Heaven help me, I missed you."

"It is good to be missed," she said, eyes stinging.

"But it is horrible to do the missing. If it is in my power, I will never have to miss you again."

Hoofbeats thundered up the road behind Phillip.

Briar looked over his shoulder and gawked. "Is that Ben, *on a horse?*"

Phillip pulled back from her, arms still around her waist, and glanced back with a prideful smile. "What good would a squire be if he could not ride?"

"You broke him of his fear of horses?"

Ben was close enough now that he heard her, and he rolled his eyes. "I was never *afraid* of horses, you dolt—"

"Now, watch your tongue!" Flora had buzzed over, Fauna and Merryweather close behind. "You will not address Her Majesty in such foul words!"

"Hallo, Mistress Flora," Ben said through a tense smile. "Still after my head, I see."

Briar very much expected *Flora's* head to pop off.

She landed next to Briar. "You will show proper decorum in the presence of Her Majesty, or I shall take no pleasure in magicking you into something truly lacking in decorum."

"Flora," Briar pleaded.

Ben gave Briar a look that said *Could she truly transform me into something?*

Briar eyed Merryweather with the same unspoken question.

Merryweather shook her head.

Briar relayed that to Ben.

And Flora threw her hands skyward at this exchange. "A *smidgen* of decorum is all I ask! The smallest of requests, the barest attempts at civility—"

"And we're back on the road!" Merryweather clapped her hands and dragged her sisters to fly around to the soldiers, vassals, and others who had enjoyed the break while they reunited with Phillip's party. "Off again! Let us depart!"

Briar, who had not left the circle of Phillip's arms, kept hold of his neck when he started to pull away. "You will ride in my carriage. That is not a question."

He splayed his hand on her back, thumb rubbing against the thin, summer-cool linen of her kirtle. "My wife is rather demanding."

It jolted through her. Those words on his lips. The way he

smiled after, and blushed, hearing himself say it for the first time.

My wife.

Ben dismounted next to them. "Me as well?"

"No," she said without looking at him.

"I— All right, first of all, Bri, I wasn't asking *you*. Second, you think I would choose to willingly subject myself to being, yet again, the invasive third party to this downright *insufferable* tension between you two? But as it happens, we have business to discuss."

Briar gave Ben a wide-eyed look of bemused horror.

"Flora is right," she said. "A smidgen of decorum from you would be excellent."

"Oh, I have been trying to extract even a fraction of that from him these past weeks." Phillip gave an anguished sigh. "It's a lost issue. I have given up."

"But he can ride a horse now, so you chose your battles." Briar cocked her head. "Now, what business do we have to discuss?"

Ben smiled. "Ah, your husband has transformed me in more ways than one, Bri. Just you wait and see."

CHAPTER SIX

They piled into Briar's carriage, the windows open to allow for a breeze in what would otherwise be stifling heat, and off the caravan set, bound for Frankfurt.

In modest privacy with Briar and Phillip, Ben dug out sheets of paper from a satchel and handed them to her.

She leafed through them, her eyebrows going up. "You can read and write now as well?"

Ben snorted. "Phillip cannot work miracles. No, one of his stewards wrote, and I dictated."

"But Ben has a remarkable memory." Phillip shifted, his arm slung around Briar's waist. She leaned into him, silently cursing that Ben had insisted on riding with them, but she fought to focus on these papers, not on the way Phillip was drawing circles on her hip.

"I merely pretended they were jousting credentials," Ben said. He tapped the top paper. "The other candidates you will be up against in Frankfurt."

Briar gaped up at him. "How do you know?"

Ben jutted his chin at Phillip. "Lorraine is not far from Frankfurt. While Phillip got the king settled, he sent me off with a steward to investigate who had arrived to put themselves forward, so we could have warning of who they are and what to expect."

Briar threw a look at Phillip. "That is brilliant! Thank you."

He shrugged away her awe. "I did feel bad for abandoning you."

"Callously abandoning."

"Callously abandoning. I had hoped this information would be pertinent and that your vassals had not already done something similar?"

"They have been, but not this extensively. Not until we are due to arrive, at least." She thumbed through the pages. Each had a name, along with details beneath, where the candidates were from and who was in their households and even rumors surrounding them. "Ben, this is *amazing.* You gathered all this information?"

True pride welled in his eyes. He had changed these past few weeks, become more himself than Briar had ever seen. Still lighthearted and the first to a joke but focused, too, with a driven loyalty to his tasks that he had only ever shown toward Frieda before.

Frieda, you would be so proud of him.

He leaned back on the carriage seat in a victorious sprawl. "You are surprised I could charm servants and attendants? You wound me with your lack of faith."

"So who am I up against?" Briar shifted through the papers, looking for the name she knew would be her first concern. "Matilda of Bavaria is the front-runner?"

"Shockingly, no," Ben said. "She was not yet in Frankfurt, but expected, as you are. The Bavarian candidate is to be her *daughter*, apparently."

"What?" The air briefly went out of Briar's lungs. But quickly, answers connected: Matilda knew of her own reputation, warlike and violent. So she was offering up her daughter in her stead, an echo of Briar's situation: all the strength and grandeur of her parent's resources but the advantage of youth and a spotless record.

Had Matilda changed her tactic upon hearing of Briar's candidacy? It was a shrewd move and showed Bavaria would be a real threat.

"Princess Clara," Ben continued. He paused. "Please do not make me recite the full titles of all these people, I beg of you."

Briar was relieved to give him a mischievous grin. "*Could* you recite their full titles?"

"I told you," Phillip said. "He has a remarkable memory. I did take him first as squire merely to please you—"

"Ah!" Briar hit his stomach with the papers. "I knew it!"

"—but now I am of the mindset that this was the true reward fate had in mind for bringing you and me together."

Briar feigned offense. "A competent squire? Not a wife?"

"Precisely."

She elbowed him, and he grunted but smiled at her, the smile that locked onto hers and drew a long, slow pull of heat from her belly.

Ben coughed. Loudly. "I swear on the life of our new lustrous queen, I will fling myself from this carriage."

Briar rolled her eyes. "Promises, promises."

"Do you wish to hear of the candidates?"

"I can read of them, can't I? What need do you serve anymore? Fling yourself out and leave me with my husband."

Ben snatched the papers from her.

"Clara, of course, is expected to be a fierce contender," Ben said. "Not much is known of her. Matilda has kept a tight grip on her daughter, but she is rumored to be Matilda's equal in every way, cunning and astute. So you'll need to watch out for that one."

Briar considered wrestling Ben for the papers. Phillip tugged gently on her hip, and she sank back against his chest with an overdramatic sigh of surrender.

Ben cut her a sharp look, a mockery of Flora's disdainful sneer. "Then there's you, of course. Frankfurt is in a *tizzy* over you, Bri. The peasant bard who went to sleep and woke up a princess, then became a queen. I tried to tell everyone I could that you are hardly anything special and not to be taken in the least seriously—"

"A competent squire, you say?" Briar whispered at Phillip.

"—but they are quite intrigued by you and your past. Then there's Landgrave Eckhardt of Hesse, as old as the stones they used to build the castle where everyone's staying, and about as interesting, too. He's nominated himself four times for emperor, which speaks to both his age and his ability to convince the Prince Electors that he is in any way a capable candidate. So, no real challenge there. But, if he does somehow win, it's still a victory for you—doubtless he won't hold the position long."

"And you *charmed* the people of Frankfurt, you say?" Briar tried to hold back her laugh.

"Then there's Duke Filibert of Lüneburg, whose best virtue is his penchant for drinking until he passes out and spares those around him his company. Followed by his brother, Count Palantine Gottlieb of Lothier, who was *otherwise occupied* my whole time in Frankfurt, the entire week, which is a remarkable amount of time to be *occupied*, given that said occupation was entirely spent in a brothel. That stamina alone may win him emperor."

Now she was laughing, unable to help it. Oh, she had missed him. *"Ben—"*

"And *then.*" He launched forward, eyes sparkling. "King Johann of Mecklenburg. Eleven years old."

Briar's eyes popped wide, shock dampening her laugh. *"Eleven?"*

"Newly king and sent here as what I have to believe is merely a way for Mecklenburg to remind the empire that they still exist. He is not expected to win, but he insists that everyone address him as zauberer—*sorcerer*—not king, and that he is a wizard, specifically an evil one."

Briar gave a small bark of surprise. "I'm sorry, say that again?"

Ben's brightness had not dimmed, so it must have been in jest, or at least less unsettling than Briar imagined. At her back, Phillip was chuckling.

"From what I can tell of his attendants, he doesn't have a lick of actual magic about him," Ben said. "They all tolerate his antics with the exhausted burden of those not paid nearly enough to pretend their charge has taken their ability to speak with vowels, which, yes, was a spell he cast on his valet while I was there."

Briar had her hand over her mouth, laughter rising again. "If I don't win, I do hope it goes to him."

"Obviously I hope you're selected to be empress," Ben said, "it'd be a great victory for Austria, huzzah huzzah and what have you, but if this child somehow *does* win, I would have an obscene amount of national pride. I mean, my God. *Zauberer.* He's a terror and fully committed to this bit and if he asked me to join his household, I'd leave Phillip in an instant." Ben batted his hand at the papers. "The remaining four candidates aren't worth mentioning."

"Meaning they are ordinary," Phillip translated. He had adapted quickly to weeks spent with Ben.

"You are making this election sound far more entertaining than I had expected it would be," Briar said, and with that admission, a massive weight lifted, a darkness that had been growing in her solitude these past weeks.

Ben grinned at her. "That's why I'm here, isn't it?"

She reached out and took his hand. Her other rested on Phillip's knee, and she tightened her grip, holding them both.

"Thank you," she said to them. The force of her gratitude made Ben sniff uncomfortably, but he squeezed her fingers.

Phillip placed his hand on hers. "Of course."

She looked up at him. His eyes were clear and soft on hers, his face open and giving, and she truly did not know how she had endured the time he and Ben were away.

Phillip, ever keeping an eye on her.

Ben, with his jokes and dedication.

Whatever happened with the election, whatever trials she would face, she would not do so alone. Not now.

"I will not fling myself from the carriage, I've decided," Ben cut in. "I will shift the topic to distract you both from making eyes at one another."

Briar rolled her eyes. "Too late, Benedikt. You *did* insist on riding with us—"

"Phillip," Ben cut in, "if animals could joust, which one do you think could unseat you?"

Phillip's laugh was sudden and left Briar dizzy.

"He has been asking questions of this sort almost nonstop," Phillip said through his laughter.

"I am not surprised," Briar said. "He once asked whether it would be better if it rained beer or cider, and the resulting argument lasted two hours and ended with Frieda slapping him."

She hadn't meant to talk of her.

The moment her name slipped from Briar's lips, she gave a panicked look at Ben and saw him flinch.

He covered it by rolling his eyes. "Do not change the subject, Bri. You lost that argument. You really should get over it."

She could not help but feel he was saying it to them both. *We really should get over it. She left. It's done.*

"Now, if animals could joust." Ben's voice was a little rushed. He flared his hand in the air. "A fox is too obvious. A badger, that's where I'd put my money on one capable of unseating you, and I have given it some thought."

"Of course you have." Phillip pressed his thumb and finger into his eyes. "A badger? You think I would lose to a badger. Spare my pride that mental image. Not a boar at least? Or an ibex?"

"Why on earth would an ibex joust? That's absurd. They have horns. They wouldn't need a lance."

"Oh, *that's* absurd, yes, but not a badger with a lance?"

"Of course not. They're wily, agile—don't laugh, I did say *if animals could joust*, so not a normal-sized badger, but a human-sized badger, obviously—"

"Burn me alive," Briar muttered. "This topic of conversation will stem fever."

But Phillip was laughing, and Ben was back to being a sun of joy, and Briar leaned her head against Phillip's shoulder and let this nonsense play out around her, her smile light and constant.

• • •

They arrived at a massive castle complex in the middle of Frankfurt when it was far too dark to see, but the grandness of the place was a dense, commanding presence that left Briar reeling. Her caravan began a flurry of unpacking. The following day would be a welcome banquet celebrating the candidates, all of whom had now gathered. It would mark the beginning of campaigning, the start of three weeks filled with trials, questions, observation, and more, all testing her mettle, poking and prodding her qualities before the Prince Electors cast their votes.

She would have to begin presenting her best self and making her presence and skills known to the Prince Electors. *Self-assured. Thoughtful. Passionate. Envisions a peaceful future for the empire. Fearless.* She would be able to put faces to the information Ben had gathered. Her head rang with all the names and details she had of people she had not met. Nine other candidates, seven Prince Electors, countless members of their households. She ached from the trip, and, in a good way: She ached from laughter, from the ridiculous conversations Ben had dragged them into during the ride.

Still, she was back with Phillip. Although travel-beaten and fending off a headache was not the way she'd imagined their first night together, as one of the castle's keepers led them, the fairies, and the vassals to the wing reserved for the Austrian delegates, Briar kept her arm linked with Phillip's.

"The king's suite," the keeper said, indicating a door. And across the hall from it: "The queen's."

Well, nearby. But before Briar could argue—

"We must review the subjects of import to the Prince Electors, Your Majesty," one of her vassals said. "It will not take long. I have received new information upon arriving, and if it comes up at the feast tomorrow . . ."

Briar sighed. Was she relieved to have an excuse to put it off? But this wasn't how she wanted it to go. With Phillip. This wasn't worthy of them.

She looked up at him, and he gave her a tired, understanding smile.

"Do not keep her up too late," he said to the vassal, without looking away from her.

"Of course, Your Majesty. Merely a quick review."

Briar ignored the vassals, the fairies yawning and twittering. She ignored everyone and kissed her husband, because she had not for far too long, and she would have this.

It was too fast, and all it did was remind her of how much more she wanted with him.

"Try to sleep," she whispered to him, though she knew it was unlikely to come for either of them.

Then she followed her vassals into the room. It was as lovely as her rooms at the Austrian castle, sumptuous and well appointed even in the low light from an already burning fireplace, but she hardly saw the finery, the touches of fresh flowers scenting the air.

She sat at a small table, two vassals diving into an explanation of how one Prince Elector, the Prince-Archbishop of Cologne, was prioritizing candidates who would commit to levying higher taxes, and it felt like a dream again.

She was here. In Frankfurt. In this stunning room, in this massive castle, presented as an equal to people who had been trained in leadership from birth.

Briar's hands clenched in her lap, nails biting into her palms, and that sting of pain grounded her.

She was here, and she would be here, and she would do everything in her power to impress upon the Prince Electors her worthiness throughout the weeks of campaigning. Or, if she could not impress them, then she would do everything in her power to impress upon them the *unworthiness* of Bavaria. She would not let her country and empire fall into the hands of a warmongering murderer. She had the ability to protect her people, and so she would.

No helplessness.

Never again.

Not for any of them.

The vassals left not long after, and after she changed into a shift,and she was unconscious before she had even fully lain down.

Blissfully, she did not dream.

• • •

As Briar followed her vassals through the castle's winding gray stone halls the following afternoon, her mind was in a fog. Phillip, his arm through hers, looked just as worn, and that was even worse, that she could not help him. Had not been *able* to help him, drawn away by duty again—and how often would that happen now? Their needs parted by the needs of Austria, and eventually, the Holy Roman Empire.

She held his arm firmly, as if to remind him she was not going anywhere, and he leaned in to press a quick kiss to her head, where Fauna had twisted her golden hair into an intricate weave of braids interspersed with golden picks. It matched the subdued golden hue of her gown, all of her set off in shades of yellow and sunset. That was the theme through her party—Phillip in golden brown, Ben too, the vassals and fairies. It unified them, made a striking declaration of their presence.

In the mirror that morning, she had fought hard to see herself in the visage of Queen Aurora in this fine gown, this elaborate hair. Dressed so outstandingly, who else but *Aurora* would be at this banquet?

But was it Aurora who was self-assured, passionate, fearless?

Was it Aurora who would succeed?

Briar's group stopped at an open set of doors. Voices chattered beyond, the murmurs of dozens of people, and the scent of food made the air savory.

Trumpets blared. They were announced within, and Briar slammed her eyes shut.

"Together," Phillip whispered to her.

She leaned into him. "Together."

They entered, arm in arm, trailed by Ben, the fairies, the vassals.

The banquet room rivaled Stefan's throne room. Towering ceilings capped the massive chamber, with huge iron windows allowing brilliant sunlight to stream through. That light caught the dozens of banners hanging from the high ceiling, one for every candidate's home, one for every Prince Elector's home as well, a fluttering display of the Holy Roman Empire's reach. So many countries and provinces represented, and still dozens more that made up this empire.

It ripped Briar's breath away. She knew the empire was large, but so many people called it home, and so did such a vast array of customs and cultures; how could one person rule it all?

She was standing in one of the ballads she sang, the lyrics come to life, tales of grand halls and highborn nobles and machinations grim and great.

The room itself was packed with bodies already, all chatting, some eating from the banquet table that spanned the length of the room. Unbidden, Briar was hit with another pang of how very much food there was: piles of treats and roasted meats and more, all just sitting there.

She could not overindulge. She was not Briar the peasant bard now.

She was the queen.

Her stomach, still, gave a hungry roil.

Köning swept in front of her. "Your Majesty, we will begin introductions. I see Duke Filibert of Lüneburg first?"

"Excellent," Merryweather said. She shared a look with Flora and Fauna, all three of them nodding simultaneously. "We shall check in with your guards around the room."

Briar looked quickly, noting soldiers in Austrian colors stationed at the far reaches alongside guards wearing colors for the other candidates. She had known, in an abstract way, that her guards would be here to watch over her, but she had not thought any threat would be present where all the candidates were gathered, and the Prince Electors, too, so very many people who all had their own security.

"Is there truly a danger here?" she asked.

Merryweather smiled at her. It was too big. Too cheerful. She patted Briar's cheek. "It is best to be vigilant" was all she said.

So not a no.

Then Merryweather, Flora, and Fauna all split off, bobbing to various sides of the room. They snagged a few strange looks from those unfamiliar with magic, but most territories had some magic users, whether their own fairies or witches or more.

Briar could not stare after them long. Köning cleared his throat, and she was off, Phillip at her side, Ben at her back.

Briar met those Ben had made dossiers about, and his colorful descriptions from the carriage were all too accurate.

Two of the candidates, Filibert and his brother, Gottlieb, were both already a little drunk. Gottlieb made a crass comment about Briar's beauty and Phillip likely would have started a war if Ben had not jumped in with a laughing comment about the strength of Frankfurt's wine and defused the whole mess.

The older Eckhardt of Hesse was asleep, draped back in a chair, a plate of half-eaten ribs on a table next to him. Köning tried to rouse him. He snored, loudly.

The Prince Electors were far more responsive. Briar met four of them at once, clustered together, and she immediately felt a pit open in her belly. *Self-assured. Fearless.*

Those traits had to have been things her vassals fabricated to appease her.

No way could she possibly emulate any of that.

Her mouth was dry, and all she could see as four sets of eyes turned to her was the vast pressure of what she had to achieve.

Briar had to speak to them.

No, Aurora, right? Briar had no place here.

But luckily, the Prince Electors did not give her long to think.

"You grew up a *peasant*, is that true?" the Prince-Archbishop of Trier asked. He did not ask offensively—it was in shocked curiosity.

"Yes," she said, facing him. "In Hausach. It's a small town near the—"

"And you lived all that time with the curse?" one interrupted.

Smoothly, Briar looked at him. She let a beat pass, anticipating another interruption, and when none came, she smiled gracefully. "Well, it did not manifest until my sixteenth birthday. My time living in Hausach was idyllic, actually." Thoughtfulness swept over her, and her smile became truer. "Idyllic and quaint. Certainly not always free of struggle, but it gave me a view of my country I would not have otherwise. Would that all of Austria—indeed, all of the empire—could be idyllic and quaint, *and* free of struggle. That is the goal we all work toward as leaders, is it not?"

The Electors shared a look, their faces showing what looked to be surprise at first, then satisfaction.

Briar exhaled slowly.

"This is your husband, is it?" another Elector cut in. "The Savior of Austria?"

Phillip's whole body went rigid.

Briar squeezed his arm. "You may also know him as the Pain from Lorraine, if you are familiar with lists."

Phillip cut her a quick look that was equal parts relief and *I know what you're doing.*

That name earned a bark of laughter from the Margrave of Brandenburg. "A jouster! You will compete in the match next week, I take it?"

Phillip relaxed with a generous smile. "Of course. I must represent my wife to the best of my abilities."

The group set off on discussions of the schedule, events and dances and more, all meant to celebrate the occasion—but to give time for the candidates to campaign as well.

As Köning expertly detached them from this conversation and pulled them into another, Briar leaned in close to Phillip.

"Do you think this is going well? I don't know how to—"

"Briar." Phillip freed his arm from hers to loop around her waist. "You have weeks yet of campaigning. Allow them to see *you*, too. Who you are will charm them more than rehearsed facts."

She let herself have one restorative beat in his arms. "I will choose to see how sweet that was and not dwell on the fact that you value my personality above facts about taxes and territory disputes, when that should have been obvious, hmm? Of course I am more interesting than *taxes*."

He pinched her side. Her cheeks flamed red and she tried to maintain her queenly composure as Phillip stifled a laugh.

"Far more interesting," he said, and she nudged him.

Ben, who Briar had not realized had slipped away, came up to Phillip and handed him something.

"Ah, speaking of your interesting personality . . ." Phillip took it, nodded his thanks, and handed it to her.

It was food swiped from the banquet table. A piece of pastry, a knob of cheese.

Briar's face lit up. She swept that joy to Phillip, who took it and smiled.

"I knew you would be unhappy not to at least try the food," Phillip said. "I can have Ben squirrel away more later. But for now?"

She kissed his cheek and reached back to squeeze Ben's arm. "I am spoiled."

"Yes, you are," Ben said with a cutting grin, and she batted him.

As she lifted the knob of cheese to her mouth, Flora appeared at her elbow, glaring first at Briar, then at Ben.

"I did not see you test the food before giving it to the queen," she said accusingly.

Ben's brows rose in sharp confusion. "Um—why?"

Flora rolled her eyes and cast her wand over the food in Briar's hands. Satisfied, she nodded. "It is safe to eat. Continue."

Then she was gone, flurrying back to the edge of the room.

Briar, Ben, and Phillip stared after her until Briar looked down at the food in her hands.

"She thinks it could have been poisoned?" Briar shot a hesitant look up at Phillip.

His lips parted, and his cheeks flushed red. "I—suppose so, yes." The expression that came over him was dark with self-recrimination, and he touched her wrist. "I'm sorry. I did not think—but I should have. This is no frivolous party. It is a deadly game, all of it. Bavaria will not be an easy competitor, nor will they fight fairly. You don't have to eat the—"

He started to take the food from her.

Briar yanked it against her chest. "No. This is mine."

"Yes," Ben agreed. "And she will eat it, because I was apparently supposed to *risk my own life* to test it, when Flora *easily* used magic to determine it wasn't poisoned instead." He gave Briar a flat look and shook his head. "She realizes that's what she implied, right? That I should've *died* for something she can do with the flick of her wrist?"

Briar again looked at where Flora now stood talking to one of her guards. "I'm sure she didn't mean . . . quite that," she said, but it was stilted.

Köning regrouped them, and as they trailed him across the room, she ate as properly as she could. Oh, the *cheese* especially, a soft white savory concoction that she had never tasted before, but it was not dissimilar to a type made by Rolf's wife at the tavern in Hausach. It sent a pang through her, of missing home, but she swallowed the last of the food and used that pang to become resolved.

This was why she was here. To protect them. Because, somehow, miraculously, she had that power now.

"Queen Aurora, King Phillip," Köning announced, gesturing to the next waiting group. "May I present King Johann of Mecklenburg."

Briar immediately sprang to attention. Behind her, she could hear Ben quietly go, "He should have said Zauberer, just you wait."

A little boy looked up from a circle of men grouped around him. He wore a heavy brocade cloak across his tiny frame, woven with a repeating pattern of the Mecklenburg coat of arms, a bull's head in a crown. His dark brown hair sat in a limp wilt beneath a crown of dense gold, and that alongside the brocade made him look like he was trying very hard to appear regal.

He glared up at Köning. "*Zauberer* Johann," he emphasized, his lip curling. "I will put a curse on your house. Locusts will swarm your bed. Your brain will shrivel into a dried apricot. Do not try me."

"Told you," Ben murmured.

Köning had gone momentarily stunned; clearly no one had prepared him for the intensity of Johann's game.

Briar quickly stepped forward and gave a deep curtsy. "Zauberer Johann, you must forgive my lord. We did not wish to reveal your true identity to the masses. But if you are making yourself freely known, then we will address you as such."

For the shortest moment, Johann looked positively *overjoyed.* That look vanished with a severe nod.

"It is wise to be cautious. I have enemies everywhere."

"No doubt. I understand more than most the negative effects that follow users of magic."

Johann's eyes became full circles, making him look every bit the eleven-year-old he was. "*You* are Queen Aurora. *The* Aurora. The Aurora cursed by Maleficent!"

One of Johann's attendants put a hand on his shoulder, tried to whisper him down off this topic, but Johann shrugged him away. Honestly, from anyone else, Briar wouldn't have even entertained the subject—but something about Johann's innocent joy had her beaming down at him and feeling, for the first time, like she could make light of it all.

"I am," she said. "You must promise not to similarly curse me while we are here, won't you? I do not know what Austria could offer you in return, but I would be most grateful if I had your allegiance and not your wrath."

Johann chewed that. "Hmm. It is a lot to ask of a sorcerer, not to curse people."

Briar fought back a smile. "Indeed. I—" A thought occurred to her. Oh, her aunts would be quite upset with her. "Do you have fairies in Mecklenburg?"

Though hers were not the only fairies that flittered around the empire, they were the only ones who had remained with one royal family and made themselves a known part of that country's rule. Briar assumed it was because of the course fate had taken them on, forcing the fairies to become unduly attached to her.

Johann's lips pursed. "No. My father drove out magic before he died. He claimed it was evil."

Well, that raised a number of questions immediately. Briar landed on "And you seek to restore what he expelled from your country?"

He blinked for a moment. As though that had in no way been his reason for assuming the mantle of a sorcerer—at least, not consciously, she thought—but now that she had connected those dots for him, he pulled up a proud smile.

"Precisely."

"What if I could offer an introduction to fairies, then?"

Johann's shock sparked on the air. "You can do that?"

"Of course. They travel with me."

"Fairies?"

"Yes."

"*Real* fairies?"

"I swear on my throne. You know the story of my . . . recent predicament. They were instrumental in freeing me from it. I am sure they would be glad to speak with you. And perhaps show you a trick or two of theirs?" Merryweather would delight in talking with the boy, and perhaps she could even convince him that trying to be an *evil* sorcerer was not the best course for his life.

Johann's gaze flicked, once, to Phillip behind her, and he must have guessed who he was, because his eyes went wide again, but he put his attention back on Briar.

"Yes," he repeated in an awed whisper. "If I can meet your fairies, I shall not curse you."

"A deal." She extended her hand and Johann shook it, giving her a large, toothy grin.

His attendants shared smiles. One nodded his thanks to her.

Phillip leaned in. "I thank you, Zauberer, for your willingness to negotiate. Perhaps I can add to the deal as well? Guarantee our safety while we're here?"

Johann looked very much how Ben had in the tavern, trying and failing to cap his excitement. "I am not in the practice of bespelling people to be *safe*"—he made a disgusted face—"but I can, for you, possibly, *maybe*, consider it. What have you to offer?"

Briar was wondering the same thing. She eyed Phillip, who winked at Johann.

"A sword created by magic that you are free to inspect," he said.

Flora's Sword of Truth.

Johann made a high-pitched whine, then straightened with the sniff and stature of someone trying to be taken seriously. "That would be satisfactory." He looked up at his attendant, gave a nod as if they had been in discussion. "We have an accord."

More pleasantries, and then Köning guided them away, Briar spinning to face Phillip with a barely suppressed grin.

"Do you think we might be able to smuggle him to Austria? I should like to keep him."

"You know, I do not think he would be opposed to it," Ben piped up behind them.

"Then by all means," Phillip said. "I have been trying to think of a way to start a war with Mecklenburg."

"After you nearly started one with Lothier, trying to punch Gottlieb as you did," Briar shot back.

"That was earned on his end and would have been well worth it. No one gets to speak about you like that."

"Ah, again, what a pair we make." Briar leaned into him. "Not at the first event yet two hours, and already considering starting as many feuds."

Phillip laughed.

Köning, who was trying very hard to pretend he had not heard their conversation, was red to his ears. "Your Majesties, the final candidate is across the room. If you will follow me?"

The final candidate.

Clara of Bavaria. With her mother, no doubt, who had murdered Stefan on the day of Briar's wedding. Matilda, whose bloodthirsty actions had shoved Briar into this competition, who ended innocent lives all for her own selfish gains.

Briar's heart twisted sharply, her lungs feeling laden with stones, by the building weight of those memories, the bloodstained stones—

All the levity fell away, the protective shield of humor, and she briefly closed her eyes.

"Breathe," she whispered to herself.

She would be gracious to Clara. She would be the picture of cordiality to Matilda, even. Because she was civilized where they were not; she was a peasant who had been wrenched into high society, and she had manners and standards and grace.

Or, at least, this queen version of her did.

This queen version would not crumple under dark, gory memories.

And so she was that queen as they wove across the room, ducking people they had met already, nodding greetings in passing.

A group stood by the banquet tables, clustered tightly together. Briar immediately saw Matilda, dressed in a luxurious gown of beaded purple, her dark hair swept back into braids, her pale skin flushed and healthy, no hint of the army-leading commander she had been in Austria.

Matilda turned at their approach, even before Köning said anything, and gave Briar an emotionless smile.

Briar stopped, her stomach knotting, knotting again, until it was all a bulky tangle, making it hard for her lungs to find room.

The Prince Electors knew Matilda had led a group to assassinate Stefan. All here knew.

And no one did a thing to bring justice for it. For only the emperor could judge a queen.

These rules were superfluous, enforced only by those they benefited, and again, Briar was struck with a resounding chord of powerlessness. Here she was, a queen in her own right, and yet she had no ability to see justice done.

It was maddening.

It was harrowing.

It was all the more reason she had to become empress herself.

It made all the sharp edges of Maleficent and the spindle and her dreams roar to the front of her mind, because if she had come this far, amassed this much power, and yet she was still restrained, what hope did she really have? What hope did *anyone* have—not even to see justice carried out, but to just *be*?

Briar ripped her eyes away from Matilda, her gaze crawling across the rest of the Bavarian group. Lords, vassals, servants—

A woman stepped out of the group, alongside Matilda.

Those sharp edges. The dreams. The spindle. All of it softened, drifted away, gauze-thin and meaningless.

Köning gestured between them. "Queen Matilda, Princess Clara, may I present Queen Aurora and King Phillip of Austria."

Briar stared at the woman next to Matilda. She stared, because her insides were collapsing, her mind playing a cold, cruel trick on her. She was sleep deprived, she was terrified and overstrung—so that was the reason. That was the reason. Because *Princess Clara*, she could not be—*could not be*—

Briar looked at Ben. He would not see what she saw, and that would confirm it, and she could take a deep breath and carry on.

But Ben's face was drained of blood, his eyes fixed, solidly, on Princess Clara.

Briar faced her again. Locking eyes with the woman wrenched a name out of her.

"Frieda?"

CHAPTER SEVEN

Frieda's face was blank, lips flat, eyes on Briar's in calm, cool detachment.

She was not surprised to see Briar.

Meanwhile, Briar couldn't get a full breath.

"What are you doing here?" she heard herself ask.

Köning gave her a strange look. "She is Princess Clara of Bavaria, Your Majesty."

No. *No.* That wasn't possible.

"Frieda." Briar said her name again, and she watched Frieda flinch but cover it by ducking her head to the side.

Phillip pressed against Briar, warm and sturdy. "Frieda? *Your* Frieda?"

Briar could only exhale sharply. None of her muscles would work. Her eyes locked on Frieda, unbelieving.

"Frieda—"

"Princess Clara," Matilda cut in, stepping closer to her daughter. She spoke to Briar, but her voice was all iron and raised to hit those around them. "I suppose it is time to announce my daughter's history. Prince Electors, would you care to hear the tale?"

Those who were not nearby quickly drew closer, and Briar was only vaguely aware of them.

Frieda straightened, meeting their eyes, defiance and resolve perfectly balanced on her face.

She had always been more in control of her emotions than Briar or Ben. More able to see the path forward, whereas Briar would react in sorrow or anger first, and only realize a more sensible course of action later.

So it was almost instinct for her to see Frieda's calmness and emulate her. That was what Briar had so often done. *Frieda is not upset; I shouldn't be.*

But that response was rusted and creaked through her chest, hauling with it pain, such pain it bubbled and rose and threatened to drown her inside out.

"You have many questions, I assume, Queen Aurora?" Matilda still only spoke to Briar, though her performance was clearly for all around. "It is simple, and a situation you yourself are quite familiar with: We believed that our future ruler would be more well rounded if she grew up among the people, left to her own devices."

Briar shook her head. Again.

No. No, it couldn't—

"It creates unparalleled strength, wouldn't you say?" Matilda's smile was sly. "Well. Formerly unparalleled. And my daughter's strength is taken even further, as I had her grow up among not only the people, but the people of our *enemy*, just so she would understand them in a way no other ruler ever would."

Dozens of things raced through Briar's mind, thoughts and emotions and horrors.

"You—" she stammered, unable to look away from Frieda. "You abandoned your daughter in the homeland you attacked?"

"She will be empress," Matilda said, and she was holding Frieda's arm now. Frieda, who was staring at the floor. "Growing up among people who are not her own allows her to understand this empire in a way no one else does, extensively, *expansively*. That it was also the village where *your* family chose to exile you—well. I am curious as to King Stefan's reasoning for just *happening* to choose the village where my daughter resided, but oh." She put a hand to her lips in faux shock. "Oh, we cannot ask him, can we?"

That snapped the sensations of the room back on Briar, as though she had broken the surface, able to breathe. But each breath was jagged and raw, air no comfort, and on each blink she saw the throne room in Hausach, blood on the floor—

Nearby, the Prince Electors were listening, and the shock on their faces matched the shock on every face around. This was the first any had heard of the mysterious Princess Clara's past. Ben had said not much was known of her, that Matilda had kept her private.

This was why.

Because she had grown up in Austria. Alongside Austria's own exiled princess.

How? *How?* It was impossible Matilda had known where Briar—Aurora—had been hidden. Even Maleficent, with all her magic, had been unable to find her until that last night. And if Austria's enemy had known all along where their vulnerable princess was, why hadn't Matilda eliminated the issue? Had Stefan known Frieda—Clara—was in Hausach? It was all too convenient, too well planned, too heavy with the twist of fate.

Desperately, Briar wondered if Matilda was lying. Maybe Frieda wasn't her daughter—

But Frieda chose that moment to look back at her. And they had the same nut-brown eyes, Matilda and Frieda. The same rich dark hair, the same frame to their jaws, the same long, thin noses.

Matilda was Frieda, only aged and cruel.

It wasn't possible. None of this was possible. Nothing had been possible from the moment her aunts had told her that she was Princess Aurora, and everything that had happened since was caught up in the avalanche that was impossibility.

"Frieda" was all she could say again, wheezing.

The crowd was abuzz now. Prince Electors pressed in, doing their best to cut into the conversation properly, but there was a growing mania around the spreading news. All knew of Briar's past, her childhood in Hausach—this was even more enticing than that. Another princess grown up in poverty and anonymity, only this one in a kingdom not her own, among people not her own.

Briar let the Prince Electors shuffle in around her. She stayed, listening to their questions, to Matilda's self-aggrandizing responses—how hard it was to send her only child off, how rewarding to know it would shape Clara into an unrivaled leader.

She heard, too, Frieda's responses. How honored she was to have been given the chance to become a leader the likes of which the empire had never known. How proud she was that her mother had had such *selfless forethought* as to send her daughter off in anonymity and poverty.

Briar had seen the bed of straw where Frieda had slept in the orphanage. She knew the frigid, hungry nights Frieda had spent huddled with the other children for warmth during winter. She remembered how she had begged her aunts to let Frieda stay with them, but they had enough trouble feeding the four of them; how could they take on one more mouth? Flora especially had refused outright.

Had Flora known who Frieda was? Had any of her aunts known? It wasn't possible. It wasn't *possible*—

"Frieda!"

Ben shouldered past Briar. While she had been standing in frozen shock, what had he been going through? The same, likely, but he was awake now, and he outright pushed aside a Prince Elector to get in front of Frieda.

A Bavarian soldier shoved him back.

The crowd went still, propriety a knotted mess.

A squire had pushed a Prince Elector and approached a princess uninvited.

He didn't care. He wouldn't, of course, and he looked at Frieda so pleadingly that Briar's heart broke.

She wasn't looking at him, though. Her eyes were on the floor, and Briar watched spots of red bloom on her cheeks. For the first time since this had begun, Frieda didn't look resolved and steady.

She looked real.

"Frieda, it's me. It's Ben."

Frieda nodded at the soldier.

Who grabbed Ben by the arm and made to drag him out.

"Hold!" Phillip jumped in. "Release my squire. I will deal with him."

The soldier hesitated, eyeing Matilda.

Frieda, though, gaped at Briar. Her lips formed the word *Squire?*, her eyes glossy. She would know how much that meant to Ben. She would *know*—

But Frieda shook it away and set her face back into that stoic, emotionless mask.

That was what broke Briar.

That Frieda could stand there, with Ben inches from her, and say *nothing*. She owed him more than that. He *deserved* more than that.

Rage bubbled up. Hot, tight fury.

They hadn't chosen this. None of them had chosen *any of this*—

She would not be powerless, and yet all around her was nothing but reminders of that powerlessness, reminders that even now, she was at the mercy of others, as were those she loved.

Phillip took Ben's arm, gently, but Ben spun away and shoved into the crowd, vanishing without a word.

"I apologize, Queen Matilda, Princess Clara." Phillip turned to the Prince Electors. "Princes. I take full responsibility for my squire's acts."

"Quite," one of the Electors said. But few lingered on it too long; they faced Matilda and Frieda with interest, fascination spiking again.

"Let's go," Phillip said to Briar. They walked away, Köning staying behind to offer further apologies. This situation had made her look weak. Had made her party look weak.

As had been Matilda's intention.

But Briar couldn't bring herself to care. She was spiraling more and more as they wove through the banquet room, down the long, twisting halls—and there was Ben up ahead, running for a door—

"Ben!" Phillip shouted.

Ben stopped, back rigid, shoulders pulsing with each tight breath.

They hurried to him. Ben didn't turn, one hand on the doorknob, head dropping to his chest.

Briar touched his arm. He jerked like she'd hit him, then whirled on her, his eyes bloodshot and tearing up with confusion that Briar had no way to soothe.

"What—" Ben started. "*How?* How was that her? How is she *here*?"

"I don't know," Briar said, and her own eyes teared as well. "I don't know. I'll find out."

"I thought she'd left because *you* left. I thought she'd left because I wasn't what she wanted anymore. I thought a hundred different things, but I never once thought *this.* She was so furious at you after you left and we found out who you were, Bri. She was *livid* at you. And all along, she was like you?"

His voice broke and he scrubbed the back of his hand over his mouth, fingers shaking.

Briar shook her head. She had no words. Nothing at all but her own pain, so similar to Ben's, and they were united in that, at least.

"We need to talk somewhere private," Phillip said softly, indicating the open hall around them, the doors to the banquet room not far behind.

"No." Ben cleared his throat. "No. I, um, I have chores. In the stables."

Phillip stepped forward. "Ben—"

"No." He ripped open the door and was gone, racing out into the bright white light of the afternoon.

Phillip started to follow. Briar put her hand on his wrist.

"Let him go," she whispered. "He needs answers, and I do, too."

Phillip turned to her, looking determined. "We will figure this out. You need answers? Let's gather your vassals and the fairies, and plan."

She could not put words to the gratitude that overwhelmed her—that he knew what to do, what she needed, without much prodding. The only one she could truly trust.

The banquet did not end for another two hours, during which Briar's vassals stayed in her stead, to keep a presence. Briar knew she was already behind, forced to catch up, but she could not be in that room again with Frieda . . . no, Clara.

Finally, they gathered in the sitting room of her suite, the fairies, vassals, and Phillip.

Briar sat on a padded bench before a window, Phillip next to her, her hands clamped on the beaded edge. She had told all present, quickly, who Clara was. Who she had been to Briar, in Hausach. The fairies knew immediately who she was when Briar had said *Frieda*; the vassals had needed an explanation, one that grated on Briar's throat like jagged knives.

Now, secrets bared, Briar waited.

The vassals were tense in their chairs, talking harshly to one another, comparing notes on information they had heard during the final hours of the banquet.

The fairies clustered by the door that led into her bedchamber, hissing at one another, until Flora spun away from her sisters with a growl.

"I always knew that girl was trouble!" Flora shot toward Briar, finger in an accusing point. "I never liked her, not one moment while you were children. Oh, I should have put my foot down the second you two met. I knew, I *knew* she was trouble—"

"Now, Flora." Fauna flew up and took Flora's hand, guiding her back down from where she'd nearly drifted up to hit the ceiling. "There is no sense in dwelling on what happened. Frieda is here. We must move forward."

"You did not know who she really was?" Briar pressed, her mouth dry.

Flora gave her a look of such horrified shock that Briar went silent. "*Of course* we did not know! You think we would have allowed you within five paces of *Matilda of Bavaria's daughter*? Stefan would have had our heads!"

"So he didn't know, either?"

"Surely not!" Flora shrieked.

"Then—" Briar wilted. "How did we end up in the same village?"

"Trickery from Bavaria," Flora said with confidence. "They accused us of subterfuge in arranging where you were exiled merely to shift the blame off them. This *reeks* of Matilda's cruelty!"

Briar didn't voice the problems that had occurred to her from that exact solution: that Matilda would have likely just killed Briar when she was a child, rather than let her grow, if Matilda had truly known that Briar was in Hausach.

There was something else at play.

"Don't you think on her more, Aurora!" Flora said, but she was barely looking at Briar, too lost in her own rage. "She is not worth the energy. She will be dealt with. Oh! She will be *dealt with*—"

"We can hardly *deal with her*, dear," Fauna tried.

Only Merryweather was watching Briar. Watching, standing by the bedroom door, and when Briar's eyes landed on her, whatever she saw in Briar's face made her own screw up in frustration.

She took out her wand and shot a stream of glittering magic up at her sisters.

It hit them in the sides of their heads, and they chirped in unison, "Merryweather!"

Merryweather did the same to the vassals, who were arguing with one another, and they, too, jumped in startled shock. It was effective, though, and yanked all attention to her, until Merryweather gestured at Briar.

"What do you wish to do?" she asked. Simple. Calm.

Briar couldn't hold her aunt's gaze. She looked at the floor.

She wanted to sleep.

She wanted to go *home*, to Hausach, and sing in the tavern, and pretend none of this had happened.

Briar could do none of those things, so she did what she had to do.

She squared her shoulders and leveled her chin. "I want to find out how much truth there is to Matilda's story. What really happened with Fri—with Clara."

"She has kept the tale secret until now," Köning said. "It is unlikely she will let slip details unless she wants to."

"Then press her to tell whatever she is willing to tell," Briar said. "She wants to brag about how this was a great plan of hers—let her brag. Fawn over her, compliment her. Find out what she did to her daughter and why Frieda was in the same village as me. Find out how much of this was orchestrated and how much was chance and—" She stopped, catching her runaway breath, and steadied herself. "Find out more. Please."

Köning gave her a small smile. "Consider it done, Your Majesty."

"And for the campaign?" Merryweather asked. "How do you want to proceed with the Prince Electors? What do you want to present to them?"

Flora and Fauna settled next to Merryweather, all three watching her now. There was a weight in Merryweather's question, in the looks they gave her, but Briar was too exhausted to make sense of their urgency, whatever it was they were trying to get her to say.

"Present to them?" Briar asked. "Why would anything need to change in that regard?"

"The Prince Electors are besotted by Matilda's story," Lord Lehmann said. "It is all anyone was speaking of as the banquet ended. She planned this. She planned *all* of this. That conniving bi—"

"Yes. Quite." Köning eyed Briar in a way that silenced Lehmann from cursing, and Briar fought not to roll her eyes, as if hearing

Matilda called no end of colorful names would be anything short of curative right now. "But what do we *do*? The basis of our campaign is Queen Aurora's history with the people. Now that is no longer the novelty we had hoped. We still have the size and strength of Austria and Lorraine combined, but will it be enough to counter whatever other surprises Matilda brings? For we cannot grow complacent that she is done with her schemes."

"We go harder with our plans to discredit Matilda," another vassal said. "Remind the Prince Electors of the lengths she's willing to go to in order to enact her will, regardless of whether she would be empress or her daughter would. With either on the throne, the Holy Roman Empire will descend into bloodshed and violence."

"Already, Matilda has begun comparing Clara's exile to Aurora's," Köning said. "Notably, in saying how our queen needed someone to ultimately save her from her peasant life, while her daughter stood on her own."

Briar rose to her feet, her posture still regal and stiff, but she felt her control fraying. "It was not *my peasant life* that Phillip rescued me from. It was a *curse*. It was magic. It had nothing to do with my life in Hausach."

Köning gave an apologetic shrug. Other vassals dropped their gazes.

"This is the game, Your Majesty," one said. "Attempting to unseat and discredit other candidates."

"It would be good, moving forward," Köning interjected, "to perhaps downplay King Phillip's involvement in your rescue. Where once it was a show of our strength, if Bavaria uses that as proof of your weakness, we may consider wedging distance between you and that piece of the narrative. Spin it that you rescued yourself."

It wasn't a *narrative.* It was her life. All of this was *her life*, and as the vassals resumed talking about how best to frame Briar's existence, she sank back to the bench, only half listening. Phillip put his arm around her.

She wanted to be angry again. She wanted to rage and storm around this room, to release these emotions.

But she was so very tired. The weight of months of sleeplessness was piling on her all at once.

"What do you wish to do, Your Majesty?" Merryweather asked again, her voice coaxing.

Briar had nothing left to give now. "Whatever my vassals believe is best."

The fairies shared a look. Were they disappointed? Let them be.

The vassals stood from their various chairs and bowed, acting on the unspoken dismissal in Briar's finality. She liked that power, at least, that she could end a meeting with merely her intent.

They filed out, the fairies lingering only enough to look like they wanted to speak more.

Briar shook her head. Silent, begging, *Not now, please.*

A thought crept up from the recesses of her brain. "Oh—"

The fairies paused, hope sparking.

"It is possible," Briar started, pinching the skin over her nose, "that I temporarily loaned you to King—no, Zauberer Johann of Mecklenburg."

She heard Flora say, simply, "Pardon?"

"He has interests in magic, and it was a way to foster goodwill with him." Briar scrubbed her face and looked at Merryweather. "If you can speak with Johann, it would mean the world to him. He seems rather . . . 'Lonely' isn't the right word. On the right path but with no one to guide him."

Flora, Fauna, and Merryweather gaped at her. Briar's face heated as she wondered what she had said wrong.

"He truly is harmless," she tried again. "A child of—"

"Of course." It was Fauna who gave her a wide, wondrous smile. "Of course. We would be happy to speak with him."

And even Flora nodded, smiling, and as they shuffled out the door, Briar was left with a sense of having done at least one thing right this day.

The door closed. She heard the lock click, and it wasn't odd; her bedroom in Austria was usually locked as well. But something about that click on the back of Flora's concern over the food being poisoned had Briar's neck prickling with awareness.

It is a game, all of it, Phillip had said.

She shivered and turned to him where he still sat next to her, the late-afternoon sun throwing the room into sinking gold.

"Would you like me to speak with Ben?" he asked.

She considered. "Is that a conversation for a prince to have with his squire?"

"I like to think I can count him as a friend now, too. I—" His head tipped, eyes wandering. "I never had much luck with close relationships. Until you. And you brought him. The circumstances of us all meeting were odd, yes, but I am very glad we were brought together."

Briar stood, needing to move, working the picks out of her hair, freeing the twisted strands and fighting back a headache that was pulsing in her skull.

"No," she decided. "Do not speak to him yet. Nothing has been found out. He deserves answers."

"You deserve answers, too, Briar."

She looked back at Phillip, still seated on the bench.

It was easier to think of all this in terms of how it affected Ben.

Because if she thought, truly, of how it affected *her*, of Frieda's callousness in just standing in that banquet room, of seeing her friend, a friend she missed so much it was a permanent ache in her soul, barely look at her, and only then with emotionless *nothingness*, as though that was what they were now, *nothing*, when in fact, they were so very, very alike . . . All the terrors that plagued Briar, the fears and worries over going from peasant to princess—Frieda felt them, too. They could help each other. They were the *same.* And yet Frieda had *stood there*. . . .

Briar pressed the heels of her palms to her eyes, trying, failing to stop tears from falling.

Phillip was there, his arms coming around her, and she buried her face into his chest, the soft rub of his shirt, the scratch of buttons digging into her cheek. His arms bracketed her, and she dug her fingers into the creases of his spine, holding on, holding on as she gasped and tears fell.

"It's all right," Phillip whispered, his head arching down to rest alongside hers. "It's all right, Briar. I'm here."

It was an echo of what she had said to him the day of the attack, the day of their wedding.

I'm here. It's all right.

"I wouldn't do that to you," she said into his shirt. She pushed back to see him, needing him to know this, to *believe* it. "I wouldn't leave you like she did him. And then to stand there, not even looking at him. If it were you, and I had not seen you in months, I . . . I wouldn't have been able to keep myself from you. I wouldn't do that to you, Phillip."

"Briar." He cupped her jaw in one strong hand. "You don't have to—"

"But I do. Because I sat there while the vassals planned to cut out your part in the rescue, as though what you did could ever be forgotten. As though you aren't an integral aspect of who I am. I want, no, *need* everyone to know how much a part of me you are. I know you do not like the accolades for your deeds, but to erase you entirely? I can't abide that. Can you?"

His face went from beseeching concern to a flash of the discomfort he showed whenever anyone spoke of what had happened with Maleficent.

"Honestly," he whispered, "I am happier not to speak of it at all."

Her chest seized. "Why?" she asked finally. "Why do you wish to forget it?"

They were alone. He could answer truthfully. He might.

Phillip leaned his forehead against hers. "It is done. It is done, and I should like to never think on it again. There are more important things—such as preparing for your campaign, and what you wish to do when you see Frieda again."

That tightness in Briar's chest worsened. "I don't want to talk about that anymore. Not now."

"Well." There was a smile in his voice. "Again, the pair we make, hmm?"

A smile rose unbidden to her lips as well.

He knotted up their hands and held them in a tangle between their chests, and it whittled Briar's focus down to that contact, the heavy silence of how very alone they were, finally.

And she should have used that solitude to get him to speak of what had happened to him the day of their wedding, why he could not sleep, what was weighing on him. But he was right—she had weights she did not want to speak of, too.

"Phillip." She said his name because she could not think of any way to phrase what was irrepressibly taking root in her stomach.

The air between them became charged, whether from him or her, she couldn't tell.

His grip on her fingers tightened. She saw him swallow.

She looked up at him from where their foreheads touched, and saw his eyes were shut.

"Don't go back to your room," she whispered.

His lips parted, a strangled burst of air. "Briar—"

"I know"—she was gasping, her heart bruising with every thud—"I know with everything that has happened, and everything still happening, that our lives are chaos, but I don't want to wait for things to settle. I don't want to wait for fate to decide when we get to be together. You are the one thing I can choose, that *we* can choose, together. I love you. And I do not know what I would do without you. But if you still want time, I—"

He laughed. An abrupt, resonating chuckle that slanted into a growl.

"Briar," he said. "Is there truly a part of you that thinks I would leave this room if you want me to stay?"

Heat dripped down her body. A slow, determined rain.

"I want you to *want* to stay," she told him. "Not because you know it is what I want. But because you want it, too."

He walked her backward a step. Toward the door to her bedchamber.

Her heart tensed.

Their foreheads were still together, and she freed her hands to grab the thick muscles of his neck, holding on for dear life.

"Briar," he whispered her name again. "We are fools. Honorable, self-sacrificial fools. Or at least, I am. *Yes*, I want to stay."

She grinned. "I didn't want to presume," she said, breathy and ardent.

"Say you love me again, and there is very little I would not want to do with you."

It was half greedy, half groveling, and it tugged at the base of Briar's stomach, her legs weakening.

"I couldn't be too forward," she said. "For all I knew, you had that lady's maid to meet again."

"Ah." She felt the twist of air in Phillip's smile. "I had all but forgotten her. Thank you for reminding me. I don't want to keep her waiting."

"No, you don't. She's been waiting quite long enough."

Her back hit the wall beside the closed door. She rocked in the jolt of it, and they froze, the ensuing silence hung with gravity that moored them both in place, forcing her to feel even more strongly the beating of his pulse in his neck, the intensifying heat in the air caged between their bodies.

"Briar," he said again, tone turning pleading. "I should like to have made this more worthy of you. Flowers everywhere—"

"Could you not be so honorable, for a few moments, at least?"

She expected him to speak again. To buffer the space, the building tension, with words, and part of her wanted to keep that buffer as well. She wanted him and he was here and they were alone and of all the impossible things that had tumbled into her life, those things rammed into each other with the greatest, most destructive impact.

But he didn't say anything.

He kissed her, a questing, worshipful movement of his lips, and when she responded with an immediate arch up into him, tongue pushing into his mouth, he answered her question.

Yes, he could not be so honorable.

He could do it very, very well, in fact.

She found the doorknob next to her, twisted, pushed the door open, half consumed by Phillip's mouth dropping onto her neck—no, fully consumed, utterly consumed—he had lifted her and was walking her into the room, and all the mismatched pieces of who she was could not sustain themselves in the radiance his mouth demanded from her skin. She felt made into a fallen angel, knowing distantly that she was bound for ruin and grief, but in this moment, she was cherished, transformed into a being of light and liquid gold by the way he worked his lips up her neck, to the curve of her ear, then back down again, down and down.

He could do that to her, the spectacular presence of him reshaping her until the awful parts slunk into the shadows cast by all the rest, and she hoped she was doing the same for him—she hoped, and hoped, until she could not gather thought at all, and then it was her and him and nothing else.

Blissful, incandescent nothing else.

Chapter Eight

The woman in blue was in a prison cell. Briar watched her writhe, bound to a chair, and tears fell down her face, hers and the woman's, so alone, so trapped.

Stay calm, *a voice said. To the woman? Briar couldn't see a source—it was not Maleficent, not her cackling taunt—*

The prison changed. Walls re-formed from stone into wood—and the prisoner became the woman beneath the five shooting stars, and she was imprisoned, too, curled helplessly on the floor of what had to be a wagon.

Empress. Wake up. *Again, not Maleficent. The same voice, though, as before.*

Stay calm.

Empress. Wake up.

Was the voice speaking to Briar?

You're stronger than this.

Your people need you.

The woman who had snuffed the fire stood in the dark, terror holding her rigid as she stared into the eyes of a soldier, eyes that glowed a sickly, possessed yellow.

I called you into existence.

How do you want your story to end?

Briar was in Maleficent's sleeping curse again.

Phillip had not saved her.

He wasn't coming.

She was these women, trapped, helpless, alone—

Stay calm.

Empress. Wake up.

Briar pleaded, begged, screamed in her own mind—she would wake up. She would wake up from this. She would WAKE UP—

• • •

Briar jolted, a scream on her lips that was only barely kept back by the realization that she was awake now. She was not in the tower, not vulnerably awaiting rescue, not victim to Maleficent's plots.

She was in a bed, in her suite in Frankfurt, shadows and warmth wrapping her in a cocoon.

She found her breath and gasped, then tried to cover it.

In the time since Phillip had saved her, the dreams had been only snatches of what she had experienced under Maleficent's curse.

But they were getting worse.

These were as vivid as they'd been when she had been fully under the spell, emotions heightened, hers and those of the women.

What was the *point* of these dreams? What did Maleficent intend by showing her these other women, and how they suffered, and how Maleficent had no doubt tortured them, too? Was she just parading her vile deeds before Briar?

Briar rubbed her eyes, scrubbing away the last of her restless sleep.

Reality came back to her, slowly.

Phillip.

Briar stretched, felt the empty side of the bed, and sat up in alarm. "Phillip?"

The curtains were drawn around the bed, but a gap at the end showed light filtering through—so morning, then.

"Phillip?" Anxiety twisted his name louder, and that echo of his absence from her nightmare had her knotting the blankets to her chest to keep herself from bolting out of bed in a frantic search. Surely he had not gone far. He would be here. He would—

The shift of movement, passing through the beam of light.

Briar's heart lurched and her thoughts ran in a quick tumble of Flora checking her food for poison, of their severity in monitoring her guards—

One of the curtains drew back.

Briar wilted at her childish fear.

Phillip smiled at her. He had dressed quickly, his shirt thrown on, untucked over rumpled breeches, his hair unkempt, and it made his smile even more dashing. She was just as disheveled, her shift askew, blond hair a knotted mess, but as his eyes held on hers in silence, she had never felt more beautiful.

He had a plate that he extended to her as he sat on the bed, letting the curtain fall back into place, closing them in.

She took the plate and grinned instantly.

"Since you did not get your usual late-night meal," Phillip said. "And it is morning, after all."

A roll of bread, a mound of jam, slices of dried sausage. She set the plate on the blanket and tore off a chunk of the bread. It was still warm, and smelled deliciously of yeast and dusty flour and something a little sour.

"I was told by the servants," he continued, "that all the food served while we are here is in honor of the candidates' homes—bread in the style of Lüneburg, sausages from Lothier, and so on. I know you will want to try it all, so we had best continue, I figure."

Her smile stretched as she ate. "You know my weaknesses too well, Sir Knight."

"You are easy to please," he whispered.

It was meant to be sweet, and it was. But her lips pursed in a barely suppressed laugh.

He blushed, even in the low light of the canopied bed, even after last night, when nothing should have embarrassed them now.

"I meant— I—" he stuttered. "Only that— Well. Oh, eat your food and be silent."

"I said nothing!"

"That look of yours speaks with its own voice."

"What look? This look? You do not care for this look? It is innocence embodied! How could you—"

He lunged across the bed, over the plate, and hauled her into a kiss. She went eagerly, him and this gift he had brought her thoroughly chasing away her nightmare until she shuddered with the fear sloughing off, shuddered more when he nipped at her mouth.

But it was morning.

Her eyes shut with a wince. "Do you know the time?"

Phillip's hand slid down her neck, down her shoulder, in a featherlight brush that left her shivering. "The fairies will be here shortly to ready you. Your vassals left a note—many of the candidates will be gathered in a garden today, partaking in games. It is meant to be a more relaxed start to the days ahead."

"Relaxed," she deadpanned.

"Yes, no doubt stress will cease to exist with all candidates and Prince Electors milling in one area."

Briar rocked forward, head going to her knees. "And Frieda."

Phillip swept the hair off the back of her neck, taking a strand, twisting it through his fingers. "What do you wish to do about her?"

Many things. She knew what she *should* do—focus on impressing the Prince Electors, fight to keep Bavaria from seizing the throne, position herself so she might keep those in Austria safe. Today's planned games would let each candidate display their cunning and calculation—qualities that, Briar knew, were not her strongest.

But what did she *want* to do?

She wanted to talk to her friend. She wanted to . . . to simply *speak* with her, to hear Frieda's story.

Was it possible that Frieda did not even want this?

Her actions yesterday flashed through Briar's mind. How Frieda had been reserved, and Briar had attributed it to her not caring—but what if it had been to cover her fear?

What if Frieda was a hostage of Matilda's?

The idea lit such horror in Briar that she bolted upright, Phillip's grip on her hair snatching tight.

She yelped.

"Sorry!"

"Did my vassals leave any other notes?" She rubbed her scalp. "Have they found more about her story yet?"

"Not that I saw."

"Then I will speak to her myself."

Phillip nodded. "I will come with you."

She took his hand, her thumb rubbing over the lines of his palm, tracing paths she knew by heart now. "Thank you, but I think it best if I speak to her alone. Or as alone as is possible in a garden full of others. No, can you see to Ben today? Ensure he is . . . not *well*, that is hardly possible, but simply . . ."

"Doing nothing foolish?"

She grunted. "That may also be hardly possible with him, but yes."

Phillip closed his hand around hers. "Of course. We have a joust to prepare for, anyway. That will hopefully distract him. I assume other jousting champions are in attendance—perhaps I can introduce him to others he will fawn over."

"I said to see to Ben, not to make him comatose."

Phillip smiled. It wasn't as true as before, and it highlighted the bruises under his eyes, sleeplessness leaving its mark.

He had not slept well. Neither had she. Even in each other's arms.

Her eyes dropped to the tangle of their hands on the bedding.

"This isn't the place I would have chosen to celebrate our marriage," she whispered.

Phillip tugged on her hand until she looked at him. "When this is over, however it ends, we will go somewhere, you and I. There is a hunting lodge on a lake in Lorraine. No court, no responsibilities.

We will spend the days seeing only each other and dozing on the shore."

The image was pure heaven.

"Idyllic." What she really meant to say was *It sounds like a dream.* And it did. A dream far out of reach—for if she won, she would be locked into duties as empress, and if she lost, she would have to prepare Austria for Bavaria's rise to power.

So she merely kissed Phillip to hide her uncertainty, though she knew he saw it anyway.

The time for dreaming would be later.

Though she knew not when.

• • •

Briar's vassals escorted her to the garden. Her aunts had declared themselves her personal guards, and today it was Flora who followed close to her while Fauna and Merryweather rendezvoused with her soldiers. It continued to itch at Briar that they were so concerned for her safety. Thus far, she had seen no actual threats, merely her aunts' fear that something would happen. But then again, they had always been concerned with protecting her, and Stefan's death was still fresh.

The garden stretched out from the castle, a series of hedges, some waist-high, others looming in wandering mazes. A crowd was gathered, the same people from the banquet yesterday, spread among gaming tables that were arranged at random through the hedges—chess, cards, dice, others Briar thought she recognized.

But the moment she exited the castle into the bright, sunny space, the blue sky wild and vibrant over her, Filibert of Lüneburg staggered past, all but shoving her aside in his desperation to get back inside. He stumbled, face a putrid shade of green, and Briar leapt away as he faltered to freedom without a word.

His attendants rushed after him. "Apologies, Your Majesty, the duke is unwell. Apologies," they said, and then the party was gone.

Briar eyed Flora, who was frowning after Filibert.

"Ben said he is renowned for being in his cups," Briar offered.

That snapped Flora's attention to her in a horrified gasp. "Your Majesty must not speak so freely of your fellow candidates!"

Oh, how was *that* a true concern, when the mother of a fellow candidate had *murdered* Stefan? But Briar let the argument drop.

She needed to find Frieda.

Briar set off into the garden. There was no formal announcement, thankfully, but eyes lifted as she passed, candidates in deep games with Prince Electors or members of their households. She spotted Johann at a table across from the Prince Elector of Saxony, face scrunched in concentration over a game of chess.

He looked up at her and gave a bright smile.

She could practically see the word "decorum" flash through his mind, and he sank into himself, switching to give her a formal, too-mature nod.

In return, Briar crossed her eyes and curled her lip.

Johann barked a laugh and slapped his hands over his mouth. Most of the others in this area were engrossed in their games, and barely flinched at his outburst; still, Briar grinned.

"Your Majesty," Flora said in chastisement, but Briar was surprised to find her usually stoic aunt fighting a smile.

She faked a sneeze as though that was the reason for her odd face. "So sorry. The flowers."

"Hmm."

But Johann had noticed Flora now, too, her wings out and wand in hand, and that joy returned to his face without pretense.

She sighed and rolled her eyes. "The things I do for children," she muttered and flicked her wand, letting a sizzle of glittery magic fill the air in front of her, temporarily taking the form of a galloping horse before it faded away.

Even across the space, Johann's wonder was palpable.

The Prince Elector playing against him said something, unaware of the magic or the silent interaction he was having, and Johann jerked back to the chessboard, stealing furtive glances at Flora.

Briar pushed on, ducking out of this area, but the weight in her chest did not much lighten, particularly as she rounded a hedge and saw Frieda.

Briar had never had the patience for games. Frieda had, though, and when days had been particularly bleak for their coin earned through song, Frieda was able to bring in handfuls of winnings through whatever game she could join in town.

So as Briar spotted Frieda at a table by a wall of blooming pink roses, a Prince Elector across from her, it was too fitting, almost as though she were watching her friend play a hand in Rolf's tavern.

Briar stopped just inside the clearing, unseen by Frieda for a moment.

Matilda was paces behind Frieda, speaking with another Elector, her smile empty and her eyes intent. Not at all subtly,

Matilda took the Elector's hand and placed a small bag of what was clearly money into his palm.

She curled his fingers around it. He inclined his head in thanks.

Briar's vassals were in conversation behind her. Some had drifted away already, mingling or seeking out information on her behalf. Flora, though, was close by, eyeing Frieda and Matilda with a scowl.

"Did you see that?" Briar asked.

Flora's scowl deepened. "Indeed. Your vassals, though, will handle any such interactions. Do *not* allow me to catch you debasing yourself by passing off bribes with your own hands. Matilda should be ashamed. Then again, I take it not much shames the likes of *her*."

Briar stood in uncomfortable stillness.

Flora was upset not about the bribery itself, but that Matilda had been the one to pass it off, and not one of her staff.

Briar should ask what other things were a part of campaigning that she would recoil at. But she didn't want to know.

Frieda was at that table still, and it looked as though she had beaten the Prince Elector. In good humor; they were both smiling.

Frieda was *smiling.*

Utterly different than yesterday, her eyes were bright and her face clear and she was the happy, observant woman Briar had known in Hausach.

It sat in Briar's stomach like a rock.

Flora nudged her. "The place at the table is free. Go—play against her. You would do well to assert yourself after yesterday."

"I—" Again, Briar's mind went blank, freezing her in place. "I had intended to, but not to *play* against her. I want to speak to her. And why are you encouraging me to interact with her? I would think you, of all people, would be set against it."

Flora's face fell. In that moment, Briar saw not a powerful fairy, but her aunt who had spent years dedicated to protecting a cursed, exiled princess, buried under a secret, tasked with an existence she had no training for. There were many things she faulted Flora for, but Briar loved her too.

"If I had a say," Flora whispered, "no, you would not interact. But it is necessary. And you will dispel any rumors if you assert yourself to her. Now, go."

Briar thought nothing at all of the campaign as she crossed to the table, the hem of her scarlet gown and gold kirtle brushing the smooth stones of the garden path.

Frieda was bidding farewell to the Prince Elector. She did not notice until Briar stood next to the empty chair across from her.

Then Frieda snapped to attention.

Her smile plummeted off her face, cheeks going vivid red. Her lips tightened into a line, jaw bulging, and Briar couldn't find a way to force air into her lungs as they simply looked at each other for a moment.

"May I sit?" Briar asked.

Behind Frieda, Matilda was watching. Not intervening. She was holding back a grin. All in the area around them, those nearby between these hedges, had paused in their games or conversations, and were watching now, too.

So no private conversation, then.

Still, Briar could question her somewhat, find out, at least, if her friend was being ill-treated or forced into this role. But her smile had been so *real.*

Briar hated, *hated*, that her next thought was to *hope* that Frieda *was* being forced into this. Because if she was here willingly, Briar wasn't sure how she could handle that.

Frieda nodded. As Briar drew out the chair and sat, Frieda arched one eyebrow.

"Though I am surprised you wish to," she said. "Given how much you hate this game."

Briar's eyes dropped for the first time to the board set before Frieda.

Damn it all to burn and writhe in the afterlife.

Rithmomachia.

A game that was equal parts chess and arithmetic with no end to the complication of strategy. The board was longer than one for chess, with pieces shaped like triangles, circles, and squares, all with a variety of numbers on them that could be stacked into pyramid pieces valuing certain sums. Those numbered pieces could influence others depending on whether they were equal to, lesser than, or greater than the numbers of enemy pieces, multiplied by spaces on the board between them, and the whole thing was a creation straight from the devil himself.

A passing merchant had brought rithmomachia to Rolf's tavern a few times. Frieda had picked it up instantly and played not merely to win coin, but because she'd enjoyed it in what Briar could only imagine was latent masochism.

Ben had bellowed laughter at the first line of instruction and spent the whole time Frieda played strumming his lute.

Briar had tried to play and come away with nothing but a raging headache.

This did not bode well, then, facing Frieda across a rithmomachia board.

Briar forced a smile. Whatever game it was did not matter.

"Are you well?" Briar asked with a smile meant to assuage any onlookers.

Frieda began arranging pieces on the board.

"We do not have to play," Briar said. "I was hoping we could simply—"

"You concede already?" Frieda's eyebrows went up. With eagerness.

She glanced to the side, at where her mother stood; but she didn't turn all the way around, more a quick flinch, a barely restrained *Do you see? I have bested her already!*

That was pride in Frieda's eyes.

She *wanted* to please Matilda.

Briar stared at that spark, willing it to become something else.

This hedge area was silent now. The Prince Electors and the other candidates alike all focused on them, on their tense interaction. Briar's vassals had gathered, and Flora too.

Still, Briar held Frieda's gaze, trying to impart everything to her wordlessly.

I am terrified for you. What did Matilda do to you? Did she hurt you? What happened?

"It has been a while since I have seen you," Briar tried again. "I want to know how you are. To talk to you."

Frieda held the game pieces in her hand. "I will talk. If you play."

"Frieda—"

"Clara." Frieda bent over the table, eyes igniting. "Princess Clara. As you should well know. *Queen Aurora.*"

She was angry. At Briar's use of her name. If she were here against her will, coerced into all this, would she be upset by that?

But that flash of anger was close to the Frieda that Briar knew.

So Briar nodded. "Princess Clara. I will play, then."

Frieda laid out the pieces. Briar was so aware of the eyes on them, Prince Electors studying, analyzing; of Matilda's bribe to one already; of the game on this table and the game being played around them and the way Frieda gave her a wicked smile that looked so very much like Matilda's.

"Your move first, Your Majesty," Frieda said.

Briar lifted a piece, moved it; it hardly mattered who started. "How did you come to leave Hausach?" she asked. She tried to keep her voice low, though the garden was so silent that every rustle of fabric echoed alongside the buzzing of insects.

Frieda, hand extended to make her move, went stiff. Her fingers arched into claws and she snapped up with a look of such malice that Briar drew back.

But Frieda transformed it into a smile, though it seemed to take effort. "You know the answer to that, Austrian queen."

The tension in the air was agonizing, a kettle rising to a boil, and Briar had no idea why it had spiked so quickly.

"I had gotten all I needed in that village, anyway," Frieda continued as she laid her piece on the board. "It was time to move on, with or without your involvement."

"My involvement? I was not even in Hausach when you—"

Frieda gripped the edge of the table. The pieces rattled. "No. You weren't. Were you?"

That too-familiar shame flooded Briar's body. "I left you. I know. I wanted to apologize. I *did* apologize—you got my letter, at least. I came down to Hausach not long after. Ben said you were—"

"Your apology means nothing." Aching vehemence tinged Frieda's words.

Because Briar had mentioned Ben.

She bit the inside of her cheek.

Frieda leaned back with a sniff. "What I am more interested in," she continued, and Briar moved her next game piece, "is how *you* left. Escorted by a trio of magical fairies, who knew the details of Maleficent's curse all along? *Before the sun sets on her sixteenth birthday, she will prick her finger on the spindle of a spinning wheel.*"

Briar set her jaw at Frieda's tone. At the look in her eyes, a hunter's look, but Briar could not see the prey.

"Yes?"

"So why, do tell—I have wondered since I heard the tale—did your fairy guardians not wait until the day *after* your sixteenth birthday to return you to the castle? Would that not have circumvented the curse entirely? They knew its stipulations. And instead of seeing it through to the logical end that would have ensured your safety, they cast you back into harm's way with hours left of your timeline."

Briar's eyes widened. She had no response to that.

She had wondered that very thing herself, though she had never voiced it aloud. She'd had too many other things to be upset over after the curse lifted.

Flora was gripping her wand and glaring at Frieda.

"I am sure their intentions were good," Frieda kept on. She moved her piece on the board, and Briar sat frozen. "But even given their failure, you have kept them on as your closest counsel. What does that say of you? That you forgive them for endangering your life, for carelessly shirking their sole duty—"

"That is not what—"

"—and then you reward them for imperiling *your whole country* by continuing to tolerate their advice and influence? What advice are they giving you that is weakening Austria, that would, in turn, weaken the whole empire?"

Briar could only manage quick, inefficient breaths. No explanation came, no arguments or counters—because Frieda was right. It was more complicated than she was implying, though, and what other choice did Briar have? How could she cast out the people who had raised her? How could she unload her anger at them—how betrayed they had made her feel, how hurt she was by their actions and lack of actions and shortsightedness?

Even just yesterday, Flora had suggested Ben *die* for Briar, as though it was a natural thing, when all Flora had to do to test a food's safety was use her magic.

Frieda did glance back at Matilda now with a wide, satiated grin. Matilda didn't bother to mask her own luminous smile.

Frieda had been cunning, before. In Hausach. It had kept them alive, and Briar had been the balance to her ruthlessness: *envisions peace*, as her vassals had noted. Whereas Frieda had gone after any who cheated them on payments or stole their earnings, Briar had more than once discovered that the thief or cheater themselves were starving, too. Frieda had called her soft, but conceded to share what little they had.

Now Briar saw the utter uselessness of her *soft* qualities over Frieda's single-minded cruelty.

Briar could barely speak.

A murmur ebbed through the crowd as the Prince Electors acknowledged the truth in Frieda's words.

But no. This had not come from Frieda. Briar's reality broke, fractured around her, as she realized she was not sitting at this table with her friend from Hausach any more than Briar the peasant bard was here.

This was Princess Clara. And she was Queen Aurora.

Briar made her next move on the board, the numbers blurring—would this piece get captured? She didn't know. Her hand shook.

Frieda was not here against her will. She was not trying to seek Briar's help; she was not trying to make amends.

She was out for blood. Out to win empress.

She had left Ben, left Briar too, with all the callousness that Briar had feared.

"It is hypocritical," Briar started, the words ash in her mouth, "for you to sit here, spewing talk of my failures in council, when your own council is so marvelously flawed."

Frieda's eyes narrowed. Her next move came, and she did capture Briar's piece.

"Were you part of the plans made to assassinate my father?" Briar snapped. "Or did that honor fall on Matilda's shoulders alone?"

"You would accuse Bavaria of assassinating the Austrian king?" Frieda gaped at her, but there was a glimmer in it, of hope that Briar was doing exactly that.

Briar absorbed her response. "You deny it?"

"I do not deny that your king was assassinated. But my mother certainly did not have a hand in it."

She *was* denying it. Outright. As though Matilda had not marched into Austria, armored and gleaming; as though Matilda had not murdered the king, at Briar's feet.

"So he assassinated himself?" Briar snapped. "Yes, I have heard that people spontaneously grow arrows out of their necks."

A harsh thing to say, and Briar regretted it immediately—Stefan had been her king, her father somewhat, and she should not speak so mercilessly of him.

A gasp sucked the air around her. Murmurs sharpened.

Frieda shook her head in a quick show of annoyance. "This false information must be attributed to your council, which we have already established is lacking. Queen Matilda had no involvement in King Stefan's death—though not for lack of your allies attempting to pin it on her."

"My allies? What are you—"

"Oh, I would not dare speak ill of any fellow ruler." Frieda gave Briar a pointed look that said *Unlike you*. "But if you took a moment to analyze the situation beyond the whispers in your ear, you would have looked into, perhaps, the quality of the Bavarian armor supposedly used by the assassins, and how the make of the plated metal was a style known to come from your newest solidified ally, and not from my country."

"Are you saying that Bavaria was framed for Stefan's murder? By *Lorraine*?"

Another gasp from the onlookers.

Why? What was she saying that was so much worse than Frieda's accusations? She could barely stomach this conversation, let alone the misplaced horror coming from the Prince Electors and other candidates.

After Briar fumbled through a move, it was Frieda's turn again, and she managed to create a pyramid piece that would trump most of Briar's remaining regular ones. "I would not make such a tactless accusation. I am saying, merely, that evidence points one way, and your advisers point another."

"There is no evidence like what you mentioned. And what explanation do you have for your mother's presence in Austria at all?"

"She was invited to your wedding, of course."

"She was *invited*?" It came as a shout, and more started to follow, screams that welled up in Briar's throat. How Matilda had marched into Austria in full armor, sword ready, and led the charge herself.

But she quickly saw what that would look like, crying *Liar* and dissolving in hurt emotions while Frieda simply brushed it off with a controlled shrug.

Briar had never been on this side of Frieda's manipulation before, her control wielded like a knife. And she realized . . . that was how Frieda had always been to others. She had been Matilda's daughter, cutthroat and focused, even when neither she nor Briar had known.

"It is your move, Queen Aurora," Frieda said with an unfurling grin, before she nodded at the table. "On the board."

Briar's chest constricted. Her vision began to go spotty, tunneling to only Frieda—Clara, this woman was *Clara*, not Frieda, and Briar could not convince herself that her friend was *this* now.

Her heart was breaking. But at the same time, that salvaging fury was rising up again, and she clenched her hand into a fist and played the next few moves in dwelling silence.

Frieda was going to win this game of rithmomachia. Briar had known she would.

As she made her last move, letting Frieda claim victory, Briar looked up and said the only thing she knew would rattle her.

"Ben would be ashamed of you. He is, in fact. And so am I, *Princess*."

Chapter Nine

Briar shoved up from the table without pretense, knocking into it. The board teetered, spilling pieces into Frieda's lap, but she didn't react to them, staring blankly at the chair Briar had vacated, finally stunned into silence.

The Prince Electors, the other candidates, Matilda, Flora, her vassals—they were all in similar shock.

Briar had to leave. She had to leave *now.* She had to find Phillip. She had to—

"The victory goes to my daughter!" Matilda's clear voice rang out behind her. "What an *outburst* from Austria. How vulgar."

Vulgar? *Vulgar?*

Briar rushed through the garden—Johann called out to her; she gave him an apologetic headshake and kept going, going, back into the castle's hall, panting, fighting for air that her lungs refused.

A hand grabbed her arm.

"Your Majesty!" Flora's tone was pinched shock, and Briar

hoped for relief, for explanation, for *something* to anchor to because Phillip wasn't here and she was spiraling.

"I am sorry," Flora said, eyes teary. "I am *sorry*. I did not think of our failure. Oh, we reflect so poorly on you—how did I not see it? We gave her this win."

That hardly mattered. The campaign, this damn *game*.

Frieda hated her. *Hated* her, and believed whatever vile story Matilda had spun about Stefan's death, and had sat there, ripping Briar apart, without so much as a wince of regret.

From behind Briar, the vassals rushed up, and they, too, looked stricken, though more somber. The hall remained otherwise empty, though it was hardly a private place for any conversation.

"Your Majesty," Köning started, winded. "You cannot leave the game in such a way. You must apologize!"

Briar staggered, pulling her hand out of Flora's grip. "Apologize?"

"You openly insulted your rival in front of the Prince Electors." Köning was fighting to keep his voice level, but true panic was in his eyes.

"She denied Bavaria's attack," Briar tried, but she could feel her resolve weakening as she spoke. Whatever Frieda had done did not justify Briar's response; if they were anywhere normal, it would have, but not *here*, not when she was supposed to be Queen Aurora. "She accused *Lorraine* of staging it—"

"She was vicious, yes, but that is the campaign, Your Majesty. She said nothing direct; *you* did. She hypothesized and laid the foundation, hoping to stoke you to what she did—anger and outburst. What she insinuated was dreadful, but what *you* said to her was openly cruel. You must apologize."

Briar's heart sank. She knew. She felt it, the wrongness in her breakdown, but she rubbed at her chest, trying to assuage the hurt.

She shook her head, incredulous, and shook it again. "I was supposed to show my strengths and speak of my skills and prove myself, not coerce and lie."

But, most of all, she had not been prepared to have to do any of this against Frieda.

Köning stepped back. "The rules of propriety you have been learning in your time first as princess, now as queen, remain in place. You cannot act outside the bounds of grace and demureness, even to unseat your opponents. We assumed you would realize that, Your Majesty, and that assumption was a shortcoming on our parts."

"Let us count this day, perhaps, as a loss for all of us," Lord Lehmann cut in. "Though you know now, Your Majesty, that you cannot attack directly. It is a subtle game. The Prince Electors will not cast their votes for someone incapable of controlling their emotions. That is the purpose of these three weeks of events, to test candidates from as many angles as possible."

"I need to go," Briar said, her jaw still tight, anger and disappointment in herself still heating her head to toe. She started to turn, but Köning made a noise of protest.

"To leave now would be to admit defeat utterly. If you will not publicly apologize, you must at least retain a presence within the garden. Play a game with another candidate or an Elector—but you must be known and seen."

No. *No.* She could not simply pretend that everything was fine. It was *unbearable*, this game, all of it. She couldn't do it.

But Frieda was doing it. And Matilda. And if Briar left, she would hurt Austria, Hausach, her people who would be at Bavaria's mercy under their control of the empire.

This was the only way to keep them safe. To make sure she retained what power she had, so that she might improve their lives as best she could.

Lehmann got Köning's attention. "We will arrange for the Electors to be in better moods for the next event. If you need time to calm down"—he looked at Briar—"be present in the garden, but you do not have to be active now. There are ways to ensure smaller victories so your reputation is not sullied entirely."

"You mean bribery?" Briar guessed, a whisper.

Their silence was confirmation. Lehmann and Köning shared a confused look, unsure of why she seemed against such a concept.

Revulsion churned in her stomach.

Flora touched her shoulder. "What do you wish to do, Your Majesty?" she asked, soft, pleading. Her eyes held an echo of the unspoken insistency the three fairies had shown in her suite, when Merryweather had asked the same question.

Briar headed for the garden again with a quick, curt nod at Lehmann. "Do whatever you think is best."

"Your Majesty—" Flora called, but Briar was back outside already. That was what she wanted, wasn't it? Queen Aurora, playing this game for empress.

What do you wish to do?

She had no idea. She only knew what she *didn't* wish to do. And it would leave her flailing in weakness, sulking about emotions she didn't want to face.

Johann was still at the chessboard, playing now against one of his attendants. The moment Briar reappeared, he waved at her, more cautiously now, and she headed for him.

"May I play the next game?" she asked, because he was the only person she could tolerate.

The attendant immediately tipped his king on its side. "I concede. Your game, Your Majesty."

Johann frowned at the man. "I do not tolerate cowards."

The attendant, half out of the chair, sighed heavily. "What curse, then, Zauberer?"

"An allergy to bread. Violent retching. For a week."

Briar gasped, half in mock surprise, half in vibrant relief at being distracted, beautifully, by Johann. "That *is* cruel, Zauberer. To be parted from bread is to be denied a reason to live."

"It is fine, Your Majesty," the attendant said. He gave Briar a helpless look, thinly veiled amusement glittering in his eyes. "A week of bread-vomiting is fair in this situation."

Johann sat back, fingers steepled, and glowered with dark satisfaction as his attendant slunk away.

Briar took the vacated seat.

"Do not let me win," Johann told her.

"I would not dream of it, nor am I much in the mood for it."

Johann huffed. "My attendants let me win."

"They fear you."

"Of course." He shifted upright, chin high. "Because I am an evil sorcerer."

The alternative was so obvious to Briar that it tripped her thoughts, and she looked up at Johann with a gentle smile. "No.

They fear you because you are king. Because no matter what acts you do to them, they are bound to you, and you have the power to upend their whole world with one command. No sorcery required."

Johann's mouth dipped open. His brows pinched together.

"I had not considered that," he said after a moment.

"It is a terrible thing to be made to do something against your will," Briar whispered, half to herself. "More terrible to be forced to do it out of fear of death."

Movement had Briar's eyes flicking to the side.

A Prince Elector stood not far, clearly listening to their conversation.

"Do you—" Johann started, then stopped, and his shoulders bent.

Briar refocused on him, campaigning be damned. "What is it?"

He peeked up at her, dark eyes vulnerable. "How do you get them to not fear you? I wouldn't—" He lowered his voice and leaned over the table. "I wouldn't *actually* hurt any of them. They know that. I think."

Briar lifted a pawn. Looking down at the carved marble, she felt the unbelievable gravity of this moment, that a king of a foreign land would ask her opinion on how to rule. Granted, he was a child, but still.

"I am new to this as well," she said to the pawn piece. "But when I was a peasant, I wished that those in power had realized that others have power, too. And that they had used what power they had to make mine stronger instead of suppressing it or manipulating it."

She set her piece on the board, starting the game.

Johann's lips screwed up in thought.

The Prince Elector walked away, and Briar watched his retreating back, unable to determine if she had pleased him.

She found she almost did not care. Though she should.

They played, Johann occasionally asking about what she had been doing since her father's death. How she was dealing with being queen.

She told him how she had sent resources to Hausach. That her vassals were compiling reports on the neediest areas, so that she might balance inequities throughout Austria—and Lorraine now. But beyond that, she had no real answers for him. She wished she did.

Her lack of answers, her uncertainty, seemed to help him. For if someone who had real magic in her life didn't know how to rule a country, then it was all right, maybe, if a normal boy didn't know, either.

Johann defeated her at chess, utterly, and he sat back with a whoop of joy.

Briar smiled, willing it to not be too hollow.

She had lost all the day's games.

But she had no idea, truly, how to go about winning, if winning meant she would have to destroy Frieda.

• • •

"You would not have recognized her, Ben. I barely did."

A day later, Phillip, Briar, and Ben were in Briar's suite, a last few moments of stillness before her aunts and vassals would arrive to strategize for the evening's ball. It was the first time she had been able to speak with Ben since the banquet, but Phillip had said he had been uncharacteristically quiet, throwing himself into chores with abandon, not even tempted by the prospect of meeting the jousters who would represent the other candidates in a few days.

Frieda would be at the ball tonight, and Ben did not have to go, but he had said he would. And as Ben sat on the window bench in Lorraine's livery, yellow and red with a white eagle, Briar pretended to fix her hair in the mirror and could not bring herself to look at him.

She had not wanted to tell him what Frieda had said over the rithmomachia game. Except he had heard, it turned out—information among servants spread faster than pollen in a wildflower field.

"It isn't her," Ben said to the floor. "Whoever she is now, it isn't Frieda."

Briar met Phillip's eyes in the mirror. She had been saying the same argument to herself, to Phillip.

"Only it is," Briar said. "And I cannot make sense of it. It was as though Matilda was puppeteering her. I don't—"

Ben's head whipped up. "She was there, wasn't she? The whole conversation?"

Briar nodded.

"Perhaps she was controlling Frieda, in a way. Perhaps Matilda's mere presence was enough to force her submission." He launched to his feet, emboldened by whatever idea was churning in him. Hope,

Briar saw in the cracks of his grief; he still had hope. She loved him for it. "I wonder if her attitude would be different if Matilda wasn't in earshot."

Based on the way Frieda had looked at Matilda, yearning for approval and pride, Briar doubted it. But she wasn't willing to let Ben doubt quite yet.

"I can distract the queen tonight." Briar moved her heavy lilac skirts. "Give you time to approach Frieda to—"

"No." His rebuke was sharp. "No. She doesn't want to see me."

"Ben, you don't know she—"

"You think I didn't try?" His voice cracked, eyes squinting with a wash of pain, and it silenced her, made Phillip dip his head. "You think I didn't spend the last two nights working up the courage to approach her, and then when I got to her rooms, she wouldn't even look at me? *Again.* Told her lapdog soldiers to cast me out, *again.* What could I do in a ballroom that would be any different? I can cause an awful scene, wailing like a heartbroken poet, but I doubt that would do much to help your campaign."

Briar sighed, chewed her words. "You know I wouldn't care if you did that."

"Ah, but your vassals surely would."

That yanked Phillip's attention to him. "Did one of them speak to you?"

Ben rolled his eyes. "Stand down, Sir Knight. I can handle their chastising—that Lehmann may be a military hero, but he's about as intimidating as a chamber pot. No, *I* also care, Bri." He pointed at her. "*I* care that in my first moments of publicly being a squire, I mucked it up fantastically. So, no, I'm not going to talk to her again.

Not until she wants me to. *You* talk to her. Phillip and I will create a distraction."

"And you can be trusted to speak cordially and not cause a scene with Matilda?" she asked.

Ben's face fell. After a long beat, he said only, "Hmm."

Phillip chuckled. "Luckily, as a squire, you have no reason to even speak to the Bavarian queen. Leave any conversation to me."

Ben put a hand to his chest, feigning a swoon. "There you are, Sir Knight, sweeping to the rescue."

"I'm not sure I like you calling him that, too," Briar said, but the weight was lifting, the shadow of Frieda's presence here lurking, though there was room to breathe. They had a plan.

Would it make a difference? Would Frieda react at all better?

Or would she find ever more potent ways to hurt Briar?

"Oh yes, Bri, you caught me," said Ben. "Phillip, my love, she has discovered our sordid affair!"

Phillip rubbed at his temples. "You're released from service, truly this time."

"That threat has ceased to have meaning."

The door opened, and in came her aunts and vassals.

It wasn't particularly funny, but something about Ben's joke and the severe expressions on her aunts' and vassals' faces clashed so potently that Briar bit her lip. Then she noticed that Phillip, too, was on the verge of chuckling; but then Ben burst out laughing, and that was all it took for the three of them to fall apart.

Flora slammed the door shut. "Decorum, please! Have you no decency?"

Ben sobered enough to say, "Decency? *Us?*"

"Oh, don't make a joke of that," Briar said. "That fruit is so low hanging it's already jam."

That set Ben off laughing even harder, Briar and Phillip, too.

It felt so good, too good, to laugh like this, although it came from a place of desperation for levity amid the harrowed looks on the faces of her vassals and aunts.

She knew what awaited her.

And in this moment, this was how she could best prepare.

"Squire Benedikt," Lehmann said loudly, over their laughter. "Have you anything new to report on the other candidates?"

They all knew by now the skill Ben had displayed in gathering information before their arrival in Frankfurt, and while the vassals did their best to get what news they could, there was always a certain amount best gotten through those who often went overlooked.

Ben pressed the heels of his hands into his eyes, steadying himself, and Briar fought to follow suit.

"News! Yes." Ben sniffed and looked up at the ceiling. "Filibert of Lüneburg is still bedridden with an illness his servants swear isn't related to drinking, though I have plenty of doubts. And his brother has not been seen since the banquet, did you know? That is hardly surprising, given his usual excursions in the city—"

Köning frowned. "They are both removed from the campaign?"

"Well, not *removed*—not formally. But unable to present themselves."

Silence fell over the room. The vassals, however solemn, were not surprised by this news, and the look they shared before shifting awkwardly may as well have been a shout.

"What aren't you saying?" Briar asked.

Köning shook his head. "Nothing, Your Highness. We have other business to turn to, with the ball in but a few minutes. If you will—"

Briar eyed Köning, not relenting. "You suspect foul play?"

The vassals shared another look.

The last remnants of laughter shriveled so abruptly in Briar's chest that she felt their deadened weight like stones.

Again, Briar got the sense that there was more they were keeping from her, the same way they had never truly explained the lies she would need to tell to win campaigning conversations.

Before they could compose a proper response, Briar looked at her aunts. "You have been overly concerned with my security, but have found nothing so far, correct?"

At Fauna's sudden wince, Briar's mouth hung open.

"You have," she said slowly. "You've found attempts on . . . my person?"

She couldn't bear to clarify *attempts on my life.* Were people here trying to *kill* her? But Filibert and Gottlieb weren't dead, merely laid low. Or, at least, Filibert was—what had happened to his brother?

Flora cleared her throat, surely to brush off Briar's concern, but it was Merryweather who flung her wand around with such an annoyed twitch that a stream of bubbles shot out, framing her reddening face. "I told you we should tell her!"

"Merryweather," Flora tried, but Fauna put her hand on her sister's arm.

"It may help keep her safe."

"Is this truly how the campaign is played?" Briar managed, her throat constricting. "Not only do candidates unseat one another through useless verbal sparring matches, but we also attempt to harm one another?"

Phillip was next to her, his hand on her waist, and she felt the dip in his mood, too.

Köning spoke, but slowly, weighing each word with care. "This is an . . . unfortunate reality of the election. Candidates have been known to suffer accidents."

"One was murdered last time," Merryweather said without padding, and Flora hissed at her.

Briar's eyes widened. "And you tell me this *now*?"

"We have your safety perfectly in hand!" Flora promised, but then her face sank, and she was no doubt remembering Frieda's accusations in the garden. Her very accurate accusations, about how the fairies had failed to protect Briar from Maleficent's curse.

Briar turned back to Ben. "Is anyone else missing?"

He shook his head. "Not that I've heard. Should I look into Gottlieb's absence more?"

"Yes."

"It'll be done."

Lies. Coercion. Bribery.

And now, threat of attack, at best poison to make her bedridden; at worst, death.

A thought occurred that threw her exhausted fear into clarity.

"Have any of you tried to attack a candidate on my behalf?" Her voice grated.

Phillip's hand tightened on her body.

Köning immediately shook his head. "Of course not, Your Majesty! Your council long ago decided that is not how Austria would best approach this campaign."

Did she believe him? They were paying bribes for her, weren't they? Why not this, too, if it was how the game was played?

"You have not been truthful about the nature of this campaign," she stated, her voice level.

"We have not." Lehmann didn't hesitate to agree. He stood from his spot at a small table near the door and clasped his hands against his back. "The messy underside of politics is ours to worry about. Especially for one such as you, young and as yet untested—one of your best qualities is that very innocence we sought to preserve. It was a calculated move not to tell you, Your Highness, not an attempt at subterfuge."

She thought back on that list of qualities. Nowhere on it had been listed *innocent* or *naïve.*

But would she still have been *passionate* and *fearless* and *thoughtful* if she had come in knowing her fellow candidates would be so vicious? Unlikely, she knew. She would have been hard-pressed to hide her disgust, her concern.

How did her vassals know that she would have reacted in such a way? Did they truly have her read so well—or was Lehmann lying, and they just simply did not believe she could handle it?

Though she could not have handled it. She *would* have reacted poorly—she was reacting poorly now. And she would have to go into the ball and pretend everything was fine, and she wasn't certain she could.

Briar rubbed her palms on her gown, the beaded designs snagging on her skin, rough and gritty.

She had told them she would do whatever they thought was best. She had told them to *do* whatever they thought was best.

How far would they go?

"We have a ball to get to," she heard herself say.

Köning shifted in his seat. "Do you wish to go over talking points for the Prince Electors?" he asked cautiously.

What did it matter? They could simply pay off anyone she did not impress, couldn't they? What need did she have to be here at all—couldn't she have stayed back in Austria and merely sent a lump sum of gold rather than risk her health and life in this vipers' den?

Briar shook her head. "I will be fine," she said, and she pulled those words around herself.

Because she *would* be, she decided.

"Your Majesty—" Flora started, but Briar cut her off when she glared from Köning to Lehmann to the rest of her vassals, and her aunts as well.

"None of you will harm anyone on my behalf," she told them. They had assured her they hadn't already, but this order would prevent any such thing happening at all. "And if you must bribe someone, consult me first. I do not sit well with the idea that Austria's money is lining pockets here, when we have so many projects to put it toward back home. Speaking of—do you yet have the information on the areas most in need?"

Her aunts made a sound she couldn't place—a gasp? A sigh? She glanced at them, but they bowed their heads to her.

Köning blinked at her, before shuffling through his perpetual stack of notes. "It is coming along, Your Highness. Riders have been dispatched to certain provinces to ask directly what resources are needed. We shall have a comprehensive report shortly after the election, I expect."

Briar nodded. She didn't look at her vassals again until they were leaving her room, trailed by her aunts.

She hesitated.

"I'll find out what happened to Gottlieb," Ben said to her.

She smiled at him. "And keep an ear out for any other suspicious happenings with the candidates, could you? Even around—" She stopped. "Especially around Frieda."

Did she mean to make sure no one hurt Frieda, or to watch out for Frieda arranging for others to be hurt?

Ben's face hardened. He inclined his head.

"And thank you," she added.

"It's easy to keep my ears open for—"

"Not for that. Well, yes for that, but I meant for making me laugh."

He smiled. "If you need me to keep your husband in check again, just give the order."

Briar grinned up at Phillip. "Oh, you can leave things of that nature to me in future, I think."

Phillip went red, but he was smiling, and Ben cracked a laugh.

Phillip offered his arm, and she took it, and they made for the ballroom.

Chapter Ten

The room that hosted the banquet had been transformed for a ball of the standard Briar had seen orchestrated in Austria, at Stefan and Leah's command. Opulence in every corner, though this theme was a repeating one of representing all the countries and principalities of the Prince Electors and candidates, so banners and colors intermingled across the designs. A small cluster of musicians held the far corner, already playing a light, simple tune as guests entered, and Briar's focus and heart latched onto them as a steward announced her and Phillip to the room.

She glanced back at Ben and nodded in their direction, and he motioned at his livery as if to say *We've come far, huh?*

Very far.

Too far.

But tonight's event, at least, was more Briar's style. Even if she would not be one of the bards playing, she *knew* this atmosphere, how to *command a room*, as her vassals said; how to *perform*. Something about this ball was so much more in line with who she was, despite every event demanding performance. Here, Briar could imagine the crowd was an audience; here, she could pretend she was in control.

Their group fell into what was now becoming routine. The fairies broke off on security; the vassals mingled with the crowd. Köning stepped in front of Briar and Phillip to make introductions while Ben hung back.

Briar scanned the crowd, and a Prince Elector turned in her direction from a group.

"Queen Aurora! Will you join us?"

"Us" was Frieda, Matilda with her; Johann as well; the Elector; and another candidate, Eckhardt of Hesse, remarkably awake and leaning his old frame on a cane.

The musicians shifted into a song made for dancing. It was not one of the fast-paced dances of villages like Hausach, but more formal. Still, Briar's heart leapt, and she considered excusing herself from the Elector's company to dance.

Köning gave her a look.

Briar sighed and put on a pleasant smile. "Yes, of course."

She needed to be in this group, anyway, to speak with Frieda. Though how to break her off from not only Matilda, but the Elector as well?

Briar and Phillip added themselves to the cluster. Tension was so thick within the group that it warmed the air, coming entirely from Frieda and Matilda the moment Briar presented herself.

Johann smiled, a large, toothy grin. Briar returned it.

And then her heart lurched when she realized: Had anyone

targeted *Johann* with poison or attacks? Surely any candidate here would draw the line at that. Competitor or not, he was a *child*.

But he was also a king. And that overshadowed any other details about him.

"I have a question to pose, Queen Aurora, and I wondered about your answer as well," the Elector said, drawing her out of her worries.

She nodded. But her eyes flipped to Frieda.

Had Matilda instigated either of Filibert's or Gottlieb's absences?

Had Frieda?

Frieda wore a deep rose-colored gown, and though it was a stunning contrast to her pale skin and dark hair, she looked horrifically uncomfortable. As they had grown, Frieda had hated Briar's attempts to play dress-up; she could rarely be found in anything other than comfortable clothes, certainly never anything this stiff.

Her discomfort hardened into challenge when Briar's eyes landed on her.

Briar looked away.

"There is a disagreement between lands," the Elector continued. "Of boundaries drawn. One duke claims a prosperous farm is on his property; a neighboring prince claims it is on his. Our previous emperor, God rest him, attempted to mediate, but the issue has again arisen, and it will be chief among the trials confronted by his successor."

He paused, a soft smile on his lips, his test hanging in the air. Briar doubted there even was such an issue; it was fabricated to see what candidates would do.

Would her answer matter, though? Or had attendants already bribed the Electors to accept any answer given by their candidate? Was that the true game to the Electors, setting the stage and watching candidates tear each other apart needlessly while they rolled in coin?

Eckhardt coughed, hacked, and spat on the floor. Briar recoiled.

"Which territory is largest?" he grumbled. "That is where the farm belongs."

Briar's disgust was tinged with confusion. How was *that* logic?

Frieda's face had the same flicker of revulsion. Briar caught it, tried to say wordlessly *He's an oaf*, and maybe, *maybe* Frieda would have responded, if not for Matilda's harsh whisper at her back.

"A possibility," the Elector said to Eckhardt. He looked markedly unimpressed.

Matilda none-so-subtly nudged Frieda. Briar watched redness stain Frieda's neck, rise up to her cheeks, but then Frieda straightened, and cleared her throat.

"It should, uh—" Frieda started, swallowed. "The duke and prince should be brought together for— No." She visibly caught herself, and Briar frowned as Frieda glanced back at Matilda, leveled her shoulders, and said, with a cold smirk, "They should be told to settle it among themselves. This is hardly a matter to be brought before the emperor. They have armies, don't they? Use them."

Briar's eyebrows shot up.

Frieda had spoken, but none of those words were *Frieda.* They were Matilda, bloodthirsty and heartless.

Frieda was trying to impress her mother.

It was one of the things she had wanted most. A family. To be out of the orphanage.

Even so, Briar could not believe her friend would willingly suggest that people get themselves *killed* for a disagreement between nobility. Frieda knew strategy well, but she knew better the ramifications of it. She had only ever learned about war from a place of wanting to understand how best to prevent loss of life.

"War has indeed happened over this particular farm," the Elector said. "War for years, in fact. It is a very strategic property, but both lands are equal in might."

Frieda's lips parted. Matilda scowled at the back of Frieda's head, and though Frieda was still facing forward, Briar knew she didn't imagine Frieda's cringe.

"Are there any magical sorts in either land?" Johann asked, drawing attention away.

The Elector shook his head. "I am afraid not."

Johann scoffed. "Then give the duke and prince sorcerers and let the sorcerers do combat. Winner takes the farm!"

"A trial by combat," the Elector clarified thoughtfully. "It is not an uncommon practice."

"Your Majesty." Köning gently prodded Briar's own back.

Briar fisted her hand on Phillip's sleeve. What did she know about smoothing arguments between nobles? She could not even get Frieda to speak plainly to her.

But it wasn't about the nobles at all, was it? The duke and the prince were the cause of this problem, but they were not the victims. The Electors would not care about the peasantry affected, would they? They had not once mentioned the common people who lived and farmed that land.

How to frame it? How to make them care through their own misguided priorities?

"How much has been spent over the years on this war?" Briar asked.

The Elector looked at her, his head tilting in interest. "Oh, it almost cannot be measured at this point."

"On both sides?"

"Indeed."

"And how much profit is brought in by this piece of land? Is it at all comparable to what has been spent in attempting to either keep it or claim it?"

The Elector's lips started to rise in a smile, his head cocking as he saw her point. "That would be a very astute inquiry to make."

"I suspect this farm, though desirable initially, has long since ceased to be worth the trouble caused," Briar said, talking with more confidence at the way this Elector was watching her, as though seeing her for the first time. "In which case, it would be in both the duke's and the prince's best interests to cut ties to the property and allow it to become its own territory. To appease any ill feelings," she added quickly with a cordial smile, "the new territory could pay equal taxes to both the duke and the prince for a time."

Disgusting for anyone to have to *pay* to not be attacked, but the Electors did so love bribes.

The Elector nodded and hummed in consideration. "An

unorthodox solution, Queen Aurora. War halted, expenses recouped, conflict resolved. Very tidy. I commend you."

Phillip squeezed her arm in congratulations. Matilda was seething, glaring at her. Frieda had her eyes on the floor.

Briar should have felt victorious. She had, for the first time, impressed the Electors with her skill, and not through bribery or coercion.

But she couldn't get rid of that filth feeling, the rub of disgust at this whole campaign.

Her vassals had, *maybe*, been right not to tell her of its true nature.

She bowed her head. "Thank you."

Dancing had long since started during this conversation, the room now half-filled with twirling, elegant bodies. Briar pretended to look over her shoulder and leaned into Phillip and whispered, "Ask Matilda to dance."

"Queen Matilda," Phillip said. "Would you do me the honor?"

The group went rigid. All here knew the oddity of the request. Well, maybe aside from Eckhardt, who lumbered off without a word of farewell. But Matilda could not refuse without breaking propriety, and so her smile was all wicked annoyance as she nodded.

"Of course, King Phillip," she said and emerged from behind her daughter.

Phillip and Matilda swept off, and that broke apart the group; the Elector pressed into the crowd, no doubt off to torture other candidates, and Johann had spotted Flora across the room and was already half running to her.

Before anyone could intervene, Briar closed the space between her and Frieda in two strides and hooked her arm through Frieda's as they'd done so many times in Hausach. It kept the Bavarian soldiers from stepping between them, and it made Frieda go stiff in shock.

She did not immediately throw Briar off, which was promising.

"That answer you gave was callous," Briar said, keeping her face pleasant. The music was loud enough to muffle their conversation to any around, and she had no stomach to handle the doublespeak.

Frieda did not respond for a moment. "It is how disputes are settled. It is the way of the world."

"What happened to you?" Briar watched Phillip and Matilda dance. Matilda's head was on a swivel, always keeping Frieda in her sight; she was grimacing at Frieda's close proximity to Briar.

Frieda huffed. "How dare you ask me that? You know very well what happened to me."

Briar ripped her eyes to her friend. They were the same height. The same in so many ways, save for Frieda's dark hair, her steadiness, her severity. Night against Briar's day.

"I really don't," she said, a plea.

Frieda glared at her, face saying she expected Briar to laugh and claim it was a joke. "You knew. You knew *the whole time.* I bought your facade in Hausach, but I know the truth now, Queen Aurora, and so you can drop this pretense."

Briar said nothing, her mouth slightly agape, and Frieda pushed on after only a beat of that confused silence.

"I know now," she said, low and hard. "I know that *you* knew who I was for *years*. That your father put you in that village solely to lure me into friendship."

"What?" The wind left Briar's lungs in a painful rush. "I didn't—"

"You were very good, I will give you that. Awfully convincing. You didn't break at all."

Briar couldn't refill her chest with air. "I have no idea what you are talking about, Frieda."

"Clara," she snapped. "My name is *Clara*, as it was then, though you knew that, even when I didn't."

"I didn't know!" Briar half shouted, wrenching her voice low at the last moment. "How could you think I knew any of this? You think it was all a lie, that I am capable of hurting you and Ben this way?"

"What was it all for, then"—Frieda bypassed the mention of Ben, though her cheeks went red—"if you weren't trying to hurt me? How do you explain that letter?"

"It was an apology. It was—"

"Not *that* letter, curse you. The other one."

Briar's mind went blank. She shook her head, fumbling, and Frieda's face contorted in rage.

"How *dare* you continue to act as if you are ignorant? The letter you sent me telling me to meet you, after your sad excuse for an apology. The letter saying you would explain everything. But where you arranged to meet me, there were Austrian soldiers waiting to kill me."

Briar jerked back. She kept her hold on Frieda's arm.

"I only sent you one letter," she whispered. Did Frieda hear? She couldn't get her voice to work any louder.

"Of course." Frieda sniffed and looked out at the crowd. "Of course you deny it still."

"That is the game, isn't it?" Briar almost regretted saying that. Except she very much didn't, and rage sparked up again, rage and confusion. "Deny events that do not suit us, such as your mother overseeing the murder of King Stefan."

"My mother." Frieda snapped one more glare at Briar. "My mother is the only reason I survived your attempt at killing me. Luckily, she was coming to find me. Luckily, she was there, with Bavarian forces, not far off, and when I managed to run, I found them."

That piece connected, made the others gleam and glow with a putrid light. "No. Oh, no . . ."

Matilda had staged it. All of it. How did Frieda not see?

"She did this to you," Briar tried. "Matilda. Do you really believe these coincidences? What she told you?"

"Coincidences?" Frieda's voice was cracking and pained. "These coincidences came because of *you* and *your* family's manipulation of my life. You had the same fairy gift as me and couldn't bear to have another princess with that possibility, so you sought to remove me from the board. You—"

"Fairy gift?" That fully broke Briar's concentration. It sent a jolt of icy panic through her, head to toe.

Frieda's rage calmed, a beat, enough that her glare turned to a sneer. "You call it a curse, don't you? That's why we're both here, isn't it? Because we were both visited by Maleficent. Because we were both given her fairy gift at our christening. Because only one of us will become empress, and I tell you now, it will be *me*."

Frieda ripped free of Briar's grasp and disappeared into the crowd, leaving her standing there, horrified, unable to move.

A presence warmed the air next to her, and Briar came to with a gasp, eyes shooting up to meet Ben's.

"Did you hear—"

"Yes." His face was gray.

Briar shook her head. "It isn't—it isn't *possible*," she heard herself say.

How many times had she said that? The words were worn from being spoken and thought, and Briar couldn't even be surprised, honestly, at this development.

She swallowed hard, tearing up.

The song ended. The moment it did, Matilda shoved away from Phillip, making a beeline for Frieda, now across the room.

Phillip, similarly, moved over to Briar and Ben. She took his hands, then forced air into her lungs.

She told him what Frieda had said, all of it, shocked that she didn't start weeping.

Matilda had told Frieda that Austria was to blame, because they were trying to get rid of the other princess who had been given Maleficent's curse. *Gift*, Frieda had called it.

Phillip was white at the end. Briar gripped his hand in earnest, fearing he would have another panic spell, but his lips parted. "She visited someone else? How did we not hear?"

"It was Bavaria. Austria would not have cared what transpired there."

"But that *witch*—" Phillip stopped. Caught himself. Color returned to his cheeks, bursts of vibrant, furious red, and he lifted the tangle of their hands to his lips. "I had thought her effects contained. I had thought her touch on our lives done with."

"Me too," Briar whispered.

"You were both in Hausach," Ben said. He had been quiet through Briar's recounting. And now he stood still as a statue, eyes on the floor. "How is that possible? *Why?* Especially if Frieda was Bavarian. Hausach is in Austria. And she was visited by that . . . *sorceress* . . . too? To what end? No curse ever befell her, did it? She was in Hausach until after Maleficent was killed, and I would've known if she'd fallen into some magic slumber. She mentioned one of you becoming empress because of it?"

Too many questions rushed through Briar's head. Too many answers now given, too many other uncertainties now revealed.

How could Frieda believe Matilda over Briar? How had Matilda managed to pit Frieda against someone she had grown up with, someone Briar knew she loved?

And how, *how*, was what Maleficent did in any way a gift that factored into one of them becoming empress?

Briar shook her head. Shook it again, because she couldn't, *couldn't* believe that there was some great plan attached to Maleficent's cruelty, that her manipulation of their lives had not ended with her death. She saw her fear echoed loud and harsh on Phillip's face, and she wanted nothing more than to haul him upstairs to their suite and block out the world. Or, better, to flee back to Austria and renounce this responsibility. If Maleficent's curse—for it *was* a curse, not a fairy gift—was intended to somehow affect her chances at becoming empress, as though Maleficent had *known* this would happen . . .

No. No. It was too fantastical, too inconceivable, too *horrific.*

She was shaking. Shaking so hard that it broke Phillip out of his matching terror, and he touched her jaw, pulled her to look at him.

He said nothing for a moment, studied her face with ever-growing heartbreak.

"Ben," he said. "You two should sing."

It was such an unexpected thing for him to say that Briar flinched. Ben did too, but the air shifted with his smile.

"What?" Briar asked. "Why? What will that do?"

"For the election? For your campaign? Nothing." Phillip's hand held the back of her neck, his thumb stroking fire up her cheek. "But this is a ball, and there is music already. Why shouldn't it be you? Singing will get you back into your element. I have not seen you happy like that since the tavern in Hausach, and I am incredibly selfish, Briar. I want, no, *need* to see you happy again."

If she had not been unendurably in love with him already, those words would have melted her thoroughly.

"And"—he threw a look at Ben—"you too, squire. You have spent weeks getting calluses with swords. Your hands have forgotten how to hold a lute, I bet."

Ben's smile went fully gleaming. Wide with challenge, with joy he could latch onto. "You insult my honor, sir, and I am forced to prove you wrong. Bri?"

He eyed her, pausing, waiting for her reaction.

Briar hesitated. The temptation was too great. Overwhelming, really, and she was nodding before she could stop herself.

Ben squeezed her arm. "I'll steal a lute off the musicians and request they stop this racket for a few minutes to—"

"I know what we should sing," she said in a rush.

"Sure. What?"

Briar shifted her gaze around the room. Frieda and Matilda were in a heated discussion by the far wall, Matilda red-faced again, Frieda bent in surrender, nodding her assent.

"'Take Me Far,'" Briar said, and slid her eyes back to Ben to gauge his reaction.

His lips flattened. He swallowed, glanced over to Frieda—Briar noted that he knew where she was—and turned back to Briar.

"For her," Briar whispered. "If we cannot reach her through talk, maybe we can reach her this way."

It was a song Ben and Frieda had often sung, requiring the overlapping voices of two lovers.

It was the song Ben had them sing the night he proposed to her. He hadn't been able to afford a ring, he'd said, but he had this song, and it was hers as much as he was.

Ben's humor slipped away, and for a moment, Briar feared she'd misstepped.

But he nodded. And gave her a small smile, albeit forced. "If you think you can handle competing with my voice, Bri. It's been a while. You're rusty."

She shoved his shoulder. He slipped away, and she stood next to Phillip, feeling the press of the people around them, the weight of her reality.

"This is not the behavior of a queen," she said.

Phillip kissed her temple. "No," he said into her skin. "But you are not only one thing."

She whipped a look at him.

No. She wasn't.

But was she allowed to let that show now? Was she allowed to still have this smallest piece of her true self?

Only one way to find out.

The musicians in the corner ended their song, but instead of another immediately picking up, silence reigned for a beat.

Then Briar heard the telltale strum of Ben's fingers on a lute, the warm-up he always did.

The crowd sought out the noise as Ben moved across the dance floor. Briar gave Phillip a parting kiss and began to weave her way toward Ben. Those who had been dancing made room for them, a small circle carved out as their stage.

Frieda and Matilda, still by the far wall, had noticed the shift. Noticed the single pealing lute.

Frieda, at least, was staring, wide-eyed, going perfectly still as Ben transitioned from his warm-up into the first chords of the song.

Briar had not sung in weeks, not since that tavern night in Hausach. It had felt like a goodbye then—so now, as her throat stretched and her lungs filled, a foggy sense of dream descended over her, as though this weren't real.

How she wanted to be only a hired entertainer at this election, no responsibilities beyond which songs to sing next and how she, Frieda, and Ben would divide their earnings.

Maybe if she could keep this piece of Briar the peasant bard, it would not hurt so much to be Aurora the queen. Maybe if she gave in to this part of her, Frieda would see, and remember what Briar meant to her, and realize that Briar would never have done any of the things Matilda had let Frieda believe she'd done.

This had to reach her, and it had to reach Briar, too, and the whole thing was so necessary that she couldn't believe she hadn't seen it until now. Phillip knew her better than she knew herself.

Ben hit a note, and she sang:

"I knew you once, now here you stand

From far across the lake

Cast out from home, I'd leave it all

If only you would take."

Murmurs rippled out that Queen Aurora was singing, who was that playing, oh, King Phillip's squire, how *odd*—

Ben played on, the tempo picking up, and Briar couldn't help the rising smile on her face, the levity of music buoying her.

"Take me, take me, anywhere, far

Into cold or fire,

Your fingers play, your lips weave song,

I become desire."

A risqué song for a queen to sing, possibly, but in this moment, Briar was hardly just a queen. She was dancing now, twirling around Ben as she'd done so often in Hausach's tavern, kicking and jumping and flurrying her skirts while his fast fingers sped up even more, pushing her voice and her legs, a challenge and a safety net in one, because she knew his talent was equal to her own, they were on the same level, she and Ben and—

Not Frieda. Not anymore.

Around them, a few nobles began clapping along.

Briar twirled again, facing off with Ben as the song shifted to his verses, and he sang, his voice light and clear:

"To you I come on bended knee,

From far across the hill

For you a plea I weave in song,

Each chord I strum, a thrill."

They danced in circles, Ben on his lute, Briar adding harmony to his parts, and all the while, she searched out Frieda as they spun. The crowd had begun to dance somewhat, attempting to mimic the kicking motions of Briar's peasant moves, and it was absurd and delightful and somewhat chaotic to see people in fine silks and jewels doing Hausach village dances.

Frieda did not move, and her face had not changed, a look of unmasked sorrow.

Briar faced Ben again and his eyes glittered. The final verse.

He gave a quick, almost imperceptible nod toward Frieda.

Briar got his meaning. They danced, twisting to the edge of the crowd, and it parted, letting them through—toward Frieda. Stationary, stricken.

Ben cut a dramatic spin, bowing his shoulders forward as the lute crooned in his hands and he finished the song.

"A thrill, a thrill, deep in your eyes

I traveled just to see

Your wanting look, your fall apart

And know its cause was me."

On the last line, he staggered to a halt in front of Frieda, gasping hard, and extended his hand to her.

The whole of the room went utterly silent. The absence of the song, the shock of his approach to the Bavarian princess.

Briar, not two paces behind him, held her breath, begging, *pleading* for Frieda to react.

Matilda was next to her, though. But Briar and Ben could *help her*, she had to know—she had to see that Matilda had manipulated her, and even if she hated Briar, Frieda couldn't blame any of this on *Ben*—

Frieda looked at Ben. Briar watched her face change, a rapid flicker of emotion—shock to anguish, longing, such potent, raging love that it knocked the air from Briar's lungs and it wasn't even directed at her. How Ben was still standing, waiting, patient, and not sweeping Frieda into his arms, Briar didn't know.

But then Frieda dropped her chin and cut into the crowd, running, *sprinting* for the doors, and she was gone.

CHAPTER ELEVEN

Over the final days of the first week of campaigning, Briar learned, with ever more sinking dread, that singing had not changed things.

Well, it had not changed things *with Frieda.*

Neither Briar nor Ben heard from or saw Frieda for a full day after. It sent Ben back into his shadow of focused work, and whenever Briar tried to speak with him, he brushed her off with a forced smile and a witty remark and excused himself.

She could not decide whether to be furious at Frieda or heartbroken; whether to storm to her rooms and scream at her or try to figure out some other way to get through to her.

The biggest praise for her performance with Ben came from, surprisingly, Briar's vassals. Briar had won over the Electors with her ability to command a room. She had held the ballroom in thrall, and that, alongside her peaceful solution for the made-up territory dispute and the way she had spoken with Johann during their chess match, meant that the Electors placed her as one of the front-runners alongside Frieda and, surprisingly, Johann. Her vassals told her he was favored entirely because of his age and the fact that it made him easy to manipulate.

Another reason to try to win, then, for his sake now, too, as he did not seem at all interested in winning emperor, and was concentrating on being more aware of the way he treated his attendants.

With each subsequent event that finished out that first week, meals and more gaming afternoons and even a performed drama, Briar found herself seeking Frieda and Johann every time she entered whatever room hosted them, only able to relax once she saw that they were both present and unharmed. Ben reported no attempts on either of their lives—no rumors of any, at least—and when Briar demanded her vassals and aunts tell her if any moves had been made against her, they averted their eyes and assured her that she was safe.

Filibert was still so ill that he had withdrawn his candidacy and returned to Lüneburg.

His brother, Gottlieb, still had not been seen, and was presumed to have returned to his home as well. Ben uncovered no new rumors about him.

Three other candidates were called back home by disasters: a burned estate, a suspected uprising, an ill relative.

Briar could not believe the validity of those explanations, seeing only the connecting thread of candidates removed through nefarious means. Each event she arrived at felt smaller and smaller, as the crowd shrank, and it began to feel as if the walls were closing in.

By the start of the second week, there were only five candidates remaining.

Her vassals rejoiced. Her aunts congratulated her. She was one of the front-runners, one of five candidates to rule, and she had no idea how to feel about that.

Relieved, she supposed; she was one step closer to ensuring that Bavaria did not seize the empire and oppress Austria with nothing to stop them. But she was feeling more and more the weight of what it would mean to be empress—events with the Prince Electors were beset with tests that showed what her life would be like in that role. Levying taxes, enforcing law, determining guilty or innocent parties, judging whether foreign slights amounted to acts of war.

These were tests only, coming from the Prince Electors, but they were *not* tests, were they? They would be real situations that affected real people if she were empress, and Briar was too aware of the fact that no matter what choice she made, people would suffer, and that kick of compassion was both blessing and curse. And alongside these tests, the threat of poisoning, attack, and death would remain, wouldn't it? As empress, she would be targeted, even more so than as Queen of Austria.

Frieda, though, was emboldened by Briar's rising prominence, and she and Matilda emphasized Bavaria's known lust for war—only now, they framed it as simply not allowing good people to be taken advantage of. As Briar listened to Frieda's responses to tests posed, she had to admit that, on occasion, it made sense to defend small border towns with shows of strength rather than let them be trampled by neighboring aggressors—that sometimes, violence was necessary—but Briar could not see when that was the case until Frieda had presented her arguments.

It was an exhausting push-and-pull. Dinners and dancing, but tension wove through every interaction, and Matilda did not let Frieda out of her sight anymore, did not allow propriety to force her to interact with Briar and her group.

This campaign was what Frieda had said it would be: a competition between her and Briar.

Because they had both been cursed by Maleficent.

Because there were forces at work on their lives that Briar did not understand, and it terrified her that she and Frieda were playing into a larger game that neither could see.

How had the curse manifested for Frieda? What had Maleficent done to her?

For all her posturing about not being helpless again, she had no choice but to try to win empress. She felt as she had when she'd approached Maleficent's spindle: hypnotically drawn to what she knew would be a violent end, but all else was dark and shapeless and there were no other options.

So she would touch this spindle.

And she would just have to hope that she would wake up on the other side again.

• • •

Little princess, my gift shall be . . .

The woman in blue faced off against a man in an opulent ballroom. She was focused in rage, hands clenched, but she was terrified, a terror that was palpable through the heave and ripple of the dream.

At her side appeared a woman in a sumptuous gown of lace and airy silk, and as the woman in blue scowled at the man, the other woman put her hand on her friend's arm—she was a friend, that was the overwhelming feeling—and the woman in blue's face relaxed.

Other people appeared around the woman in blue as the dream shifted and flickered. Men in fine clothing, a portly chef in a knit cap, a child, too; others, all with the same overwhelming feeling: friendship, companionship, support.

Tiny princess, my gift shall be . . .

The woman under the five shooting stars stood on a battlefield, her face sweaty and dirt-streaked, a sword at her side. For a moment, she alone faced an army of thousands, their bodies stretching into the horizon as one solid mass of impending consumption. The woman was fierce and ready, but she would be destroyed by this army.

A flash, and people appeared around her. Women by the dozens; soldiers armed and determined.

They all faced the army now, together.

Sweet princess . . .

Creatures half-man, half-beast corralled a screaming group in a grand ballroom. Serpents appeared, lashing scaly tails, smoke thickening the air as the people cried out for help. The woman who had snuffed the flames stood among them, one of them, and she would make a shield of herself to save them—

Until others appeared with her, broadening that shield, protecting her as well. A man with a cockeyed grin; a tiger, fierce and snarling; a . . . flying carpet? That couldn't be right—and there were women, too, one who bowed low and mouthed, "Your Majes— Your Majesty."

What will you do with these visions, Briar, Aurora?

Little princess. Little princess.

Did I give you a gift after all?

• • •

Briar came awake, not with a jolt but with a smooth emergence into awareness. She lay still for a moment, curved against Phillip's chest, her eyes closed, feeling the lingering threads of her dream, as always. The dreams haunted her every night now.

And there had been other emotions—not merely fear and threat and terror. Under the curse, and up until now, there had only *ever* been fear and threat and terror, things to torment her.

But this time . . .

There had been support. Encouragement. Things that left Briar reeling, her mind aching.

Her first thought was that this couldn't have come from Maleficent. Maybe her mind had finally broken free of that curse, and she was formulating her own dreams now, taking those pieces left behind and building them into something grand.

But . . . she had heard that voice still.

Maleficent's voice.

What will you do with these visions, Briar, Aurora? Did I give you a gift after all?

Briar lay in the dark, eyes still shut, her breath quickening yet her pulse sluggish.

Had her other dreams shown positive things, too, only she had been too blinded by the fear to see them?

Briar clenched her jaw, refusing to answer that question.

Frieda's words were getting to her. That Maleficent's curse was not a curse, but a *fairy gift.* It couldn't be real. It couldn't be true.

There was nothing positive she could gain from these visions. There was nothing to be gained because of the agony Maleficent had caused, and even if there *was* a gift in these things, Briar did not want it.

Even so, her mind pulsed with the memory of the women standing tall against their struggles, friends at their backs.

They felt the same things she did: fear, anxiety, terror, *loneliness.* And yet they had friends, they had victory, they had *support*, and that was what helped them overcome the darkness.

Beneath her cheek, Phillip's chest twitched. "Are you all right?" came his soft whisper, gently coaxing in case she still slept.

She arched up, nestling her face into the bend of his neck. By the dull light slitting through their bed's drapes, she knew it was morning, though only just.

"Of course," she said into his smooth skin there.

Phillip curved his arm across her shoulder, toying with the lace edge of her shift's collar where it gaped over her shoulder. "Liar."

She stilled, lips to his skin, and in lieu of trying to convince him of what he well knew was, indeed, a lie, she kissed the tendon that bundled in his neck when he tried to look down at her.

"Go back to sleep," he told her. "We have a few hours yet."

"A few hours," she echoed, and laid her cheek back on his chest, her mind working—what was today? "You joust this afternoon."

"Mm."

"You should be the one going back to sleep," she said, lethargic, exhaustion potent and relentless, and she wanted to sleep without dreams, she wanted to sleep without fear, she wanted—

Phillip had already been awake.

She leaned up on her elbow, blinking down at him through the gray atmosphere of their curtained bed. "Have you slept?"

He ran his fingers through her hair, and after a long moment of silence—again, silence as an answer; she hated it from her vassals, hated it more from Phillip—he propped himself up on his elbow to match her posture and kissed her.

She groaned into his mouth. "I know what you're doing."

He rolled them both, trapping her beneath him on the bed. "I am kissing my wife in our bed. I should hope you know what I am doing."

His teeth pressed down on the lobe of her ear and she momentarily forgot everything—the dream, the question he had not answered.

"One day," she gasped, "you will answer my question, Sir Knight."

He stilled over her, lips resting on her ear, now brushing the sensitive skin there. "Not now," he whispered, and it was too raw, too pleading. It altered the mood entirely, drowsy teasing to a scrambling handhold at something solid and fortifying and real.

She knew that desire too well. To find solace in him.

"Not now," she heard herself agree before she could think it through.

It had been *Not now* for weeks. He had avoided any mention of his discomfort or why he did not sleep or the way he still occasionally got that look on his face, a suggestion of the panic that had incapacitated him.

"Phillip," she tried. "You can—"

But he kissed her again, more intently, open mouth and soft tongue, a wordless reassurance as he slid his arm beneath her hips to hold her against him.

I am fine, the kiss said, the motion of his body, the resolution in his touch. *I am fine, I promise.*

And so she made her kiss a response. *I am here. I am here, and I'm not going anywhere.*

• • •

The jousting list was impressively large, spanning the whole width of the castle, with multiple areas for competitors. It spanned the whole width of the castle, multiple areas for competitors to face off, all of it rimmed by stands for the crowds that even now packed the arena. The event had been opened to the people of Frankfurt, with one section kept exclusively for the election candidates and their parties.

That was where Briar stood, at the edge of the balcony box, with Merryweather next to her.

One of her aunts was always with her now.

She'd asked them about this change. They had forced smiles and told her not to worry.

One morning, Fauna had been whispering with Flora over Briar's breakfast spread. Briar had been leaving her bedchamber, and her aunts had not spotted her yet, so Briar heard Fauna choke out a horrified "*. . . found poison—*" before Flora noticed her and gave another masking smile.

She knew she would be targeted. She knew she *had* been targeted, and that her aunts and vassals weren't telling her.

But she couldn't make the reality settle in her mind. It felt absurd, as fictional as a tavern song. She was starting to move through her days in a state of delirium; she felt hysterical most of the time, on the edge of dissolving into laughter.

She was a top candidate for empress.

People were trying to hurt her. Kill her, even.

Frieda had been cursed by Maleficent, too.

How was she expected to handle one of these things, let alone all of them?

From this balcony, Briar could see to where Ben was helping Phillip adjust the last few pieces of his armor, off to the side. There would be five rounds for the candidates to show off their athletes. Phillip was part of the third pair to ride, with the two others ahead of him mounted already, horses dancing in anticipation of the crowd's peppered cheering.

Briar's dreams rang through her. The women, standing strong because of their own internal fortitude, but backed by support.

An attendant banged his foot on the floor of the balcony and she jumped. "The joust will commence—candidates only, please stand at the railing."

Briar, already there, gave Merryweather a tight smile. "Presentation for the crowds, I suspect?"

But Merryweather only took the barest step back from her. Staying close.

Too close. Her face was severe.

Briar's gut twisted as the other candidates filed into position. She felt exposed. "Merryweather?"

Her aunt shook her head. "You focus on your campaign, dear. I've got it."

"It?"

Merryweather's eyes flicked to the other candidates lining up. Briar followed her gaze.

She had seen Frieda and Johann here when she first arrived, and so had dismissed the rest.

But now she did a count.

Counted again.

There were only four candidates present. Eckhardt of Hesse, Johann, Frieda, and Briar.

"What happened to the fifth candidate, Merryweather?" Briar whispered.

Merryweather grumbled. "Blasted business, this whole damn thing. I can see why Flora wanted to keep you locked in that cottage during your early years."

Briar had the odd, humbling realization that she would have gladly consented to being locked in that cottage now, if it meant being back in Hausach.

"What happened?" she pressed again.

Merryweather relented with a sigh. "Injured. This morning. An attacker tried to kill him but only managed to stab his side."

The breath left Briar's lungs in a huff, like she'd been punched. "What? How?"

It had all been subtle thus far. Candidates called back home. Vanished. Ill.

This—this was a *direct* attack. A violent one.

“His security was lax.” Merryweather’s voice was barely audible, low and hard in Briar’s ear as the area around them hummed with the energy of the coming joust.

“Who did it?” Briar tried. “Do you know?”

Merryweather hummed. “The attacker was not found. No evidence remained. But don’t you worry, though. No one will touch you.”

Briar nodded, because Merryweather would expect her to agree, but it was a hollow gesture.

Was it one culprit behind all of the sabotage, or each candidate’s team prepared to do whatever it took for them to win? Was it one threat, or many? Did it matter? The campaign was nearly halfway complete and that made this castle no longer just a den of vipers, but of hornets and snarling mountain cats and poison-tipped thorns.

Her heart wrenched with each bruising beat.

Frieda’s words in the garden came back to her. How easily she had pointed out Briar’s aunts’ flaws.

And with Frieda in her head, and thoughts of the candidate being stabbed, and memories of Stefan bleeding on the throne room floor, Briar threw a panicked look at Merryweather.

What of Johann? She kept her voice almost silent, mouthing the question so he wouldn’t hear. If he had not been told of this campaign’s truth, she did not want to worry him.

But Merryweather smiled, reassuring. “He is well looked after by his people.”

“Someone has been *stabbed*, Merryweather. He’s a child. If anyone—”

“Briar.” Merryweather put her hand on Briar’s arm. “We will

keep an eye on him as well. We are using what magic we can to monitor you, and we are stretched thin as it is. At least, I am. Flora refuses to look after—" She stopped.

Briar frowned, but then caught the spark in Merryweather's eye. "Frieda?" she finished. "You watch out for Frieda, too?"

Merryweather gave a little shrug.

Briar faced the list. She didn't say anything else, afraid she would fall apart into questions about whether Frieda and Matilda were at the center of the attacks to begin with. Did Frieda need protection, or was she the only one immune to attack?

Just down the railing, on the other side of her from Johann, Frieda looked as sleep-deprived now as Briar felt, haggard if not for her painted face and vivid, lively gowns. The aura of wanting to be here, of being wholly on her mother's side, had faded. Now, as Briar glanced at Frieda, she noticed her friend was watching her already, and she saw, for a moment, a flash of grief.

But the flash held. Frieda's eyebrows bent in regret.

Briar forced a steadying breath. Tried to shift her face into something like a question, a plea of offering. She did not expect Frieda would receive it.

A horn blew, an announcer introduced the first pairing of jousters. One rode for Eckhardt of Hesse; another was a career jouster from Frankfurt.

"Your king rides today?" Johann shifted closer to ask.

Briar looked down at him. Frieda faced the list.

A man had lifted a flag. It came down, and the jousters took off from opposite ends, long lances outstretched before them, horses thundering the dirt. A fence separated the two paths, over which they would meet in the middle and attempt to either unseat each other or break their lances on the other's body.

Briar had never seen a joust, much less seen *Phillip* joust, and as the first pair clashed with a violent spray of wood and metal clanking, she jumped, biting the inside of her cheek.

"My husband, yes," Briar said. *Oh, he will be bruised tonight.*

"Ah." Johann was barely tall enough to see over the railing, and he rested his chin on it. But the moment he did, an attendant hissed a warning of *Posture, sire, please*, and Johann straightened. "How long are jousts? Terribly long? I have new spells to memorize."

"Spells?"

The question came from Frieda.

She looked at Johann in honest confusion.

"He is a sorcerer," Briar explained.

Frieda's eyes lifted to hers. There was a beat of *Truly?* and Briar smiled, because this was such a normal conversation, but bare and fragile.

"Yes." Briar smiled at Johann. "Are the spells from Flora?"

The jousting pair reset; three matches, three lances, would determine the winner.

Johann nodded. "She said she could teach me how to make a coin vanish."

Now it was Briar's turn to think, briefly, *Truly?*

Merryweather, at her back, whispered, "Sleight of hand."

Briar didn't drop her smile at Johann. "Formidable. As long as you can make the coin reappear, I should think—no sense magicking away your kingdom's funds."

Johann scratched under his crown. "I wish I could magic myself away from *here*. Everyone is dreadful. Well, not you." He looked up at her. "But everyone else."

And he surprised Briar by giving a pointed grimace at Frieda, who was still watching him.

The jousting pair completed their round. A winner was declared, not Eckhardt's jouster, but all celebration would be reserved for the end, when the remaining candidates would present the prizes.

Frieda's face went red. But she nodded at Johann. "That is earned. I have not given you reason to like me, have I?"

Johann scowled. "Your mother is devilish."

Briar choked a laugh, half horrified, half impressed. He was not wrong.

Frieda's eyes went wide.

Matilda, who had been clustered not two paces back with vassals and attendants, must have heard, for she crossed the space and positioned herself behind Frieda, a mirror of Merryweather to Briar.

"Face forward, daughter," Matilda snapped with a look of distaste for Johann.

Briar had been very good about not openly glaring at Matilda. She was cordial and proper, even if Matilda was barbaric.

Now, though, she couldn't help a snarl from escaping her throat.

"How like Austria," Matilda muttered, and put her hand on Frieda's shoulder as she faced the list.

Something shifted in Frieda's attitude, in her bearing. Briar's longing to speak with Frieda had not been alleviated, had merely gone dormant, and it raged now, awake and desperate.

"See?" Johann whispered to Briar. "Devilish."

Briar edged closer to Johann, keeping her gaze on the side of Matilda's face for one beat longer.

Matilda's presence cast a shadow over any conversation. They watched the next jousting pair play through their three matches in silence. One of the contenders this time was a jouster for Johann, going against a man who represented one of the Prince Electors, and when Johann's man proved victorious, he whooped and clapped and spun around to point at the Elector.

"I have bested you!" Johann cried, not a gracious winner, but Briar couldn't help smiling at his excitement.

Frieda, too, had a smile on her lips. But Matilda was still at her back.

Merryweather was right—this was blasted business, this whole damn thing.

The next pair was announced.

"King Phillip of Austria, more commonly known as the Pain from Lorraine"—the announcer paused for a cheer from the crowd, and Briar couldn't help but grin at her husband's notoriety, for letting other riders pummel him with sticks, but still—"rides on behalf of Queen Aurora of Austria."

Phillip cantered Samson into place, lance in hand, the face shield up on his helmet. He was armored head to toe, the heavy metal glossy and gleaming in the high afternoon sun. There was distance between him and the balcony, and Briar tried to catch his eye, but he kept his focus ahead as Samson stopped at his mark.

Ben hung back by stacks of extra lances. He, at least, looked up at the balcony.

At Frieda.

He turned away to cup his hands around his mouth and shout something at Phillip, who nodded back.

"And his contender," the announcer continued, "Lady Corinna of Munich, riding on behalf of Princess Clara of Bavaria."

Briar didn't move. She wanted to. She wanted to see what expression Frieda's face held, but she could only stand in stunned absence, feeling her stupidity. She had not asked whom Phillip would ride against, and no one had offered the information.

But of course it would be this.

Had Matilda arranged it?

That question led to a revelation, one that soured her stomach and had her muscles turning to stone: If she had, was this a trick of some kind? Had Matilda planned something far more menacing?

Briar's senses became raw and alert, sweat breaking down her spine. She briefly considered shouting to stop the match, but how would that look? And besides, Phillip had jousted many times before; he knew what he was doing. It would be fine.

It *had* to be fine.

With each blink, Briar envisioned knife wounds, blood . . .

Lady Corinna directed her horse into place opposite Phillip. Her visor was down already, her armor black, her lance done in black to match.

There was a green dragon painted on her breastplate.

Was Munich's insignia a green dragon? Briar didn't think so; she *knew* Bavaria's was not.

What was the purpose of that dragon?

"Oh-ho!" the announcer cut back in, bellowing from a place in the stands nearby. "Our contender ups the challenge—we have here a re-creation of King Phillip's famous clash with the dragon Maleficent!"

No.

No, no—

Briar's lungs emptied in a gasping rush and she grabbed the balcony's edge, her eyes fixed on Phillip, begging him to look up at her.

She spun toward Merryweather. "I need to go down there."

Merryweather's eyes widened. "In the middle of the joust?"

She couldn't do that, could she? Of course not, but this was cruel. Any mention of Maleficent set Phillip off in a panic, and for it to be here, like this, in an already heightened situation—how did Matilda know? How had she found out this weakness of his?

Was this a calculated move against him, or was it merely as the announcer said: a reenactment of what Phillip was well known for?

The crowd cheered and Briar spun away from Merryweather to see the flag drop.

The joust began.

Her heart lodged between her ribs, too big, the beats too painful.

Lady Corinna took off, lance poised, dragon insignia gleaming.

Phillip didn't move.

Ben shouted at him, the noise muffled and lost beneath the cacophony of the crowd and the thundering in Briar's ears.

Finally, he kicked Samson and started to gallop down the path.

His face shield was still lifted.

"Your shield!" Briar shouted. She didn't care if it broke decorum; she cupped her hands in imitation of Ben and shouted again, "Phillip, *your face shield—*"

Samson carried him, gaining speed. Lady Corinna's horse matched his, and what should have taken only rapid seconds stretched out, and all Briar could see was that dragon, racing toward her husband.

Lady Corinna's lance was angled perfectly, the easy effort of a seasoned jouster.

Phillip should have been just as composed. But his grip shifted, lance jostling, and Samson's gait faltered with the motion.

The lance slipped from Phillip's grip, hit the ground with a hollow clatter of wood on packed dirt that Briar could hear even over the crowd.

He looked down at it, then back up at Corinna, and Briar could see the whites of his eyes with a pulse of fear—

Corinna's lance crashed into the center of his chest in an explosion of splinters and chunks of wood.

Phillip grasped at the reins, the saddle, but the action only heaved his body around so he didn't drop back behind the path his horse had taken; he hit the separating fence, the impact so hard his helmet flew off, and momentum carried him up and over so he dropped to the dirt directly in front of Lady Corinna's still-galloping horse.

Briar screamed. She nearly vaulted the balcony's railing, but Merryweather grabbed her and hauled her back into place.

Lady Corinna rode hard. This had happened in seconds, less

than that, and Briar watched those hooves tear up mounds of earth mere yards from Phillip's supine body.

Corinna pulled hard on the reins, veering her horse, at the last moment leaping over Phillip so her mount and its hooves cleared his body in one arc.

Phillip did not react to it. Did not stand.

Briar shoved away from the railing, through the people pressing close behind her to see. A few cried out to her, apologies or worry, but she ignored them all, only managed to see Merryweather, who flew in front of her and began bodily heaving people aside.

Down they went, two long sets of stairs, until Briar tore out of the stands and sprinted across the list's packed dirt, skirts in hand, legs straining.

Ben was there already, reaching Phillip now.

She slid to the ground next to Ben. Phillip lay on his back, and she took his head into her lap. "Phillip!"

His eyes were open. They locked on her, and she would have wept relief if not for the immediate spasm of anguish that contorted his face. "I can't—can't breathe—"

Ben dove into action, rapidly undoing the straps of Phillip's breastplate, yanking it up and off. Briar helped, trying to be gentle, but Ben was on a tear, careless for kindness, and he ripped away the padding beneath until Phillip was left in only his sweat-stained undershirt.

"Surgeon, we need a surgeon!" Ben shouted off toward the entrance.

"One is coming," Merryweather said, and took off toward the man who was racing across the list for them.

Phillip rolled out of Briar's lap, onto his elbows, gasping between Ben and Briar, his whole body shaking, sheened in sweat.

"Don't," Ben said. "Don't move. If you've broken anything—"

"Nothing broken," he managed to say. "Can't breathe."

"You could have cracked a rib. You might not feel it yet. The shock of it— Don't *move*."

"Nothing is broken," Phillip snarled. "I can't *breathe*, I just need to—to—"

He swayed. Briar grabbed his shoulders.

He pushed her away.

She sat, hands extended, her body not yet feeling the full force of these last moments, but she felt this.

Ben was just as still as she was.

"Phillip," she tried.

He crawled, swaying as he did so, his gasping, grating breaths coming too fast, not deep enough. He reached the fence that divided the paths and clung to it, using it to pull himself to his feet.

The surgeon arrived, but Phillip bowed away from him, too. Everyone around was silent, listening to him try to breathe as he bent over the fence, shoulders wound tight with strain, body shaking.

Briar stood, Ben with her, and she wanted to go to Phillip, to touch him, but she paused, waiting, a crack slithering up through her chest.

"Phillip," she tried again.

"I'm sorry."

Briar spun. Frieda was behind her, winded from running.

Matilda was far back, not running but approaching them all the same. Two Prince Electors were coming as well, hurrying as fast as decorum allowed.

"For my jouster," Frieda added.

That made Briar's worries roar back on her.

Matilda had planned this.

She had known, somehow, that it would affect Phillip this way.

"She shouldn't have struck him once his lance dropped," Frieda was saying. "It was a surrender, and she continued the match anyway. I'm sorry, on behalf of her—"

Matilda grabbed Frieda's arm. "We offer no such apology!"

Attendants and the Prince Electors stopped at Frieda's apology, eyes widening briefly.

"What a rare show of empathy from Bavaria," one said.

It cut like a knife. *That* was why Frieda had apologized? To garner favor? Briar's rising anger changed into disgust, but Frieda made a cry of objection.

"That is not my purpose! Bavaria shouldn't have—" She noted the pressing crowd, the gathering people. "Back!" Frieda shouted at them. "Everyone, back! Give them room!"

Briar blinked, dazed, as people hesitantly obeyed Frieda's gravelly shout.

Matilda stepped in front of Frieda, speaking half to her, half to the Prince Electors. "Bavaria offers no apology and admits no wrongdoing. This is jousting! And *this*—"

She glared at Phillip where he was still curved over the fence, his back to them.

"How is *this* the prince who killed a *dragon*?" Matilda sneered.

Briar's whole world funneled to the fixed point of Matilda's snarling face. All else evaporated.

She was aware of moving.

Her hand curled into a fist, lifted, winding—

Ben's body in front of her, holding her back.

"Calm down, Briar," he said. "Hey, look at me. *Look at me.* Calm down."

"I will not," she heard herself growl. "Let me go, let me *go*."

"Briar." Ben shook her. "That will not fix anything. Breathe. All right? Breathe."

She tried, but Phillip was paces from her, hands over his face, elbows planted on the fence.

Briar pushed Ben aside and slowly walked toward Phillip. Jousting attendants were trying to shuffle everyone off the list now, at Frieda's command.

"Phillip," Briar said, because she couldn't think of anything else to say, just his name, a brittle plea.

He lowered his hands. He was breathing normally now. But he did not look at her.

"I'm all right," he said to the fence.

"No. You're not."

His tense shoulders went even more rigid. "Briar. Please. Not now."

Not now had turned into him getting thrown from a horse. Because she hadn't tried harder to get him to talk to her. Because she had let his problems sink into the background, and now her heart was breaking and she could only agree, again, because they were in the middle of a jousting arena.

She pressed a hand to her mouth, pushing away the tears while she was in public .

Merryweather floated over. "Will you stay? The candidates are expected to crown the champions."

Briar's body jolted. "That hardly matters!" she hissed.

"What do you wish to do?"

Go with Phillip, of course, but he still wasn't looking at her. Everything about his posture was a silent entreaty not to press, not to make it more of a scene than it was.

And, though it nauseated her, she wondered what the Prince Electors thought of Austria now. Did she need to stay to improve whatever opinion they had? In that moment, did she *care*?

She knew what Briar would do.

What would Queen Aurora do?

What path should she take when those two actions diverged so wildly?

"I—" She couldn't think. She wanted too many things, and she stood there, hating it all.

"Go back to the balcony, Bri." Ben put a hand on her arm. His face was calm, when every part of Briar was shredded. "I've got him. I promise. Finish the joust, and I'll get him settled by then."

"But—" Briar started.

"Not now," Phillip said again, but it wasn't angry; it was desperate, tear-pinched. He twisted toward them, but still didn't make eye contact with anyone. "Ben. Please."

Ben swept in. He hooked one of Phillip's arms around his neck and helped him limp away from the fence. He was injured, but not badly enough that he couldn't walk without help, and the two began to make their way out of the arena.

The crowd erupted in cheers for him. Phillip stumbled; Ben kept him upright.

Briar stood in their wake, feeling lightheaded, feeling numb.

Chapter Twelve

The candidates' box was overcrowded now. Briar was vaguely aware of Matilda and Frieda in a tense one-sided argument in the corner, Matilda berating her, Frieda with her head bowed in submission—but her eyes occasionally drifted to Briar.

Briar ignored her. Ignored the Prince Electors who tried to offer condolences or words of comfort. Ignored Merryweather, who grumbled about how long jousts took, and why wouldn't they wrap it up after such a traumatic turn?

She ignored everyone.

Until Johann touched her elbow.

"I will use my magic to help you," he said gravely.

Briar's eyebrows drew together.

He leaned closer, conspiratorial. "I will make you disappear from the balcony."

A soulless smile pulled at her lips. "Thank you. But that is unnecessary."

Ben must have gotten Phillip back to the suite by now. Was the surgeon with him? How wounded was he?

"It was not an offer. It was a warning," Johann said, a beat before he grabbed the edge of the balcony and heaved himself up to stand on the railing.

Briar blinked at him.

His attendants chirped in alarm.

Johann whirled, brocade flaring like a sorcerer's cloak, facing the crowd on the balcony. There was a quick, stifled gasp.

"Begone," he mouthed at Briar, and flicked his fingers, then looked at the Prince Electors. "My vassals told me that you only want me to be emperor because you think I'd be easy to control. Which is just *stupid*."

"Zauberer—" one of his attendants tried, but Johann kept on, red rising in his cheeks.

"Have any of you Electors spoken to those who are tasked with guarding me? Why would you have made the assumption that I'm easy to manipulate? Mecklenburg is grossly offended and I hereby declare a curse upon *all* the houses of those who underestimate me—"

Queen Aurora would stay.

She would stay and ensure the reputation of Austria.

Briar started walking.

Merryweather was briefly stunned by Johann's ever more impassioned speech that was now rolling into a list of his strengths, Mecklenburg's resources, the things they truly had to offer. Briar had to admit it was an impressive display. She hadn't heard Johann speak so maturely yet, had not seen him have this presence before.

Merryweather came to and slipped off behind Briar. "I am surprised you lasted that long," she whispered as they headed down the stairs.

Briar stopped and whirled on her. "I was supposed to stay. You told me to stay!"

It came out winded, desperate.

Merryweather's face slackened. "I asked what you wanted to do. I reminded you of the options before you."

"You implied—"

"Briar." Merryweather set her soft hands on Briar's cheeks. "What do you want to do? Right now? What are you doing?"

"I'm going to see my husband," she said, and was surprised at how confident, how definitive her voice came out.

"Then go. Go, and let that be your choice."

That question beat in Briar's mind as she went. As she lifted her skirts and started running, propriety be damned.

What do you wish to do?

What will you do, Briar, Aurora?

So far she had been incapacitated by uncertainty, and that was far more grotesque than making the wrong choice. These versions of herself had been at war for so long, neither side gaining ground, and the casualties were now spreading out beyond her. How long until more than those closest to her suffered? How would Austria fare thanks to her indecision? Or the empire, should she be elected to rule it. What events would she allow to happen while she was alternating between a past and a future that didn't feel like hers?

Tears welled in Briar's eyes as she wound through the halls and stairs of the castle, up, up, until she burst into her suite. "Phillip?"

The door to the bedchamber was open, and as she hurried across to it, Ben came out. Behind him, she could see Phillip seated on the edge of the bed, a surgeon tying off a bandage that wrapped around his stomach and shoulder.

"He's fine," Ben told her instantly. "Some bruised ribs, nothing broken, miraculously."

"Thank heavens," Merryweather said. "I will update the vassals. Briar, if you have need of me—"

"I'll be fine." Briar gave her a tight smile in dismissal. She shouldn't be angry at Merryweather. But that question lingered in her aunt's gaze now. *What do you wish to do?*

Briar turned back to Ben as Merryweather shut the door behind her and it clicked, locking.

"Is he—" Her mouth hung open. She wasn't even sure how to finish that question.

Ben glanced back into the room for a beat, then stepped closer to Briar, angling so they were out of earshot of the door.

"Do you remember when Viktor came back from the eastern border skirmish?"

Viktor, one of Ben's older brothers.

Briar frowned. "No, I don't think so."

"You might not. We'd just started our little trio in the woods." Ben sniffed, and Briar noted his shirtsleeves rolled to his elbows, the spare bandage he was knotting and unwinding around his hands. "Viktor wanted to be a soldier, so he went off to war. It was only a few weeks, that battle. But still. When he came back . . ."

He trailed off. His eyes wouldn't hold on her, his face sunken.

She had never seen Ben serious like this. It sent prickles of warning up her spine.

"When he came back," he said again, and twisted the bandage, around, around. "When he— Damn it." He released an exasperated huff, and Briar saw his eyes were sheened with tears. "Rolf said battle changes soldiers. Everyone said that. Everyone *knew*. But Viktor—it was like part of him didn't come back from that border fight. He'd be fine sometimes, and then something would happen, a loud noise or a strong emotion, and he'd snap. Just start raging, breaking things, yelling. These violent, horrible outbursts."

"Why are you saying this?" she whispered.

"Because . . . I'm not saying Phillip's the same, he isn't being violent, but it *feels* the same. It feels like he went somewhere when he battled Maleficent, and part of him didn't come back. I mean, I didn't know him before whatever it was, but that's why I said that stuff about Viktor—because it's an awful lot like that."

Briar steadied herself and asked, "What happened to Viktor?"

Ben shrugged one shoulder. "He's still in Hausach. Rolf tries to keep an eye on him, soldier to soldier, but how do you get back that piece that got left behind when you don't even know what it was?"

The surgeon came out of the bedroom. He bowed at Briar, medical bag on one arm. "I recommend rest, as much as possible, Your Majesty. No physical exertion for at least a week."

"Thank you," Briar said absently.

The man left, and Briar put her hand on Ben's arm, squeezed hard.

She didn't know what to say. About Ben's brother. About any of this.

So she looked up at Ben and smiled through her tears. "Thank you. For being here, for helping him. I don't want to do any of this without you."

Not *I couldn't do any of this without you.*

Ben pulled her into a hug, quick and harsh. "There's nowhere else I'd rather be. Now go see your husband. I'll be in the stables. I'm sure Samson is rattled, too. Call on me if you need me. Or, no, I'm sorry, *summon* me, should you have anything further to ask of me, Your Most Exalted Majesty."

He said it to make her smile. So she did, even though she didn't feel any of it, and Ben saw that, too.

He gave her arm another squeeze, and left.

Briar walked into the bedroom, heart knotted excruciatingly, and saw Phillip, still sitting on the edge of the bed, facing the window with shades pulled open, showing the afternoon sky over Frankfurt. Sharp rooftops peaked into the distance beyond the warped pane, a haze of ripples and spikes.

Briar sat next to him on the bed. She kept her eyes on the window, her hands in her lap, though she wanted to touch him, to initiate contact; she wasn't sure what he needed.

"Who's here still?" he asked, a croaked whisper.

"No one." She looked down at her hands, nails that had been shaped and smoothed, no longer dirty, fingers no longer calloused.

Phillip reached out to take one of those hands, threading their fingers together. She twisted to face him, and he curved toward her, and then they were sitting with foreheads together.

"The dragon," he whispered between them. It was all he said.

Briar stifled her need to gasp or sob or have any strong emotion, focusing wholly on Phillip. "I don't know how Bavaria knew that would unsettle you so much."

"I know."

She pulled back to look at him, but he kept his head down, eyes shut, hands interlaced with hers.

"I know," he said again. "Because I make it easy to see. I do not hide that weakness as I should. I've tried, I've tried day in and day out since it happened. But it's everywhere, all the time, and everyone can see, and that confirmed it. I may as well introduce myself as the prince who slayed a dragon and will always be mortally terrified because of it."

She tightened her hands on his. Tightened and held on and stayed quiet.

"I see it, still. Whenever I try to sleep. A forest of thorns, engulfed in green flames that don't burn it, but they burn *me.* I'm burning up, swallowed in green fire that becomes Maleficent's dragon mouth, the thorns her teeth, and there's thunder cracking and lightning and her *laugh* . . ."

He stopped, tears slipping down his cheeks.

Briar held on to him, silent, breaking.

"I thought everyone was dead," he continued after a moment, voice pinched, tears coming stronger now. "I rode into the castle, and everyone was unconscious I know now, and I know it was the fairies' doing *now*, but then? I thought Maleficent had killed everyone. I'd fought her and defeated her and this was what I came back to? To be the only person to survive her attack in the *whole country*? And so I went up to that tower, because the fairies told me to, and

I knew you were there. But I had no idea what would happen when you woke up. Would you even remember me? Would you be terrified and start screaming because a stranger had kissed you awake? And then we would be the only two living people in Austria, heirs to an empty land. Or would saving you bring everyone back, too? I didn't know. What would have happened if I'd failed? I'd never fought in a battle before that day. Lorraine never had need for me to. But there I was, the sole defender of both your country and mine, against a *dragon*. Against a curse. Doing these impossible feats like I was meant for it. But it turns out I didn't win, did I? She did. She won, because I *can't* . . ."

He sobbed, freeing his hands from Briar's to press the heels of his palms to his eyes.

"Any time I think about it, any time I try to fight, have to stand up as I should, I can feel myself withering. And I scream at myself not to, to be stronger than that, but I can't stop the rise of it, and then I watch myself disintegrate and all I can think is how weak I am."

Briar couldn't take it anymore. She grabbed his wrists to peel his hands away from his eyes, then took his face in her palms, thumbs brushing the tops of his cheekbones, wet with his tears.

"You are not weak, Phillip," she told him. "You are *not*."

"I can't protect you." His eyes slammed shut. "I can't fail you, I can't fail our people, but I *will*, I know it."

She tilted his face so his eyes met hers.

"You are not weak," she said again with as much surety as she had ever felt. "Fear is not weak. What you endured was more than anyone should have ever been asked to take on, and if you had come through that unaffected, it would have been disturbing, honestly. Of course it changed you. But it did not make you weak."

Her words to him doubled back on herself.

If you had come through unaffected.

Of course it changed you.

She teared up. She had been changed by what had happened to her. She had been changed and she assumed that was it, that she was either Briar or Aurora with no option to meld the two.

What if it was not one or the other?

What if she was still *her*, only altered? Not someone new. Not someone old. Someone braided from both.

Phillip swayed, fingers encircling her forearms, and her mouth stayed open, willing a great solution to come forth, a way she could help him face these fears and overcome them.

But there was no easy fix. No easy fix for what had been a massive, terrible destruction.

"I'm here," she said, softer. "Fate brought us together, over and over, and so whatever you are bearing now, let me bear it, too. I cannot fix this for you, but I will carry the weight with you as it heals. You've let me in by telling me this. So let me stay there, with you, and maybe, we'll be able to breathe under this weight. Together."

After a long moment, he took a shaking breath, and his tension began to ebb.

"Together," he whispered.

Briar convinced him to lie down. Not that it took much prodding—he was exhausted, physically and mentally, and his eyes were closed the moment he leaned back on the pillows.

She gently stretched out next to him, not wanting to risk hurting him more by putting her head on his chest, and settled for splaying her hand flat on his stomach.

He took her hand, eyes still shut, and tugged. "I won't break."

Briar scooted closer, body alongside his.

"No," she told him, resolute, "you won't."

And neither will I.

His eyes cracked open and caught hers. He held there, watching her, until his eyelids fluttered, exhaustion sinking down his features.

"I don't know what I did," he started, "to deserve you."

"Deserving has nothing to do with it." She rested her lips on his bare shoulder, feeling it rise and fall. "I'm yours whether you deserve me or not. There is no getting rid of me, no matter what you do."

His lips slanted in a smile that faded quickly. "I love you," he said, as expected as his next heartbeat.

She smiled. "I love you, too, Sir Knight."

His brows pinched, and she thought he might have tried to say something else, but he was, finally, asleep. Deeply so, his face relaxed, hand going heavy where it rested over hers on his stomach.

Briar stayed there next to him, watching him sleep, and even with all that had happened, she felt lighter. He did, too. She knew now what plagued him, what weight he bore, and he would no longer bear it on his own. Much like her own burdens—she did not know how she would endure any of this without Phillip, without Ben.

Some things were impossible to suffer alone.

The thought hit her, memories of her dreams from Maleficent. All those great women, all their supporters and friends.

Whom did Frieda have now?

• • •

Briar waited until she was sure Phillip was in deep sleep, making certain he didn't jolt awake from nightmares. After a while, she gingerly pulled her hand out from under his, tucked the blankets up over him, pulled the curtains around the bed, and slipped out.

What do you wish to do?

What will you do with this, Briar, Aurora?

She wanted to confront Bavaria. She probably should have had more far-reaching plans, but in this moment, she wanted to scream at Matilda for the trick she'd pulled on Phillip, and get some semblance of vengeance for the constant barrage of cruelty.

But that was how wars continued, wasn't it? An attack masked as vengeance, another masked as reprisal, and on and on, and when did it stop? That was how the fighting between Austria and Bavaria had carried on for years.

Briar had gotten halfway to the main door of her suite before she realized Merryweather was sitting in the corner. She stopped, eyes going to her aunt's, and a cool sense of calm fell over her.

"You and your sisters magicked everyone in Austria to sleep," she said without pretense.

Merryweather jolted. "Y-yes? What does that— How is Phillip?"

"Asleep. And he will be fine. No thanks, as it turns out, to you and your sisters."

Merryweather walked forward. Didn't fly. "Briar—"

"You magicked everyone in the country to be asleep. Why? What purpose did that serve except to leave him alone in that final battle? The whole *army*. There was a whole army that could have stood by him, and you left him alone."

"We didn't know how long you would be under Maleficent's curse," Merryweather said. She wasn't defensive, but she was fighting to keep her voice level. "We kept the kingdom in stasis to hold them in place with you."

"And Phillip? Once you had freed him from Maleficent's dungeon, why did you not awaken at least the soldiers? Why did you give him a sword and a shield and send him off against a sorceress dragon *alone*? Why, *why* is everyone else capable of seeing the flaws in your actions except for *you*?"

She tried not to shout, so aware of Phillip sleeping in the other room, but her words were snapping and vicious and she was so *angry*. At Matilda, at Frieda, at this whole blasted campaign, but this, she could control. This, she could resolve, right now.

Merryweather nodded, her eyes glistening. "We did what we believed best."

"So did Maleficent."

The words were out of Briar like an arrow from a bow. She saw them strike Merryweather physically, her chest caving in, her eyes widening. But it was not hurt she saw—it was fear.

"What do you—" Merryweather stopped. Breathed. "What do you mean?"

"Maleficent did what she thought best," Briar expanded. "In cursing me. To get whatever convoluted result she wanted. Stefan and Leah did what they thought best in sending me away and having all spindles destroyed. Matilda has done what she thought best for Frieda, in twisting all our interactions so she distrusts me. Doing *what you believed best* does not absolve you from the pain your actions inflicted."

"We are not the same as Matilda and Maleficent," Merryweather snapped. Her cheeks reddened. "Do not group us together. The choices we made were out of love for you."

"And that makes it worse, doesn't it?" Tears pricked Briar's eyes. Merryweather saw, and her anger deflated. "Because you claimed to love me, and hurt me anyway. At least Maleficent and Matilda only ever claimed to hate me, and so I *expect* them to hurt me. But you, and Flora, Fauna, Stefan, Leah—all of you gathered around me and heaped love upon me and then *gutted* me."

Her voice was rising. She felt the rip, the strain of it, and she rolled her eyes shut in a wince and paused, listening to the bedroom. Phillip didn't stir.

So Briar exhaled, and opened her eyes to see Merryweather with tears running down her cheeks.

"I don't know how to reconcile that," Briar whispered when Merryweather said nothing, merely sniffled. Then Briar laughed, dry. "I don't know how to reconcile much of anything. Briar Rose with Aurora. Your love with the pain you inflicted. How can all of these opposing forces coexist without tearing me apart?"

Merryweather considered that. And she finally spoke, though she said only, "Sometimes they don't."

Briar frowned, her eyes heated, but her own tears didn't fall.

Merryweather looked out the window, sucked her teeth. "Sometimes forces oppose each other so greatly that they do tear apart their bearer. And what is left are . . . shards. Shadows of what should be. And those shadows make mistakes and they flounder because they are *incomplete.* That is what we should have taught you." She faced Briar again, apology ripe in her expression. "We should have prepared you, every day, to endure all of the conflicting forces you would be at the mercy of. We should have—"

Briar lurched forward, rage iron-tinged and bitter. "I am at the mercy of *nothing*," she spat. "Not again. *Never* again. That's why I'm here at all, fighting like hell to win a crown I don't even want. That's why I concede to petty propriety and play these stupid games. It may seem like I'm at the mercy of these larger forces, but *I am not.* I am *choosing* to do these things. You misunderstand what I have been saying—I will *not* let any of these things destroy me. I am done being the victim. I am the hero now, Merryweather."

Hot, heavy tears streamed down Briar's cheeks, and she only felt them when she sucked in a quaking gasp, her lungs prickling like they were full of needles. She felt every ounce of the pain that the past few hours had thrown at her. She felt every minute of lost sleep.

But Merryweather stared at her in awe and adoration, and it didn't fit at all with the conversation they had been having. The argument.

"We thought—" Merryweather's breath wavered. "We did not know that was why you were giving in to your vassals and us as well."

Briar scrubbed the back of her hand across her damp cheek. "You think I'm weak. That I'm bowing to you all for lack of a spine."

Merryweather pressed her lips together.

Briar shrugged. "Sometimes, a little. But mostly it is because I don't know what the *hell* I am doing, here or in Austria. I am not too proud to admit that. And so I *will* listen to suggestions—from my vassals, most of whom have ruled their own provinces longer than I have been alive, and from you three. When I do what you say, it is not simply because I have no other ideas; it is because the ideas you present have merit, and I trust you. Should I do all this on my own? Should I ignore the support I have? *What do you want from me?*"

They had been asking her what she wanted to do, and each time she had felt she didn't know.

But she realized: She had known all along.

She was here, fighting to be empress. Facing the ghosts of her past. Yes, she still had moments of doubt and indecision. Yes, she still wrestled with her instincts versus the choices advised. But she was making choices, learning from those choices, and growing. She was taking pieces from each mistake and each horror and all of the people in her inner circle, and she was evolving.

She wasn't the old Briar Rose anymore. She hadn't been for a long, long while. Yet neither was she this new Queen Aurora.

Perhaps all these labels only hindered her. Perhaps it was far easier than they had all made it out to be.

Perhaps she was simply Briar, and what that meant could change daily.

Merryweather placed her palms on Briar's cheeks, hesitating for a moment, as though she expected Briar to shove her away. But her aunt's soft touch felt like her childhood and safety and always would. Briar closed her eyes, a few more tears slipping free.

"I think," Merryweather started, her voice frail, "that we have misjudged you, Briar. We owe you an apology. Many, in fact, so let me begin with this: I am sorry we have not seen what you have been doing as queen and candidate. I am sorry the expectations we placed on you clouded your truth."

That apology may have been meant for this one wrong, but it branched out, became a connecting web over every pain in her life. It touched bruises she had learned to avoid, prodded wounds she had never expected to close. It was more painful than soothing in this moment, and Briar did push Merryweather away now.

Bleary-eyed, exhausted, Briar turned for the door. "I'm going to speak with Matilda."

Merryweather choked. She might have argued, but the reality that their conversation had uncovered hung in the air around them, thick as smoke, and so she did not question Briar.

Briar ripped open the door to her suite and went stock-still.

A figure pushed off from the wall opposite the door. A beat before Briar could cry out, she recognized it.

Frieda.

Briar glanced up and down the dark hall. Evening was coming in, and the windowless gray stone was lit by torches against the coming night, but Frieda was alone.

Merryweather moved over to glance around Briar, and gasped. She tried to yank Briar back, but Briar resisted, fingers anchored on the doorframe.

"What do you want?" Briar asked, hollowed out.

Frieda stepped forward, her palm rubbing against her skirts. "I wanted to make sure your husband was all right."

Briar stared at her.

Frieda's eyebrows peaked. "King Phillip. Is he all right?"

"He's fine. Sleeping." Briar wilted. "Finally."

"I'm jealous."

It came so softly that Briar almost didn't hear it. When she frowned, Frieda shrugged.

"Well." She smoothed her skirts awkwardly and looked once, quickly, into the suite behind Briar. She saw Merryweather and straightened. "You are heading out. I won't keep you."

"What do you mean?"

Frieda's lips parted. "I meant that I won't hold you back from—"

"Not that, you fool." Briar had no patience left, not for anyone. "When you said you're jealous of him sleeping."

"Oh." Her eyes held on Briar's, silence stretching, and a mask fell. Slipped, really. "I have dreams. Plaguing, restless dreams."

"You said she gave you the same . . . gift," Briar stated.

Frieda hesitated, before nodding.

"She was dead, though," Briar said. "Phillip killed her before your sixteenth birthday."

Their birthdays were a week apart. It had been one of the things that had bonded them early on.

So if Maleficent gave Frieda the same curse—to die on her sixteenth birthday—it would not have taken effect, because Phillip destroyed the sorceress before Frieda turned sixteen.

Frieda's head tipped, and she smiled, sad, tired. "Matilda was furious about that," she whispered. "She heard what Phillip did, and thought it meant the gift would not come, that it would all have been for naught. But . . ." Frieda shrugged and looked away, but not before Briar saw the sheen across her eyes. "My sixteenth birthday came, and as it ended, her *gift* came upon me even in her death. I collapsed and could not be woken. In that state, I dreamed. I awoke on my own, after some time had passed, and I had dreamed so much I could hardly distinguish truth from fiction." She sighed. "And I dream still."

When Phillip killed Maleficent, it hadn't broken the spell Briar was under. She hadn't immediately woken up—she had only done so once Phillip had kissed her.

So maybe it was not unthinkable for Maleficent's curse to take Frieda regardless of whether Maleficent was alive.

"What do you dream about?" Briar asked. She heard some of the tension leaving her voice. Behind her, Merryweather kept all that same tension, but Briar was talking with Frieda, talking about this impossibly terrible thing someone else had experienced, too. And not just someone else, but someone she loved, someone who had once known her soul.

Frieda's shoulders stiffened, her lips parting.

Briar continued before she spoke. "A woman in a blue dress. Another under shooting stars."

"And one throwing a pail of water onto a fire," Frieda finished, her face blank, but with the unpleasantness of a repressed memory. She said nothing else. Set no foot upon the bridge Briar had built.

They had the same dreams.

Maleficent *gave them* the same dreams.

Frieda had come here to her suite, *she* had chosen to come here, and now she was acting antsy and like she would bolt, like Briar had been the invasive one.

Briar's jaw set. Frieda stayed silent, her eyes on the floor and feet shifting, and Briar rolled her eyes.

"Why are you here? Why did you come? You've made your opinion of me very clear, *Princess Clara*, and if this is a ploy of your mother's to go after my husband, I will destroy you both. Mercilessly. That is a promise of war you can take back to Bavaria."

Merryweather screeched behind her, but Briar didn't care.

Frieda whipped a look back up at her. "That's not why I'm here. She doesn't know I'm here, in fact."

Briar was done forging connections. Let Frieda fight for her, for once. "I'm shocked you're still able to think without her say-so."

"That's not fair."

"Is it? You broke my heart. You broke Ben's heart. And now you care, when my husband was nearly killed by your mother's cruelty?"

"Yes."

Briar stopped up short. She had a whole argument building up in her throat, but she snapped her jaw shut.

Frieda folded her arms, glanced around the empty hall, and whatever anxiety she'd had in her bearing overwhelmed her. "I *know* what my mother did with the dragon and the jouster was wrong. I know that. And so I acted on it. Because so much else is uncertain. And I *know* that you were visited by Maleficent, like I was, and given the same cur—gift. The same gift. I'm trying to act on what I *know* now, instead of what I've been told, and it turns out . . . I know so little."

"You don't," Briar snapped. "You know me. You know Ben."

Frieda's eyes went watery, bloodshot. "But you don't know me."

"Of course we—"

"I died. Under Maleficent's gift. I died, because no one amended it for me when she gave it."

Briar went so slack her hand slipped off the doorframe. "What?"

"And no one woke me up; I came back to life on my own. I was *dead*, and then I rose out of my deathbed. Do you know what it feels like to die and come back, Briar? It isn't like sleeping and waking. It . . . *hurts*." Frieda's voice dipped, went jagged with remembered pain, and she took a beat, swallowing down the emotion, before she spoke again. "And I'd seen these intense visions of women I didn't know—and heard cackling laughter—and then my mother was there, this woman I had never met. She told me it was all right, that this was meant to happen. That the pain of dying and coming alive again, that me growing up in poverty among the people, was *worth it* because Maleficent had told her that was how I would become the greatest ruler in the empire's history. That's why it happened to us both, you and me—because one of us is a backup. A spare."

"And you believe that's me, I assume?" Briar's tone was deadened.

Frieda snorted. "My mother believes so. Your gift didn't take all the way, did it? You didn't actually die, just slept, and Phillip woke you up. According to her, that makes me more worthy. According to her, you shouldn't even be here, and I should be revered as some kind of goddess. So, Briar"—Frieda lurched forward, but her tone was not accusing; she was beseeching—"there are a great many things I don't know, but I *do* know that you don't have to do this.

You aren't fated to it like I am. You can leave. You can stop this and protect yourself and your husband and *go*."

Briar rocked backward, letting Frieda's words process. She quickly saw through them, saw past the sincerity, and it was a knife straight into her stupid, fragile hope.

"Clever, really," Briar forced herself to say, instead of scream. "Tell your mother I commend her on this turn of phrase."

"This isn't—"

"Aggressive tactics aren't working, so you come at me with empathy and compassion? As though I would believe a word of it from you now. *Clara*."

Frieda winced. "You don't have to believe me. But you realize you aren't chosen for this role, don't you? You didn't complete the curse. You woke—"

"So now you say it is a curse?"

"*Gift*, I mean, Maleficent's *gift*—"

"No. It was a *curse*. It was a curse, for us both, and she *destroyed our lives*. All these outside forces have done nothing but destroy our lives, and you've given in to them all rather than believe in Ben and me and the fact that we're here for you. You've chosen all this over us, over the man who loves you still, and what *I* know is that does, indeed, make you Princess Clara. So do not try to seek understanding with me. You and Queen Aurora are not friends, we have no history, and I do not have to listen to a word you say."

Frieda gasped, hands tightening into fists crossed over her chest, eyes tearing, but she didn't cry. She didn't try to speak again, and Briar watched her mind work, wondered what thoughts were racing through her head.

She was so close to understanding what Briar saw. That they were the same and could help each other.

But not like this. Not with Frieda thinking that *anything* good could come from what Maleficent had wrought.

Briar turned to tell Merryweather to get rid of her just as a clatter of armor and booted feet thundered up the hall.

Frieda's shock at the sound was all that kept Briar from calling her a traitor, but moments later, soldiers of the Frankfurt castle rushed past, angling around them both for a wing farther up.

"Candidates." One soldier stopped, giving a quick bow. "We must ask you both to return to your suites and stay in place. There has been an attack."

Briar's chest lurched. "Who? Where?"

"It is isolated and appears to have ended, but please, for your safety, stay locked in your rooms." The soldier hurried off with the rest of the men.

Merryweather took her arm. "Come, Briar—"

But Briar watched the path the guards took. And dread welled up, toxic in her chest.

An attack.

Another assault, another attempt to remove a candidate from the campaign. One had just been stabbed, as Merryweather had told her before the joust—was it the same attacker? The victim wouldn't be the same candidate—

There were only four left now. She and Frieda were here.

Which left Eckhardt of Hesse.

And Johann.

Briar shot into the hall.

"Briar!" Merryweather plunged after her. A beat, and Frieda's fast footsteps followed, too.

The soldiers' armor left a noisy trail that Briar followed, begging her instincts to be wrong.

Two halls over, the group of soldiers melted into others already pouring into and out of a suite with the door thrown open.

Beside the door, an insignia hung on a banner. A bull's head in a crown.

Mecklenburg.

Chapter Thirteen

Briar shoved through the armored soldiers, heedless of their cries. When one tried to stop her, Merryweather sprayed him in the face with a stream of bubbles that shocked him enough to let Briar slip by.

She elbowed her way in, past further cries of "Halt!" and "Don't, Your Majesty," until she stumbled into the front room of a suite.

It was dark, soldiers trying to coax a fire to life, others holding unsteady lanterns that cut beams of orange and yellow over the dark stone room. There was a dense table, chairs pulled out; food abandoned mid-meal; an armoire beside a trunk.

Briar slipped on the smooth stone floor, catching herself on an arm—Frieda's.

Her mind went blank. A weird, absent refusal of disconnected thought.

Why had she slipped? The stones weren't that smooth.

Briar looked down. The flashing lantern light shone orange and yellow, orange and then scarlet. Blood.

"No." A gasp ripped out of her, a visceral, wrenching tear. "Johann. Johann!"

She staggered forward, through the pool of blood, and her eyes caught on the source: one of his attendants, clutching a bandage to a giant slice through their arm while another tried to stop the bleeding.

"Where is he?" she asked helplessly. Soldiers were in the process of searching the rooms, and other attendants and vassals huddled in a bedchamber farther in, weeping and explaining to a guard what had happened.

An attack, quick, brutal, one masked man had forced his way in as they were settling for the night, so it had been dark. The flash of blades. Panic.

They didn't know where Johann was.

They didn't know what had happened to the attacker.

If he had taken Johann—

Briar spun, eyes leaping to each corner of the front room, searching, fruitlessly, because Johann *had* to be here still. The alternative was too horrific, unthinkable.

Her hand was still on Frieda's arm, holding tight. Briar whipped a furious glare at her.

"Your mother did this," she snarled.

Frieda gaped at her. "I would never sanction an attack on a child!"

"You said there is a lot you don't know. Do you know what other measures your mother is taking to go after candidates? Rumors?

Poisonings? What won't she do? What do you *know*, and how will that help us here, *Clara*?"

Frieda's face paled. The fireplace was coming to life, illuminating the room more fully.

"Bavaria did not do this," Frieda said again, and a pulse of fight lit within her brown eyes. But it lessened, and Briar expected her to say something to the effect of *It could have been Austria*.

Instead, Frieda surveyed the room. "Where would he have gone? What enemies did Mecklenburg have?"

Briar ripped her hand off Frieda's arm. "You don't care. *Get out*."

"No," Frieda said.

Briar looked at Merryweather, at first wanting her aunt to throw Frieda out, then realizing—

Agony broke. Its splintered pieces stabbed into the fresh, raw wounds their argument had made. Briar had thought she was hollowed as much as she could be; now she knew the true depth of grief. "You said you would watch him, too."

Merryweather shuddered. She was flying, wings beating hard, her short stature making her eye level with Briar.

"We'll find him," she promised. She glared at Frieda, then pushed away, fluttering to the nearest soldier, asking for more details.

Briar tore her hands through her hair, blond strands snagging on her fingers.

"He's eleven," she whispered. "He's eleven, and your mother tried to have him killed."

Frieda was silent a moment. "Where would an eleven-year-old go if he was afraid?"

Briar looked up at her, scowling. "I went to *you*."

Frieda's face fell slack. She tried a smile that didn't reach her eyes.

Then it blossomed, and she was grinning at some memory.

"You came after a storm. Remember it? It ripped the roof off the blacksmithy. You were sure it was a dragon come to eat the whole village. Your aunts didn't believe you, so you came to me, because you knew I would."

Briar curled her arms around herself. "Don't. Not now—"

"No. Wait." Frieda held a hand out. "You came to the orphanage. It was the middle of the night, and the priest would have been furious to find you there, so when he came in for morning prayers, we hid you—"

Briar's eyes widened.

"In the armoire." She spun, scrambling forward.

Her fingers fumbled the knobs on the massive armoire, taller and broader than the fireplace, and she yanked the doors wide.

And cried out in shattering relief, plummeting to her knees.

Johann was curled in the base of the armoire, hands over his ears, eyes shut, humming softly to himself.

At the cut of light over him, his eyes flared open in panic.

But then he saw Briar. And . . . Frieda behind her, the soldiers too, and the blood on the floor, and his terror pitched into a sharp, warbling scream.

Briar held her arms out and he toppled into her, clinging to her, screams turning to sobs as his remaining attendants heaved themselves out of the far room, racing to him with shouts of relief. He was pulled out of her arms quickly, and she let him go, releasing him into the comfort of his people. Through their mess of questions and tears, his voice was small and so very, very young as he apologized, over and over.

"I'm sorry," he whimpered. "I'm sorry, I'm sorry, I won't do it anymore."

"Do what?" one attendant asked, smoothing Johann's curls back from his tear-slicked face.

"Magic. I won't do magic anymore. It didn't stop that man and it was foolhardy and childish and I'm sorry, I'm sorry. I should've done something to stop it, something *real*—"

Johann was gathered into a series of arms and bent heads, a tangle of hugs as people cooed over him, reassuring him, promising him it wasn't his fault.

Briar straightened upright, muscles stiff. She felt Frieda next to her, watching Johann and his group, and without a word, Briar left the room.

She walked, in a daze, her panic receding in a stupor until she was halfway back to her room and came to with a shivering wheeze.

"Briar—wait."

"Don't. Don't talk to me. Not now." Briar leaned against the wall, the cold of the stones bleeding through her sleeve. She couldn't breathe for the relief of knowing Johann was alive, couldn't breathe for the onslaught of horror this day had brought.

Frieda stopped next to her. "Bavaria didn't do this. My mother is not the monster you think, and I came to talk to you because—because I do know you. And I know this campaign, this *life*, is crushing you, and I wanted to give you a way out. I can do this. Lead. I can *do* this."

"So if I concede to you," Briar said, staring at the floor, "and Bavaria takes control of the empire, I am expected to believe you will leave Austria unscathed? That my country, my people, will be protected?"

Before Frieda could answer, Briar laughed. She laughed and it hollowed her out.

"Listen to us," Briar said. "Talking about leading and empires and duty like we weren't both singing for our meals a year ago. Do you really feel you could, in any way, contribute to bettering this empire, Frieda? That if it were in your hands, you would not be manipulated by your mother, you would not make choices that harmed others, that you would have all the skills necessary to rule? *Really* rule? Because I don't. I don't, at all, and I am not fool enough to believe I ever will, and it's ridiculous, idiotic, that the Prince Electors expect one person to bear this."

Frieda's face was gray in the low light. She blinked quickly, eyelids fluttering. "That is why Maleficent cursed us. Or—gave us those dreams. To prepare us in ways that other emperors were not."

"You think the scenes she gave us are meant to prepare us?" Briar blanched.

"Yes." Frieda nodded. "Those women were all leaders. The images we see of them, the things they went through, the choices they made—all of it is information, examples, showing us how successful leaders endure."

Briar couldn't rationalize that. Yes, some of the images in her dreams had shown her beneficial things—but she refused to accept that anything good could come from Maleficent.

"Why us both, then?" Briar asked instead. "Why two of us, if it would only ever be one?"

Frieda's lips parted. "A spare, I told you. Or to prove which of us is truly worthy. Or—"

"I don't know about you," Briar said, "but I am tired of outside forces determining my life's course. Especially ones that tortured me and hurt people I love. I don't care what Maleficent's intent was. *I* determine my future. And you should start thinking about what *you* want out of yours, too. And"—she paused, gasping—"you should ask your mother who ordered the assault on Mecklenburg. And the poisoning of Lüneburg, and all the others, and who really killed Stefan, if you so wish to *know* things now."

Briar heard the flap of wings, then Merryweather's startled "Away from her! Briar—you cannot leave alone! What if—"

"We are done," Briar said, and walked off without another word to Frieda.

She walked, faster and faster, until she raced back to her suite and shut the door on her aunt.

In the bedchamber, Phillip was still asleep, now curled on his side.

Briar shut that door, too, and leaned her forehead against it.

What do you wish to do?

In a wild, limitless world. No rules, no restrictions.

She wanted to protect Austria, to know the people she loved in Hausach and villages like it were safe and cared for. She wanted to rule, but only alongside those she trusted and could depend on. Phillip. Ben.

Frieda.

Who, even after these months of pain and separation, still knew Briar's deepest wishes. Who was headstrong and confident where Briar could be uncertain and hesitant.

That was what she wanted most.

To be whole again.

Her knees trembled, gave out, and she slid to the floor, not crying, just staying there, bent in half, trying not to fall apart.

• • •

The next day, Johann withdrew his candidacy, and his party set off to return to Mecklenburg. Briar went to say goodbye to him, Ben and Phillip in tow.

Johann was somber now, not in his crown or brocade, just a boy, gaunt and small and scared.

He promised to write to her, and his attendants assured her that he would be well watched over. Their attitude toward him had changed in recent days—honest affection was now unmasked, and Briar knew, hoped, that he had the support he needed for what his future would hold.

Ben crouched in front of Johann with a flourish as he produced a thin wooden rod.

"Every zauberer needs a wand," he said.

Johann hesitated. "I do not think I want to be a sorcerer anymore."

Ben leaned in, his grin sly. "It is not a real wand. I am not paid enough for such trinkets." He shot a look at Phillip and rolled his eyes at Johann in shared annoyance, and Johann finally managed a smile. "It's actually a piece of a broken lance that I sanded down. You can have it as a reminder that there is power to be found even in small, broken pieces. And, failing that, you can use it to greatly annoy your attendants by jabbing them in the stomach."

Johann grinned but tried to stifle it.

Ben handed the rod to him. Johann took it.

And immediately jabbed it into Ben's side.

Ben flailed away with a startled cry, lost his balance, and landed hard on his back.

There was a pause throughout the room, Johann's attendants halting their packing to gape at Ben on the floor.

And then Johann *howled.* He giggled so hard his eyes teared up and he bent double and wheezed.

Ben looked up at Briar and Phillip with a grimace.

"How did you not see that coming?" Briar asked, unable to stop the hiccup of laughter that escaped. It set Johann off laughing even harder, and Ben's head flopped back on the stones.

• • •

There were only three candidates left.

Eckhardt of Hesse.

Clara of Bavaria.

Aurora of Austria.

A day of lockdown was declared to search the castle for the attacker who had assaulted Johann and the candidate before him. None was found. Even Ben, who threw himself into investigating, could not find any information tying the attack to Matilda, or even Eckhardt, or anyone else.

Another day was given to allow the remaining candidates to rest and recuperate.

Phillip slept more now. He still awoke, but the mere fact that he *could* sleep now, even in few-hour snatches, was a marked improvement. Briar, by contrast, slept worse than she had since just after the curse, lying awake next to Phillip most nights, unwilling to see her own dreams.

When she did, she saw the women. She saw their supporters and friends. She saw them standing in grand halls or on battlefields, faces determined, mouths shaping words she couldn't hear. But she knew the intent—they were leading. Directing. Making choices. Confident and strong and *powerful.* She had seen their origins, too. How they had all started scared and uncertain, like her.

These images, stories or history or things yet to come, did have lessons in them that she needed.

And she hated that.

She hated that Maleficent had, in fact, given her a gift. That Frieda was right. Their curse had been a blessing, a thing meant to build them into better rulers.

It made her want to abdicate her throne and run away, if only to escape whatever plot Maleficent had forced her into.

She feared her unworthiness. But she *knew* others were unworthy, too, and they held their positions without flinching. Like Matilda; like the Prince Electors who rolled in bribes; like Eckhardt of Hesse, who had not said more than a handful of words the whole campaign and was more often than not asleep during events. These were the people she would leave to rule the empire, all because she didn't feel like she had anything to contribute?

The game was corrupt. The players, corrupt. The whole lot of it *corrupt.*

And as Briar woke one morning, knowing another banquet awaited her and, in only a few days, the Prince Electors' vote, she was oddly numb. She moved in a fugue state, letting her aunts dress her and style her hair. Phillip escorted her down through the castle, Ben behind them, and they spoke to her, but she only managed monosyllabic responses, and they shared a concerned look.

The banquet was smaller. Only three candidates and their retinues. The Prince Electors, all seven of them, were clustered together, already in deep conversation with Frieda and Matilda.

Eckhardt of Hesse was asleep in a chair by the window.

The Electors welcomed her into the circle with smiles that didn't light their eyes. They had some test to present, no doubt. Another test, while their hands reached behind their backs for money her vassals were paying. While Matilda plotted to send her attacker after Briar next. Or Eckhardt, even, and why not? He was an easy target. Johann had been, too.

Briar stopped before them, her arm through Phillip's.

They posed a question to her.

"The empire deserves better than this," she said to whatever they'd asked.

A few exchanged looks. Frieda, across from her, cocked her head, eyeing the Electors, then Briar.

Matilda already, always, smoldered with anger, knowing Austria was up to something, waiting for them to unseat Bavaria, to attack. Everything was about Matilda, of course.

"Pardon, Your Majesty?" one Elector pressed.

"The empire deserves better than this. Than us. Than *you*," Briar clarified. It earned a hiss from Flora, behind her, but Briar ignored it. "Look at the candidates left. One is asleep at ten in the morning—has anyone checked whether Eckhardt is even still breathing? Has he been a corpse simply moved and posed for days? What good would he do as emperor?"

A stifled gasp rang through the banquet hall, peppered with cries of restrained outrage. "Your Majesty!" and "I dare say!"

"And another candidate," Briar said, "is puppeted so thoroughly by a warmongering murderer that I am shocked she has not been throttled by the strings."

She said that with a pointed glare at Frieda. Whose face was, for the first time, full of emotion, not held in furious blankness.

She was horrified. Hurt.

Good.

"You would *dare* accuse me of *murder*?" Matilda shrieked.

That shone clarity through Briar's building fury. She could so easily eviscerate her own decorum, but she breathed, breathed deeply, and reached for her poise.

She would speak, and she would be *heard*.

"And then there's me," Briar continued, "who has fallen too easily to these superfluous games. What other tests will the Prince Electors run us through for entertainment while we fill their coffers with gold from our kingdoms? While we risk our very lives being here? The people of this land deserve better than a ruler selected by the amount of gifts bestowed. Meanwhile, seven candidates have been driven off, threatened, poisoned, and *attacked* as this game plays on."

An Elector scoffed through pale shock. "The road to emperor is paved with—"

"I was not finished speaking," Briar said calmly. Commanding the room. "I have heard nothing but excuses of that sort all along. *This is how things are. Dangers are expected. This is how it's done.* I will no longer be part of it. This is no way to determine the next ruler of our empire, and if you cannot find it within yourselves to choose a leader through worth, merit, and heart, then I do not want to be considered."

She hadn't known she was going to say that.

She truly hadn't planned to.

But that was the choice that had started to grow in her, the roots digging down into her soul.

She didn't want this. Had never wanted it. But now she didn't want it because it was vile and cold, and she refused to be a part of a system that was so blood-soaked.

The moment her declaration lit the air, Electors gasped again, dismay and offense. Matilda's face curved in a devilish smile. Briar's vassals cried out in shock.

And Frieda watched her, eyes watery, but not relieved, as Briar would have expected. Frieda looked concerned, still, the way she'd been when she'd asked Briar to concede.

Briar turned without another word, Phillip falling into step beside her, Ben scurrying ahead and spinning around to walk backward in front of her.

"Well," Ben said, wincing with shock and humor.

"Briar, I—" Phillip's lips parted. He looked down at her as they crossed the banquet hall, and she shrugged, her heart racing, aching.

"I didn't plan to do that. I—I had to do *something.* I couldn't take this anymore."

Phillip stopped them once they were in the hall. He pulled her into his arms, and a tremor started in the base of her spine, reverberating up her back, down her arms and legs, and she felt what she had done.

She had withdrawn her candidacy for empress.

Bavaria would win. They would have the empire's resources at their disposal.

Austria would suffer. Maybe Frieda would restrain her mother's bloodlust. *Maybe.* But Briar knew better; Frieda was under her mother's control now.

The vassals and her aunts were moments behind them, all open-mouthed.

"Your Majesty," Köning croaked. "What did you *do?*"

She squared her shoulders at him. "I will not play their game anymore. I will not play *anyone's* game anymore. We are going back to Austria, and we will fortify our borders against whatever Bavaria inevitably throws at us, and I will focus on making my country the strongest, healthiest, happiest it can be. As I should have done all along."

Weight was lifting from her shoulders, from her soul. She could *breathe* again.

Köning's lips flapped, but he shut his mouth and nodded. "As you wish, Your Majesty."

Flora, Fauna, and Merryweather looked at her with teary eyes. She expected the same anger and confusion, so seeing it on them should not have been so jarring.

"You would not be empress, Aurora?" Fauna pressed.

Briar's shoulders went tense. "No."

"But," Flora protested, cheeks reddening, "you are capable of such greatness! You are destined for *more*—"

Merryweather put a gentle hand on Flora's arm. "We must accept her choice and trust her path. We must trust *her.* We owe her that, and more."

Merryweather met Briar's eyes. The echo of their conversation vibrated in the space between them. Had Merryweather told Flora and Fauna what she and Briar had spoken of? They had not offered similar apologies or mentioned it, and their shock now said they still clung to their prior expectations of her.

Flora looked like she was going to burst. "It's her, though. It's *her.* How can she give it up?"

It's her? What did that mean?

Merryweather guided Flora away.

Briar shook it off. With the weight lifting, she felt other things now, like a grinding discomfort in her chest, in her eyelids.

She thought she might actually sleep tonight. Soundly, dreamlessly.

"Let's go home," she whispered to Phillip.

He kissed her temple and they began walking again, back through the halls.

Only Ben lingered.

Briar glanced back to see him looking into the banquet room, where Frieda still was.

The next time they saw her, if they ever did, would likely be on a battlefield, or over war negotiations.

She and Frieda had playacted such things in the forest. Frieda, wielding a stick that became a sword in her mind. Briar, drawing battle lines in the dirt, begging for mercy for her captured soldiers. Frieda laughed and agreed, and they had celebrated their pretend war's end by splashing in the cool water of a nearby brook, drenching each other silly.

What memory was in Ben's mind? What ache was he stuck in?

"Ben." Briar stopped.

She held out her hand to him.

A pause, and then he joined her. She looped her free arm through his.

They were going home.

But, like the lance piece Ben had given to Johann, a part of them was separated from the whole, and Briar felt it as strongly as a gouge in her heart.

CHAPTER FOURTEEN

The note arrived as they were packing.

Merryweather accepted it from a messenger as Briar went over travel routes with Köning. It was Merryweather's sharp gasp that drew her attention.

And then the look on her face, one of staggering worry, and Briar stood from her chair, feeling like her aunt would try to hide the letter, would lie about its contents.

"What is it? Who is that from?" Briar held out her hand.

Merryweather pressed it to her chest. "From . . . Frieda."

Ben and Phillip, packing by the window, looked up simultaneously.

Briar snatched the note from her aunt.

"She wants to meet with you," Merryweather said as Briar read.

Heart in her throat, Briar read the letter twice. It was short, but her eyes blurred, and she sniffed hard, fighting for composure.

Briar—

Meet with me before you leave for Austria. Just the two of us, as it began, no guards on either side.

I will be in the garden at nightfall should you accept.

Frieda

Briar had wanted a letter like this from the moment she had first seen Frieda in Frankfurt. She had wanted Frieda to reach out.

Now she had.

And she had signed the letter *Frieda.*

Something about it was odd, though. The tone, maybe. Briar couldn't place it, or maybe she was rattled by everything that had happened the past few days.

Ben was already at her side, and he took the letter before she could stop him, but he couldn't read, and he stared at the ink, his eyes wide.

"What does she want?"

"She didn't say." Briar's throat was dry. "It's a trap. From her mother. It has to be."

"Why?" Ben frowned at her. That flicker of hope was still in him. Would always be in him, she knew, and her heart broke all over again. "Why would she care to threaten you now? You stepped aside. It has to be from Frieda. It has to be *real*."

"What if it is not?" Köning stood from the table. "It is an unnecessary risk to take, Your Majesty. We know where Bavaria stands. Nothing will come of this meeting that you have not already decided."

His words were a little colder, insinuating that she had taken this path and so must stick to it.

She glared at him. "I do not appreciate the tone, Lord Köning."

He reddened.

Ben took her arm. "If this is from her, if this is real— Bri. You have to try."

Briar looked up at him.

And she knew.

She'd known the moment she'd heard it was from Frieda. Because she had the flicker of hope, and it would always be there, and she was breaking her own heart, she nodded at Ben.

"The letter asks that you go alone?" Phillip was closer, his face worried.

"I will not leave the castle grounds."

"Johann's people were within the castle grounds, too," Phillip said. "As well as the other candidates who were attacked or poisoned. To plan the place and time ahead, and know you will be there . . ."

"You can scout it if you like."

Phillip's face set. He wanted to say more. But he bowed his head in surrender.

He and Köning were right, though.

It was an unnecessary risk.

What if this was not about Bavaria? What if this was *Frieda*, and Briar could, somehow, reach her? Not to reclaim her friendship—she wasn't sure they could, not after everything—but maybe to bridge any future clashes between their countries.

That was how a ruler thought, wasn't it? To put logic and reason first for the well-being of their people. To resist getting distracted by the selfish part of her heart that was still a child and wanted her friend back even now.

"If Matilda plans to attempt anything," Briar said slowly, "we could make it more difficult for her. Call for one last meal before we leave—a feast at Austria's expense. Tonight, during the arranged time. Ensure that Matilda and most of Bavaria's party will be in attendance, so we can keep an eye on them should any slip away, other than Frieda."

"Won't that make it harder for Frieda herself to slip away?" Ben asked.

Briar shrugged. "Possibly. But I would like to control some of the situation, however we can."

Köning made a grunt that might have been approval. "We can certainly do that, Your Majesty."

"Good." Briar rubbed her face, breathing hard into the cave of her palms. "We will leave tomorrow, then." It was not yet the afternoon, hours to go until her meeting with Frieda, and she felt as though she could lie down and sleep for years.

Where was a spindle when she needed one?

She laughed at her own bad joke, an empty, hollow laugh that had Phillip frowning in concern.

He held his arm out to her. "You should lie down," he prodded.

And Ben, bless him always, shattered what remained of the unbearable tension by looking straight at Phillip and saying, "Married for what, not even two months, and that's the best proposition you can muster?"

Ben cut an encouraging grin at Briar, gauging her reaction, her need to smile, and when she looked at him rather vulnerably, he pressed on with all the determination she loved in him.

"Oh," Phillip said, a small plea of warning, "don't start—"

"Without even putting effort into it," Ben plowed forward, "I can think of several far better ways to lure your wife into the bedroom, most of which involve some veiled reference to your lance."

Flora choked.

Köning rushed from the room with an excuse about arranging the last-minute banquet.

And Briar laughed. She laughed harder when Phillip's whole face went red and he shook his head in annoyed resignation.

"Death by embarrassment from my squire," he said to the ceiling. "This is not how I foresaw my end."

"Oh, I've embarrassed you in ways far worse than talking about your lance," Ben said.

"And you shall stop now!" Flora snapped. "Decorum—"

"Decorum, yes, I was being nothing but decorumed! Decorated?"

"Decompressed?" Briar offered. "Deconsecrated?"

"Oh, I was deconsecrated when I was about fifteen, Bri."

She cracked a laugh so loud it hurt.

Flora's face was purple. Fauna was humming over a flower vase, arranging buds, wholly oblivious. Merryweather was laughing.

"Point is, my dear Flora," Ben said, "I am Phillip's squire, and I was merely discussing one of his jousting tools. I have no idea why you are looking at me in such horror over what is a perfectly innocent, not at all cheeky topic of conversation."

"He is nothing if not a humble squire," Briar said, smiling.

"The humblest!" Ben declared. "Thank you! Someone realizes. I am too good for the lot of you. Now out, all you who do not see my worth, for it is truly no concern of ours how my lord uses his lance, except for his wife, because she is famously such a fan of jousting."

"God help me, Benedikt." Phillip covered his face with his hands, not fast enough to hide his smirk.

Ben did serve, at least, to get her aunts to leave, and when he followed them out, Briar and Phillip were alone.

He crossed to her and gathered her into his arms.

"Do you think I should not go to meet her?" Briar asked into Phillip's chest.

He tightened his grip on her. "I want you to be happy, Briar. And I am beginning to think you will never be truly content until you resolve whatever you need to resolve between the two of you. If it means risking your safety . . . I cannot say I am thrilled at the prospect, and I will not even try to hide my contempt for Matilda in the banquet hall while you are gone. But I think you would not forgive yourself if you did not try."

"I'm afraid to hope."

Phillip held her so tightly she couldn't feel the sag of her body, the weight in her chest. There was only him, his steadfastness, his strength.

He kissed her cheek. "Don't hope, then. Just rest."

When she twisted to look at him, he caught her up in a kiss, so he was not just steadfastness and strength now, but mouth and tongue and fingers on her back.

And she thought, as if down a long, echoing corridor, that

maybe she could have all she wanted. Maybe she would meet Frieda tonight and they would reconcile and all would be as perfectly happy as she hoped.

But why did that hope feel so tainted?

• • •

Night approached both too quickly and not quickly enough. Her vassals pulled together a fabulous last-minute banquet under the guise of Austria apologizing for Briar's brusqueness. She did not condone that apology but let them use whatever excuse they needed. As Ben and Phillip joined the vassals in the banquet hall to represent Austria, Briar snuck down the castle stairs to visit her friend.

It was almost how she had done so in Hausach. Sneaking out, bursting with things she would tell Frieda. Only now she was flanked by Flora, Fauna, and Merryweather, on alert, though they would not go into the gardens with her.

"We can magic ourselves to be small," Flora whispered as they headed down the cold stone stairs. "Hide in your pocket, should you have need of us."

The door she would take out of the castle was paces ahead, but Briar paused in the shadows, and her aunts stopped around her.

And she realized that this *didn't* feel like how she would sneak out to see Frieda; it felt like the night her aunts had escorted—dragged—her from Hausach, to the castle, clad in the finery of a princess. They had plunked her in front of a dressing mirror in a room that was too grand to be hers, put a crown on her head, and given her such a look of confusion when she'd started crying that she couldn't bear to even try to explain why it hurt.

But they had raised her. And they loved her, and she loved them, and she didn't know when that had stopped being enough.

"No," she said to Flora in the darkness. "Thank you. I must do this without you."

She paused, though.

And threw her arms around the three of them.

"Thank you," she said again. *For giving me Hausach*, she thought, willing them to feel it, but she couldn't say it aloud. They had hurt her in ways she was still uncovering, but they wouldn't understand that the best gift they had given her was not a fairy blessing or her return to a throne; it had been her simple life, her humble origins.

Then she pressed on, leaving her three aunts behind, their eyes tearing up.

Outside, evening had only just fallen, a warm, damp summer night that threatened rain. But the sky was clear for now, alive with speckled stars, a full moon giving pale white light to the rows of hedges and flowers set before her.

Briar wove into the garden, passing gray-washed plant life, until she reached the area where she had played rithmomachia with Frieda.

It was quiet.

And empty.

Briar's heartbeat thundered in her clenched jaw, in her fists, rocking jerks she felt quicken with each passing moment of vacant stillness.

The tables had been cleared, so it was a normal garden now, a stone path, the walls of shrubs stretching over Briar's head. In the play of dark and moonlight, her eyes made movement of everything, so a pulse of wind might have been Frieda coming from beside her, or a knot of flowers might have been a Bavarian soldier, crouched, waiting.

But no one was there. Anywhere.

Briar turned in slow circles, holding her breath for any sound, but that only let her thudding pulse rock in her head.

And when her eyes drifted up to the moon again, seeing how far it had shifted—

The sky was . . . gone?

She blinked. It was darker, as though a storm had moved in. It was certainly humid enough, but had she missed clouds rolling overhead? She squinted, fighting to make sense of the darkness, that shape—

Beams?

Wood beams.

A ceiling.

What—

Briar spun, shock leaching urgency into her veins, and she staggered at the wrenching shift of her surroundings. The garden, the garden was gone, dissolved entirely, rocking out from under her—

Briar toppled to the floor, catching herself on her elbows.

She felt wood beneath her.

She looked up and saw an old table, a fireplace, stairs twisting above. She saw walls decorated with painted Lüftlmalerei—mural art that Fauna had done, flowers and happy dancing villagers who pranced all over the cottage.

The cottage.

Her cottage.

Briar scrambled to her feet, skirt twisted around her ankles, breath coming hard and fast, and panicked.

She had passed out. That was the only explanation. She had been hit on the head, hadn't she? Struck from behind.

Light flared in the fireplace.

Briar whirled.

And knew she was dreaming.

Knew she was unconscious.

Because she was looking at a pointed heart-shaped face that only existed in nightmares now. The face was matched with a coiling black horned headdress, draping black cloak, long fingers set with thick onyx rings. And a curling grin, red lips, and arching black brows.

The nightmare leaned against the fireplace, eyes slitted in appraisal, and when Briar faced her head-on, she gave a rattling cackle.

"Well, my dear," Maleficent crooned. "How nice of you to join me."

CHAPTER FIFTEEN

PHILLIP

Phillip hated this.

He should have convinced Briar to allow him to wait with the fairies outside the garden, armed and ready to help her, instead of being in the banquet room, uselessly glaring at Matilda of Bavaria. He'd even strapped the Sword of Truth to his waist, despite how much carrying that sword unsettled him. It was an undeniably powerful weapon regardless of his hesitation.

But one of the first things he had noticed about his wife was how she needed him not to press matters—it was a trait he shared with her, albeit an infuriating one when he found himself on the other side of it. She needed space to think through her plans, and he was usually glad to give it to her—except for now, when those plans put her in danger, and he had submitted too quickly to her plea that he serve as Austria's presence at their impromptu parting banquet.

Which meant that now, she was out in the garden, meeting

with Frieda, alone, quite possibly held at swordpoint by Bavarian soldiers—

"Flaying or drawn and quartered?"

Phillip rocked to face Ben with a startled frown. "Pardon?"

Ben nodded across the banquet room. Most of the Bavarian and Hessian contingents were present, and the Prince Electors, all milling about, minstrels playing a light tune from the corner. Frieda was not here, which boded well, and Phillip had counted and re-counted the number of soldiers around Matilda.

Four were missing, which could have merely meant they were off duty.

Or.

Or.

"You look like you're trying to torture Matilda through the power of thought," Ben explained. "So I was wondering what method you were hoping to magically visit upon her. Now, personally, I wouldn't be opposed to a breaking wheel."

Phillip had gotten used to sensational things coming out of his squire's mouth, but they were always accompanied by a bright smile or at least that glint in his eye. This one, however, came with a tension around his mouth, and he was looking straight at Matilda, unsmiling.

It was remarkable that Ben had kept any of his levity after Frieda's appearance. Remarkable and concerning, and Phillip had learned quickly, just as he had adapted to Briar's needs, that Ben often said straight out what he was thinking, if one looked beneath the humor of his words.

"You still believe Matilda is pulling Frieda's strings?" Phillip clarified.

Ben blinked at him, then rolled his eyes. "Heaven help me, it's annoying how quickly you picked up on that."

"Picked up on what?" He knew what.

"How I—" Ben waved his hand, encompassing something intangible. "Say things with far more flair than others. It took Bri years to figure out how to get to the root of my meanings so effectively. You're infuriating."

"Yes, communication is infamously the bane of your existence."

"Let me have my brooding, sarcastic comments in peace, would you? You don't adore talking about your feelings, either." Ben poked Phillip's rib cage in demonstration, still wickedly bruised from his fall during the joust, and Phillip bit down on a bark of pain.

His father might have said a better king would not allow a squire to treat him so familiarly.

He would be wrong.

Phillip rubbed his ribs. "That is precisely why we both should make a greater effort. Especially given our return to Austria." He paused, eyeing Ben. "You won't be all right leaving her."

Ben held Phillip's gaze, lips working, but he gave a resigned shrug. "I'll have to be. And she'll be empress, right? It'll hardly be the first time an unsuitable match ended in heartache."

"*Unsuitable match.* That is an oversimplification, and you know it."

"What, you think she and Bri are making good right now? They'll sweep in here, back to being the best of friends, and Frieda will apologize for . . . everything, and I'll grovel a bit, and happily ever after, there we are. That's what will happen. Right?"

Phillip didn't dignify that with a response.

Ben sighed. "Look, I tried, all right? I tried to talk to her. I tried to *sing* to her. She asked to see Briar, not me. So that's that, isn't it? Even if they make up. I don't know what else I could do, but she reached out to Briar, so yes, maybe— I don't know. I don't know. I don't like any of this."

And there it was, confirmation that this whole situation was *wrong*, and Phillip truly had no idea how Briar had any faith that Frieda would be there, alone, waiting for her to talk things over.

Köning appeared beside Phillip. "Everyone is gathered, Your Majesty. Would you care to open the banquet with a few remarks?"

An unspoken command was woven into the words; Phillip would need to formally apologize for Briar's outburst. Over his dead body, honestly; she'd had every right to eviscerate the Prince Electors like that. He was damn proud of his wife.

But he gave Köning a cordial smile. "Of course."

A prickle ran up the back of Phillip's spine.

Instinct flared, shooting out to the tips of his fingers, and he was clutching his sword hilt before he even knew why, the surge of a threat cocooning painfully around his lungs. *No, damn it,* no—

Breathe. Breathe fully.

Ben's focus caught at something behind Phillip, his face dropping into concern.

Phillip spun.

Frieda had entered the banquet room, walking calmly across

to her mother. Unbothered. No look at Phillip or Ben—and no Briar with her, not even as Phillip waited, sword still sheathed, hilt gripped in his opposite hand.

The door to the banquet room remained empty.

Another long moment passed.

Briar did not follow her in.

Everything shifted in that moment.

Sharpened.

Like he'd emerged to the surface and scrubbed pond scum out of his eyes and could see more than grime. He saw one thing, and it was the only thing that had ever truly mattered to him.

Phillip started walking toward Frieda and Matilda, Ben with him.

Matilda was buoyant tonight. Phillip had yet to see her anything but furious, so to see her laughing with a Prince Elector and sipping wine only added to the sense of wrongness that thickened the air.

At Phillip's approach, her smiling face took on a look of cutting malice. She threaded her arm through Frieda's, pulling her daughter close, and raised her wine goblet to the room.

"Let us give a cheer," she started, voice bellowing out. "To the next empress of the Holy Roman Empire."

That made the Prince Electors, who had been enjoying yet another luxurious event in an endless series of luxurious events, straighten, moods shifting.

"What do you declare, Queen Matilda?" one asked.

Eckhardt of Hesse, who was awake and seated at a table, halfway through a plate of gravy and roast boar, glanced up with a frown.

Matilda grinned. "It is what *you* will declare, good sir. That my daughter is empress. Austria has withdrawn. We all know you will not vote in Eckhardt. Thus, Clara is our new empress, and you will announce it as such."

Eckhardt scoffed and sputtered, wiping his hands insufficiently on a napkin. But when no one of import spared him a glance, he did not rise from the table, merely slouched in his chair and continued to grumble to himself.

The back of Phillip's throat constricted.

Honestly, though, he didn't care at all who was crowned.

Where was Briar?

He glared at Frieda until she looked at him in confusion.

"The election is not yet come to pass," an Elector said. "Clara and Eckhardt are not the only remaining candidates. In fact . . ." He cast his gaze around the room, frowning, and landed on Phillip. "Where is the Austrian queen?"

"I was wondering that very thing myself," he said. To Frieda.

Frieda's confusion deepened, her lips parting.

Wait—what was the Elector saying?

"Her absence does not matter!" Matilda's voice went a little shrill. "It further proves her ineptitude, that she could not even appear, to spare you a proper farewell and apology. You would do well not to linger on these last days out of ceremony. Clara is empress. Make it so."

"The terms of Queen Aurora's concession were only if we could not *choose a leader through worth, merit, and heart*," recited one Elector, a quiet older man who leaned on a cane. "Given her impassioned speech, we are quite eager to keep her in the running. She has proven herself a thoughtful, competent candidate."

Phillip gaped at Ben, brows lifted, not sure whether he should argue that Briar had withdrawn her candidacy, or agree and accept her continued nomination on her behalf, or—

Where was she?

Her absence beat into him, became as close as his pulse.

What has Bavaria done to her?

It beat, and beat, and Phillip opened his mouth to shout at Frieda and Matilda, when another *beat, beat* caught his attention so aggressively he felt grabbed by the throat.

He looked over his shoulder.

The flutter of wings. That was what had caught him.

The fairies dove into the banquet room—without Briar. Their faces were haggard and terrified.

Frieda was here, and so were the fairies, and Briar had not returned.

That was it.

Phillip closed the space between him and Matilda of Bavaria, towering before her, his vision entirely red. It centered him enough that he couldn't be overcome by panic or anxiety—he was a being beyond himself, pushed out of his own shaking body to be wholly at Briar's call.

"Where. Is my. *Wife?*" he snarled at Matilda.

The Bavarian queen wasn't one to cower. She sneered up at him, the amusement in her eyes saying she was hoping for such a confrontation, either to be able to fight back or to prove even further Austria's weakness.

"A king who cannot keep track of his own wife," Matilda spat.

That redness spiked, overwhelming his vision, drowning him in single-minded focus.

A body moved next to Matilda—Frieda.

"What are you talking about?" Frieda asked in the demanding, level tone used in training yards to exact attention. "Why is she not here?"

He very nearly drew his sword.

He whirled on Frieda, and he would have held the Sword of Truth to her throat if Ben had not been suddenly between them, hands up, eyes wide.

"Whoa there, all right, let's— Frieda, where is Briar?" Ben asked. He was only looking up at Phillip.

Frieda shook her head. "Why would I know?"

Phillip's body went cold.

It had been a lie.

But Matilda was here. Most of the Bavarians. The Hessians.

Who . . .

Who sent the letter?

"You sent her a letter," Ben said. "You asked her to meet you in the gardens."

Matilda gave her daughter a fierce glare, but Frieda was believably confused.

"That is what we came to tell you!" Merryweather cried. "The gardens—something has happened in the gardens. They swallowed her up!"

"What did?" Phillip's voice was like sand in his throat.

Merryweather's face fell. "Vines. Magic. Dark magic."

That coldness filling his body transformed into pure ice, freezing him in place.

Frieda flicked her gaze to her mother. "What did you do?"

Matilda scoffed. "Nothing! Why would I have gone after someone who *conceded*?"

Frieda heard something else in Matilda's words. Something that turned her a bit green. "You have targeted candidates, though."

It was not a question.

Matilda stared at Frieda, narrowed her eyes, and snorted. "Do not get righteous with me, child. We are nearly to the end. Be *grateful*."

"Grateful?" Frieda's voice rose, her face set in a furious scowl. "Grateful that you ordered an attack on a child? That was you, wasn't it, who targeted Mecklenburg?"

Matilda put her hands on Frieda's shoulders, her whole bearing shifting with skillful ease. "Sweetheart," she said, voice suddenly gentle and prodding. "I forgive you for not understanding our ways. Do not be so cross now, darling. Do not be so—"

There was a moment where Frieda might have melted into her mother's act. And Phillip could see the effect it was having, had been having, on Frieda. A softness in her eyes, yearning for exactly what Matilda offered.

But Frieda dropped a boundary over her own emotions, shutting down her reaction with a harsh glare.

Matilda didn't let more than a beat pass of Frieda's expression before she rounded on the Prince Electors, back to her rigid, callous self.

"My daughter is empress," she stated. "Declare it. *Now.*"

Things were unspooling. Here, there. The whole of the room felt events beginning to fall apart—or maybe that was just Phillip. *He* was both unspooling and frozen, forced to stand there motionless and watch himself disintegrate.

His hands shook. Vibrations in his arms, in his lungs. He couldn't breathe, and his vision was going spotty, narrowing—

No, damn it, *no*, Briar *needed him*—not now, please—

In the corner, one of the banners cast a shadow.

But it wasn't a shadow.

And as Phillip stared, it became the only thing he could see.

That shadow took flight, the force and weight of its movements shaking the banner in a ripple.

The bird banked and dove out into the hall.

A raven.

Dark magic in the garden.

No. No, *no*—

He'd killed that witch.

It couldn't be her.

Phillip started walking, then running.

There was a bare sword in his hand. When had he drawn it?

He was near the door when Ben gripped his arm. He heard Ben's words through the muffled fog of his own fervent barrier.

"Phillip—wait—"

"Maleficent."

The name was knives and hooks, and it ripped pieces of his soul out as it came from his mouth so that he held a hand to his neck, sure it would come away covered in blood.

Ben went white. "Here? How?"

Phillip didn't have time to explain. Briar had been gone for too long as it was.

"It's *Maleficent*," Phillip hissed at him. "It's her. Again. Somehow."

"All right. But you're not going into this alone. This is not like last time. I'm coming, too."

Phillip tasted the burn of green fire on the air. Felt the bite of a thorn that had ripped through his shoulder.

The whole kingdom had been dead. Briar had been cursed. It was on him, wholly on him.

"Phillip," Ben said again, harder. "I'm with you. I'm still hopeless with a sword, but I'm with you."

"Me too."

Phillip twisted, the oddity of the voice jerking him around, a pause long enough that his vision centered.

Frieda stood behind him. Eyes ablaze.

Farther back, Matilda was shouting at the Electors, caught so wholly in their argument over the passing of the crown that none had even noticed that Phillip, Ben, and Frieda were at the door.

The fairies were hovering over Frieda's shoulder. Merryweather nodded at Phillip and held up her wand in a sad offer of whatever help they could manage.

"Can you fight?" was the first question that came out of Ben's mouth.

Frieda's gaze turned to his. She paused for a moment, then smiled, but her eyes were still hard. "Yes, I can fight."

Ben's face went red. He bit his lip and looked to Phillip, his gaze weighted and fearful but determined.

Phillip adjusted his grip on the Sword of Truth and didn't recoil from its density in his hand.

"Come on, then" was all he managed to say, and he shot off into the hall.

CHAPTER SIXTEEN

Briar had had this nightmare before.

Maleficent was alive and Phillip had never saved her and she was trapped again, helpless and at this sorceress's mercy.

So an odd sense of calm fell over her like heavy wool, fuzzy and dense.

This wasn't real.

It couldn't be.

But a stab of fear: Her dreams had never been this *real* before. She could smell the damp wood of her cottage, the earthiness where Fauna had spilled a bag of flour once and the scent had never gone away. She could taste it on the air, powder and mildew and the endless rich greenery of the forest just outside the window. Chill bit into her arms, rising up her limbs to the back of her neck, and somewhere deep beneath this protective shield was a voice, her voice, whispering *This is no dream, is it?*

Numb, moving as if it were, in fact, a dream, Briar stumbled to the door of the cottage and tried the handle. Locked. Her fingers were so cold suddenly, she could barely bend them, but she fought to grab the lock and twist.

It didn't budge.

Trapped.

Helpless.

The curse is taking me again.

It took Frieda even after Maleficent was dead—it isn't finished with me yet—I'm asleep again, and Phillip won't save me—

Or maybe.

Maybe the curse had taken Frieda anyway because Maleficent had *not* been dead.

Every reason was equally horrifying, and Briar tried the door again, again, unable to come up with anything other than the consuming instinct to get *away.*

"No, darling," Maleficent cooed from behind her. "You will not leave quite yet. You and I need to have something of a talk."

Briar stayed facing the closed door, tugging hard enough to rattle the wall, shaking dust from the wood beams over her head. Her heart thundered, aching fear constricting her like vines, and she realized, distantly, that this was how Phillip must have felt in his panic episodes.

That centered her.

Don't think about your own fear—think of Phillip.

If Maleficent had Briar . . .

He would have to face her again.

But he *wouldn't*, because this was a *dream.*

"Let me go," Briar begged, no louder or more forceful than a whisper.

Maleficent laughed. "Yes, that is what you want, isn't it? To leave. Back to Austria. After everything I have done for you, the path laid out perfectly, you would give it all up without a fight. I did not train you to be a coward, Briar Rose. Aurora. I did not train you to be a *fool*."

Briar whirled on her. "You did nothing. Everything I am I have become in spite of the things you subjected me to, and I owe you no explanation for the choices I make. Now *wake me up*."

Maleficent's red lips stretched in a smile that contrasted with the malice in her eyes. "Oh, you are awake. This is very real, darling. You forced me to take drastic measures."

Briar's breath went out in a sharp gust.

Maleficent was lying.

She was a *liar*. She was a sorceress and a villain and she was *lying*.

Maleficent smirked at Briar's rising breaths. At her shaking head.

Briar blinked quickly. "No. No, I'm not discussing anything with you—you gave me *nothing*, nothing I will accept. *Let me go!*"

"You don't have to accept it. What I gave you were not *gifts*. Not in so many ways. They were pieces arranged on a board. Paths forged. Luckily for you, I never expected gratitude for what was necessary."

A cold horror chilled Briar's limbs, froze her irrevocably in place.

She turned back to the door, banged on it with her fists. "Help!" Again, harder. "Help!" Again, again, bruising herself, pain rippling up her arms. "*HELP!* I'm in—"

"Darling, really. You have to know that won't be in the least effective."

"I will not listen to anything you have to say!" Briar swung on Maleficent, fury raging through her, breaking apart her fear so that she focused only on being *angry*, on being filled with vengeance. "I don't know why you thought I would even for a moment tolerate *any* explanation you have to give—"

"Because it's your fate, Briar Rose Aurora. And your aunts did not have the strength to see it through."

That did stop her.

Her aunts?

It's her, though, Flora had said. *It's her. How can she give it up?*

Briar paused long enough that Maleficent's smile went wicked, a hunter bending over a triggered snare, gazing at the rabbit caught in its loop, knowing there was no escape.

"You have seen," Maleficent said in that voice that curled like smoke. "You have guessed. Your aunts have lied to you about many things. Do you want to know the full extent of their betrayal? Do you want to know how spectacularly they have failed you?"

Briar didn't speak. Not to refuse. Not to scream for help again.

She had hated silence for months. The silence after she asked a difficult question, the silence after she did something improper. But this silence was the worst yet, a silence she created, a door she opened.

Because as much as she railed, as much as she fought, she *did* want answers. And Maleficent was the only one able—willing—to give them to her.

Self-hatred became another constricting tendril around her heart, squeezing, squeezing.

At her silence, Maleficent's grin faded. She did not tease. She did not torment. She looked at Briar in one long, drawn-out moment of . . . understanding.

"I am not the villain you have created me to be, Briar Rose Aurora," Maleficent said. "Your fate is such that you would have drawn the attention of things far worse than me, had we not intervened. I am but one part of a force connected to guiding the fate of powerful women rulers," she said. "And that force foresaw an empress of the Holy Roman Empire who would unite the whole of the land in an unmatched age of peace."

Briar waited for Maleficent to sneer at that. But no—she said it as though it was an outcome she wanted. It left her a little breathless, and Briar watched Maleficent inhale deeply, steadying her shoulders. The motion made her . . . made her *human* in a way Briar had never seen.

Briar tightened her hands into fists. Widened her stance.

She would listen, she would be here, but she would not be unprepared.

"But the vision we had," Maleficent continued, "was unlike ones we had been given about rulers of other countries before. It kept *changing*. One day it would be a girl with dark hair and a stoic manner; another, it would be a girl with hair of sunshine gold and a demeanor of pure joy."

Briar flinched. "You had visions about Frieda and me?"

Maleficent pulsed an eyebrow. "And they overlapped and changed so often, so viciously, that the Queen's Council could not pin down precisely who the empress would be."

"The Queen's Council?"

A gentle nod. "The force that guides powerful women rulers. The force I am a part of, darling."

Briar glowered.

She and Frieda were in a prophecy of sorts? Fated by this *Queen's Council*?

At least she had a name for the force that had irrevocably altered her life. But knowing the name of the thing did not make Briar any more likely to obey it.

"The vision changed." Maleficent kept talking. "And kept changing, and ripped apart and changed back. The magic of the Queen's Council allows us to take the form that will most benefit the ruler we need to guide. But with each change of the vision, the Queen's Council began to change as well. We . . . *disagreed.* We were one being, but with each shift of the vision, we began to split. Part believed this girl would be empress, part believed *that* girl, then part changed its mind again; part believed neither and it would all come to ruin, part believed the two must be tested. We could not decide on a path nor a form to take. The magic got so vigorously knotted in its own uncertainty that it sundered us into pieces."

Maleficent spoke of pieces, and Briar saw some come together before her next words formed.

Magic.

Broken pieces.

A trapped breath welled in Briar's lungs.

Her . . . her aunts?

No, she thought again, *no, this is absurd—this isn't even real—this is a dream—*

But nothing had ever been a dream, had it? Not from the start. It had always been visions, had always been real women in situations just like Briar's. Had always been Maleficent's real cackle, because she had been alive the whole time.

"I am one such piece," Maleficent said with a sweep of her arm, as though giving an introduction. "And once I had been severed from my sisters, I saw the purpose of that vision clearly: that *both* girls needed the tools to grow to their fullest potential. To that end, I took it upon myself to give you both the tools you would need."

Briar's stomach sank. "You're the reason we both ended up in Hausach."

Maleficent nodded.

She'd known. The whole time. Maleficent had *known* where Briar was, where *Frieda* was, and she hadn't attacked, she hadn't swept in and enacted her curse early—she'd led them both to Hausach intentionally. To *each other* intentionally.

"I gave you the chance to learn each other's strengths and weaknesses in preparation, so you could ultimately face each other and determine once and for all the course of the visions themselves," Maleficent said. "That is the only end, the only *possible* end."

Briar sank back until her hip bumped a table, the anger briefly evaporating out of her in shock. "You want Frieda and me to try to kill each other?"

"Of course. One must win. Why have you taken so long to realize?"

"Because I won't do it," Briar stated, winded. "Because it is barbaric! You would think I would be at all driven to *murder* my closest friend?"

Maleficent sighed, that look of understanding still on her face, but it was heartless now. "You sound like the remaining council members. They disagreed with my methods as well. Claimed they were *harsh.* But the results will—"

"Harsh?" Briar shoved upright. "They were—are—more than harsh. You are cruel and a villain, no matter what heroic honor you think you've earned for *bravely* cursing two women and manipulating our lives. You tried to kill me. You *did* kill Frieda. You were—"

"I did that to give you the visions you now know were to your aid." Maleficent was unfazed by anything Briar said. "Visions of other rulers that the Queen's Council has helped, their strengths and weaknesses and successes and mistakes, so you would come armed with all the knowledge it was possible to provide. Frieda was only on the other side of life for a few moments; as such, she was able to receive the visions far more easily. *You*, though, needed to remain asleep for far longer to receive them, thanks to that nuisance of an amendment to my curse. *Not in death, but just in sleep. And from this slumber you shall wake, when true love's kiss, the spell shall break.* Vile annoyances, easily remedied. That man of yours did make it a particular challenge to keep you from rescue."

Briar surged forward, hands in fists. "Do not speak of him."

Maleficent waved dismissively. "I was never going to *hurt* him, and I was never going to hurt *you*, or Frieda, or anyone in your miserable little lands. Why do you think I let your prince think he had killed me? I did not *want* to torment you. All of this was *for* you, and you are here now, on the cusp of the prophecy coming true. One of you will become empress."

"Yes," Briar said. "It will be Frieda. I conceded."

"Aha, no. That is not how this works, Briar Rose Aurora. I did not arrange these pieces and set up this board to perfection for you to take the coward's way out. That is not a woman worthy of a prophecy so strong that it *shatters* a mighty force into pieces. Do you understand the gravity of what your destiny has done?" Maleficent's eyes glittered, with awe and hatred and that vile pity. "You *broke* a force that has existed for time immemorial. You and Frieda—your fate was powerful enough to nearly destroy us. So do not think your little wants and wishes are capable of combating what is coming for you. If the Queen's Council could not stand against it, you are but helpless to be carried in its grip."

"Helpless."

The word was a sparked flame. It was a knife dragging up her spine. It was enough to ground her and infuriate her, and in this moment, Briar was anything but helpless.

"You have seen me grow," she said, her jaw tight. "You have watched me become who I am. What makes you think I will not fight every moment to break free of this?"

"Fight if you want," Maleficent said with a shrug. "I am saying you will be ineffective. Your destiny lies here, facing Frieda, until one of you emerges as the true empress."

"An empress determined through bloodshed will bring about an age of peace? Do you hear how contradictory that sounds?"

"Peace does not come without sacrifice. Do not be naive." Maleficent finally took a step away from the fireplace, the first movement she had made at all, and Briar matched her with a step backward, hitting the table again.

"Now." Maleficent's faintly amused expression turned wicked.

"You will return to the castle and see through the path to fate I have made. My time grows short—I have outrun my own fate too long. And besides, we have other rulers to aid than *you*. Don't be so selfish, darling. Do what must be done."

Briar could only manage enough control of her senses to keep breathing. Quick, shuddering breaths.

Maleficent would make her return to the castle and *kill* Frieda?

It didn't make sense. None of this did. Not Maleficent claiming this was the only way to achieve *peace*; not her explanation about a force breaking, a Queen's Council rendering, and her being one part of it.

Other things made no sense, too.

They had not made sense for months, but Briar had ignored them, pushed them all deep down, because to truly confront the inequities and failures of her aunts, she would have broken apart herself. Frieda had declared their flaws at the rithmomachia game, but even then, Briar had barely begun to acknowledge how her aunts had failed her. How they had shoved her back into harm's way the final night of the curse. How they had let Phillip go into the fight against Maleficent alone. All their little mistakes over the years of living in Hausach that Briar had shrugged off as *her bumbling aunts*, even when their mistakes cost her food and security.

For as powerful as they were, it *made no sense* that they had failed at what should have been simple, obvious things.

Her aunts were the other parts of this council.

Maleficent, Flora, Fauna, Merryweather—they had been one magical force that was rendered to pieces.

And now, separated as they were, they were incomplete, and

that incompleteness made them unreliable and dangerous and shortsighted, well-intentioned but imprudent.

Briar remembered the visions she'd had in Maleficent's dreams. The women, their power and strength, and, at the base of it all, their supporters and friends and advisers.

None of them were alone.

Indeed, when these women *had* been alone, they had been at their weakest.

Maleficent had given Briar these visions so she would learn from other rulers.

But the biggest thing Briar saw in them, the solution that came raging at her full and bright, was not one that Maleficent had intended.

Or perhaps she had.

Perhaps, somewhere in the brokenness that was Maleficent and the Queen's Council, this was what Briar had been meant to see all along.

And she knew, as she stared at Maleficent, surrounded by a magical illusion of her childhood home, how this mighty story between her and Frieda would end.

CHAPTER SEVENTEEN

PHILLIP

Phillip burst out of the castle, battle-ready, *focused*—

And stopped.

He wasn't aware of why he stopped, his body feeling it before his brain made sense of what he saw.

Thorns.

Tangled, arching branches of thorns, trunks as thick as his body, tips razor-sharp and glinting in the moonlight. And smoke, smoke from enchanted flames somewhere, burning, green fire that ate the thorns but didn't destroy them, though it would destroy *him*—

For a moment, he was back at the castle in Austria, the one outside Hausach, facing down an endless forest of thorns that might as well have been blades.

This was what had become of the garden.

The hedges were gone, all greenery and flowers taken over by knotted arches of wood splintered by thorns the size of spears, the invasion wholly sealing off the garden from the castle.

Phillip knew, immediately, that was where Maleficent had Briar.

"Are we going in *there*?" Ben asked next to him, voice clipped.

Phillip took off.

He couldn't linger.

He had to keep moving.

If he stopped . . .

He hacked at the vines, the Sword of Truth slicing through trunks with terrifying ease. It had been some comfort then to have such a weapon on his side; it was no comfort now. He didn't feel anything, in fact, just the rub of the hilt on his palms, the sweat starting to gather down his spine, the tight lump of mingled panic and fear in the center of his chest, beating where his heart should be.

Don't stop.

Briar needed him.

Don't stop, don't feel it, don't think—

Someone grabbed him by the shoulders and heaved him back.

Frieda threw herself in front of him. She was glaring, but not at *him*, just furious in general, and he couldn't help holding the sword out at her, as though he might attack.

"Step aside," he ordered.

"So you can hack your way through what might be *miles* of thorns?" Frieda snapped. "How far do these go into the garden?"

She angled the question at the fairies hovering behind them, their wings beating in nervous, fluttering lurches.

"We—we don't know," Fauna said meekly.

Frieda's glare turned to pure ice. "Then maybe you should use those wings of yours to fly up and *find out*?"

Phillip's sword tipped to the side as Merryweather shot off into the sky a beat ahead of her sisters.

Frieda pointed at Phillip. She looked like she might use that same tone on him, but then she dropped her hand.

"I never got a chance to thank you, King Phillip," she said.

That shocked him. "What?"

Frieda cut a fleeting look at Ben. "For killing Maleficent."

"It doesn't look like I did," he whispered.

Her eyes snapped back to him. "We should fix that, then."

The fairies returned in a rush of wind. "The thorns wrap in a complete circle around the bare center of the garden," said Flora.

"And she has—" Merryweather stopped, panted, her plump face sheened with sweat. "She has our cottage there. Our old cottage, from Hausach."

"Briar's in there." Phillip advanced on the thorns again.

He would get inside. He would rip that cottage apart if he had to, however magical it was.

But it was Frieda who jumped into action first. She turned to the fairies and asked, "What's the extent of your magic? Could you fly us all over there?"

Merryweather squealed triumphantly. "Yes! We might be able to—"

"Can we?" Flora cut in. "Our magic is only in goodness! How would we—"

"Oh, do let me *try*, Flora." Merryweather waggled in the air, settling in, and gave a mighty flick of her wand.

A tidal wave of bubbles materialized under Frieda, Ben, and Phillip, and without further warning, the three of them vaulted into the sky, moving so fast Phillip didn't have time to process what was happening before the fairies lowered them into the center of the thorns, a small clearing in the middle of the garden.

There, surrounded by the thickest vines and thorns, was a cottage he had been to once. Months ago.

Maleficent had been lying in wait for him.

It would have taken him far, far too long to cut his way through all this, as it had the first time. He hadn't thought to ask the fairies for such a thing; he hadn't thought to ask them for *anything*, assuming that what they had given was the extent of their abilities.

As he landed, stumbling to his feet, he looked at Frieda, and at Ben, and felt how this fight differed from the last.

He was not alone.

Not now.

Not again, if he could help it.

Ben's face went white in recognition at the cottage, but he said nothing, no quip or joke or anything to lighten the mood, as though he knew nothing could. Merryweather was scowling, and she turned to Flora.

"Why didn't we do that the first time?" she asked.

Flora folded her arms. "We have our tasks. Our *goals*. Nowhere does it say we must do this or that."

"That is nonsense, sister," Merryweather snapped. Her eyes

drifted to the cottage. "And I think," she said slowly, an odd look of fondness easing her, "that it is time we stop with all this nonsense, indeed."

Merryweather started to fly for the cottage, when Phillip darted ahead of her. It was instinct to protect; the moment he did, he faced that cottage, and his throat tightened.

Briar was inside.

He approached the cottage, raised his sword, and kicked in the door.

It burst open with a shower of splinters and dust.

The darkness beyond the shattered door looked the same as it had months ago. Only—there was an orange glow, a lit fire, and as Phillip took a tentative step inside, shapes materialized. Briar was standing, unharmed. A cascade of relief drenched him—

The other shape was Maleficent.

She was standing too close to Briar, and it confirmed what he had known all along.

Maleficent was alive.

He had failed.

He had never killed her.

Phillip had imagined, in his darkest dreams, facing her again. In those nightmares, he was unable to move, weaponless, standing on a cliff as she approached in her full dragon form. He always awoke as she was killing him and he was standing there doing *nothing*, because that was what he would do—panic would take over, pin him in place so he was a target rather than a person. It was how he felt any time he had to fight outside of dreams since then, an overwhelming sense of freezing in place.

So he expected that now. He was watching outside himself, and he waited to choke and stand there helplessly.

But he kept walking forward. Somehow.

Behind him, he was aware of Frieda releasing a trembling breath.

He kept walking into that cottage, toward where Maleficent stood with Briar by the table, and his sword stayed lifted, gripped in both hands, and his arms didn't shake.

He stopped once Maleficent's neck was within range of his sword.

"Back away," he started, with a snarl, "from my wife."

"Phillip," said Briar. "I'm all right. Really. I'm all—"

Maleficent cackled. That laugh haunted the edges of his dreams.

His arms shook, once, a vibration that he stifled by gripping his sword tighter.

"Oh, little prince," she cooed. "Still driven by honor, I see. It hasn't been your downfall yet?"

"Pride will be yours," he promised. "You should have stayed under whatever rock you crawled out from."

Her grin dropped. Her mockery. Her scorn. All of it fell away, and she looked at him studiously.

"I knew you would be an important part of our dear Briar Rose Aurora's life, little prince," she said. "You should know that I never wanted to hurt you."

He drew back. Just a beat.

Then resettled, sword still up.

"You have one chance to surrender," he told her, knowing—hoping—she wouldn't take it.

"Phillip," Briar said, her voice quaking. "You don't have to. This is different now."

Maleficent's grin returned. "You should listen to her, little prince. Besides"—her eyes flicked over his shoulder, to the open door—"there is a far more powerful force coming to get me."

CHAPTER EIGHTEEN

Briar took a step closer to Phillip, then another, with Maleficent merely watching the door. Briar walked more confidently until she reached out and touched Phillip's shoulder.

He flinched, blinking quickly, and something shifted in his gaze, the hardened wall of focus softening as he saw her.

"Briar," he gasped. "Are you all right?"

She nodded. And, just as important, *he* was all right. He was afraid, yes; but he was *standing*, and there was a clarity in his eyes that lifted a weight from Briar's chest.

This realization happened in a flash, and Briar had barely managed to squeeze his shoulder when a flurry of movement crowded through the door. Frieda and Ben were just beyond the threshold, but pushing past them came Flora, Fauna, and Merryweather to enter the cottage.

The three of them stopped yards back from Maleficent, the whole of their small cottage between them.

Maleficent's grin was all levels of darkly unamused. For a moment, her hands twitched at her sides, and Briar wondered if she might try to run or fight back.

But all she did was look one more time at Briar.

"I know it will be you," she said, a threat and a promise.

Then she faced the fairies again and, her arms out in surrender, walked toward them.

The moment they were within feet of each other, the air in the cottage flipped inside out, a great void.

Briar shouted, her body ripping toward the force, Phillip's sword clattering to the floor in his scramble to grab her. Frieda and Ben dropped to the dirt outside the cottage. Wind whipped in torrents through the open door, blasting so hard against the windows that they burst inward; screaming gusts whistled down through the chimney, billowing the flames hotter, scattering embers and ash. That debris built, built, coalescing with starbursts of glitter and sizzles of flame, and it was magic, magic cleaving the air, all of it gathering and knotting around Maleficent, Flora, Fauna, and Merryweather.

The force of it grew and grew, a hum building, and some pitch of the whine served as warning—Briar and Phillip dropped into a huddled crouch as the rising shriek of magic and wind hit its peak in a percussive explosion that knocked them both to the side.

As quickly as it had come, it stopped, and only dead silence remained.

Briar twisted, hand a shield, muscles knotted against the need to run either for cover or into whatever fight might await.

But there was a deeper sense of calm.

What had happened was not a threat.

Indeed, as the dust settled from the now absent wind, the cottage was gone. The garden stretched around Briar, hedges and flowers washed gray under the midnight sky. Off to the side, Ben and Frieda were rising from where they had fallen, their faces shades of hesitant and wondrous.

At Briar's feet, bent over in a trembling, panting ball, was a woman.

She looked up at Briar slowly. In the dimness of the moonlit garden, Briar had to squint to focus her eyes.

The woman was Flora. No, Fauna. No—those were Merryweather's eyes. Fauna's smile. Flora's brow.

Maleficent, too. Her chin, her hair, pieces of them re-formed now.

Briar stood over the woman. She opened her mouth but nothing came out, nothing that would encompass all the questions she had, the realizations she had come to.

The woman stood, too. She was in a simple black gown, her long dark hair tumbling to the middle of her back, and as she inclined her head at Briar, her eyes sparked with something so close to regret that Briar's shoulders bowed.

"You are whole now?" Briar asked, hesitant.

The woman's lips quirked in a sad smile. "It would seem so." Her gaze drifted out, seeing something in the ether, memories congealing, perhaps, pieces of all the fairies and Maleficent at long last reconnecting.

"I owe you an apology, it would seem," the woman finally whispered.

"Only me?"

The woman's eyes met hers. She frowned.

And that confusion broke through Briar's mask of calmness.

She moved around the woman, and Phillip came to his feet behind her, giving the woman a wide berth as Briar crossed the garden stones to Frieda.

Briar stopped next to Frieda but faced the woman. "You owe us both an apology."

The woman's eyes flicked between the two of them. "Yes. I suppose I do." She brushed her hands down her skirt, and Briar caught the shake of her fingers, the nervousness and discomfort in her stance.

Without looking away from the woman, Frieda leaned toward Briar. "What is going on?"

Briar quickly explained what Maleficent had told her when they had been alone, about the prophecy of an empress who ushered in an era of peace. About how that prophecy changed and warped so much that it broke the magical force connected to it, the Queen's Council, and created four separate entities all driven to see that prophecy fulfilled, albeit it in their own misguided, incomplete ways.

As Briar spoke, she watched the woman. So much about her was familiar, yet so much was strange, and Briar realized that the twist of pain in her chest was because her aunts were gone. But they were also here, in this new person. Or sorceress? Or fairy?

This *Queen's Council.*

Frieda shook her head at the end of Briar's explanation. "Maleficent wanted us to kill each other?"

She didn't ask Briar maliciously—she was curious, confused. Heartbroken.

Briar felt her lips form a soft smile. "She would have been disappointed."

And Briar was relieved to see that echoed in Frieda's eyes.

After all she had gone through—the curse, Matilda's influence—Frieda was still here.

"But we both had an equal chance of the prophecy being about us," Briar said as she turned back to the woman. "Why me? Why did the three of you protect me but abandon Frieda?"

When the woman looked at her again, she was more Merryweather than anyone else. "Because you are compassionate and bring people together. You are precisely the type of person who could beget peace."

"And Frieda isn't?" Briar's voice was hard.

The woman glanced at Frieda. Uncertainty tinged her face. "We thought—*I* thought of her as brash and military-minded. Not someone who would bring about peace."

Frieda's expression was of barely restrained hurt. Her jaw worked and she dropped her eyes.

Likely she had heard that daily since becoming Matilda's daughter again. And all those things were part of her, Briar knew; even before their lives had been upended, Frieda had been passionate, but that came from her unwavering sense of right and wrong, and her eagerness to see those wrongs corrected.

"To expect peace to come without conflict is shortsighted,"

Briar said. "I see that now, too. I see a great many things now, first among them being how this prophecy will come to pass. And you helped me with that, actually."

The woman's eyes widened slightly. Cautious wonder.

Briar stepped closer to her. "As Maleficent, Flora, Fauna, and Merryweather, you were disjointed. You—all four of you—were singularly driven. But seeing you come together now—you were always meant to be this, weren't you? You were always meant to be one. United. *Together.*"

Her eyes shot toward Phillip on that word. He smiled at her.

"But that is how I've been seeing myself, too." Briar faced Frieda. "Disjointed. Each part of me kept separate."

She held out her hand to her friend.

"Somehow, Briar Rose the peasant bard has the capacity to make this empire a better place," Briar said, lips quaking as she tried to smile, tried even harder not to cry. "Somehow, I can stand here and honestly say that I do want to be empress, if only because I see the injustices that others overlook. And I know you do, too. I know you want to be empress to help this land and its people. So why can't we both do it?"

Frieda's eyes held on Briar's, face breaking with—

Hope.

It was hope.

Briar lifted her extended hand, making it an offering. She hoped, too, hoped so hard her fingers trembled.

"Why can't we rule together? Jointly?" Briar smiled on a huff of suppressed tears. "The prophecy showed the two of us ruling, didn't it? That was why it was so hard to interpret—because it wasn't talking about *one* ruler. It was talking about two. You and me, together."

Frieda didn't appear to be breathing. Briar wasn't, either. Her eyes teared up and she smiled again and she kept her hand out. In this moment she wasn't a woman standing in a castle's garden; she was a child, and she was lonely and scared and hungry, and she wanted her friend to come play with her in the woods so they could chase away their loneliness together.

On a shaky exhalation, Frieda lifted her hand and pressed it into Briar's.

They were each alone in their own way, thrown unmoored into a vast, wide world, two little girls making flower crowns and coming up with nonsensical songs. The fact that they had met had been fate and it had been magic, and Briar didn't need a Queen's Council to tell her that. Because from this, she had found Ben, and Phillip, and now Frieda was holding her hand again, and nothing had felt this right and whole since the night before her sixteenth birthday.

"All right," Frieda said with a startled laugh. "Empresses."

• • •

While Briar and Frieda had forged unity out in the gardens, those in the banquet room had not.

Matilda's anger had spilled over. Bavarian soldiers filled half the room, their weapons drawn; the other half was given over to soldiers of the Prince Electors and Austria. Eckhardt appeared to have vanished entirely, and while Matilda stood in the center of the room, at the head of her contingent, the Prince Electors were huddled by the rear wall of windows, shouting their disdain to her from behind their protectors.

Matilda held a sword aloft. Still dressed in her banquet gown, she made a fearsome sight, a warrior-queen demanding the throne. "—as it should have been all along," she was shouting over the Prince Elector's objections, over the clank of shifting armor on both sides. "Name Bavaria the victor and *be done*!"

The swirl of tension was a similar building force as the magic in the garden. Only this force was driven by revenge and bloodlust and power-hunger, which after Maleficent's vileness was almost a relief.

This, Briar knew how to deal with. Or rather *not* deal with, because she was fully *done* with the games and lies and coercion. Even the similarity of facing a battle-ready Matilda in a grand room did nothing to discomfit Briar—she saw only vengeance, the opportunity to right another wrong that had sent her off on this path.

No one would die by Matilda of Bavaria's hand this time.

The woman had opted to stay in the garden, or rather, Briar and Frieda had told her to stay, to allow the two of them to take the first step toward their joint rule. No magic, no manipulation. Just the two of them.

As the prophecy had foretold.

Briar walked straight up the split that the soldiers made of the room. Matilda alone stood in that empty space, and when she saw Briar approaching—with Frieda at her side, Ben and Phillip behind them—she lowered her sword a fraction.

"Daughter." Matilda held out a hand and smiled in a way that was more a scowl. "You have brought the Austrian queen to surrender? We will take our victory to—"

The Prince Electors shouted in outrage.

"There is no need of surrender!"

"We will not name Clara empress!"

"This behavior is—"

"The only surrender," Briar said, her voice hard and loud, "will be yours, Matilda."

It cracked over the room.

Frieda gave a sudden roaring laugh that seemed to catch her off guard. She gaped at Briar and slapped a hand over her mouth. "You have stayed the same in many ways," she murmured.

"Clara," Matilda said immediately. "Come away from her. You are empress now, and I won't—"

"Yes," Frieda said with a flat smile. "I am empress. And Briar will be as well."

That silenced the room even more effectively, until one Elector cleared his throat.

They were still behind their cluster of soldiers, but the Elector pushed through, armor and weapons jangling until he stumbled free, dabbing at sweat with a handkerchief.

"That is— I don't— What do you mean, Your Highness?"

Briar tried for a cordial smile. How she hated these damned cordial smiles.

"The campaign is over," she said. "Princess Clara—"

"Princess Frieda," Frieda corrected her.

Briar grinned and looped their arms together. "Princess Frieda and I have agreed to jointly rule the Holy Roman Empire. Provided this decision pleases the Prince Electors—but I think you will come to realize such an arrangement is the only possible solution. The strengths both Frieda and I possess complement each other's weaknesses, and together, we will unify two of the most fractured and warring kingdoms in the empire."

"This is—" the Elector babbled. Others joined him, equally stunned. "This is *highly* irregular—"

"Frieda and I both grew up at the very bottom of the system that we have been campaigning to rule," Briar cut in. "We have both experienced the worst of this empire's inequities. You have seen our abilities over this campaign. You have placed us already at the forefront. You only have things to gain by allowing us *both* to rule."

The Electors eyed one another, quietly whispering among themselves.

When their whispers stilled, and an air of acceptance permeated, Briar wanted to smile—but her attention was on Matilda of Bavaria, who was seething, her sword still gripped relentlessly in one hand.

Frieda let go of Briar's arm and stepped forward. "Mother, this is for the best. For Bavaria's sake, and the empire's."

"She has manipulated you," Matilda spat, glaring ferociously at Briar. "She has *corrupted* you—the throne is Bavaria's! The throne is *mine*!"

She lunged.

Briar barely had time to exhale in shock, let alone move, as the sword reared back.

Phillip dove, naked blade before him, poised to intercept.

But Frieda moved, too. She threw herself not just in front of Briar, but *at* Matilda, and grabbed her mother's hands around the hilt of the sword. She shoved them both backward, back again, until they careened into the slack-jawed group of soldiers.

"*Stop!*" Frieda commanded. She shoved again, and the sword broke from Matilda's grip, clattering across the stone floor. "Stop. I will only do this with Briar. I will only—"

"Then you are not my daughter," Matilda snapped, and pushed her away.

Frieda's face, red with exertion, hollowed briefly. "That does not stop me from being princess of Bavaria. And you have attacked my joint empress in broad view of the Prince Electors after Bavaria extended promises of co-rule and peace."

"You have no right to speak in this manner." Matilda was fuming. "You are *nothing*, no better than a peasant. You should be grateful for everything I have given you. You would bring us to ruin, you conniving rat!"

Briar's whole body went red-hot with anger.

But she didn't have to intervene—because she hadn't even seen Ben move. Suddenly, he was there, and Briar gave a startled shriek as she watched King Phillip of Austria's squire slap Queen Matilda of Bavaria.

The crack of Ben's palm on Matilda's cheek echoed through the perfectly silent banquet room. It stunned Matilda enough that she went immobile, head thrown to the side, arms stiff.

Ben, twisted in the motion of having smacked one of the most powerful people in the empire, stumbled back and coughed roughly to clear his throat.

"Well." He tugged down his tunic and nodded at Frieda. "I've had quite enough of her."

Frieda, eyes wide with shock, managed to nod back. "Quite." Then, gathering herself quickly, she faced the soldiers. "Place my mother under guard. She has crimes to answer for."

The Bavarian guards glanced at the Prince Electors. Who still held the power to tip this all into chaos.

But one waved them on. "Well, get on with it. Your empress has given you an order."

A smile bloomed on Briar's face. Was it of relief? Gratitude? Shock? She couldn't tell, only that something had clicked rightly into place.

Briar raced forward as soldiers wrestled Matilda of Bavaria across the room, ignoring her snarls and snaps of command.

Frieda was gaping at Ben when Briar stopped next to her.

Ben's cheeks went scarlet. He looked pleadingly at Phillip, who sheathed his sword.

"Did I just help stage a coup?" Ben asked.

A slow-growing smirk bloomed on Phillip's face. "Possibly."

"Oh." Ben scratched his jaw, clearly on the fence between alarm and vague acceptance. "A lot's happened in the last hour. Why not end with a coup? That makes perfect—"

Frieda grabbed the collar of his tunic and kissed him.

Briar clamped her hands over her mouth, but it did nothing to stop her squeal.

Phillip laughed and pulled Briar back. "Give them a moment to—"

"Wait!" Briar tried to wriggle out of his hold, but he was strong and determined, and half of her wasn't even trying to fight.

Frieda peeled back from Ben in enough of a pause to gasp, "I'm sorry, I'm so sorry I—"

"Forgiven, forgiven, of course you're forgiven." Ben was frantically shaking his head, his arms around Frieda's waist, his face a wild falling apart of need. "Kiss me again, my God I've missed you—"

And then they were fully assailing one another. In the banquet hall of the Frankfurt palace. While the Prince Electors watched on in unmasked shock.

Phillip managed to wrestle Briar back a few yards, giving Ben and Frieda what amounted to privacy in this utterly ridiculous place for a reunion, but Ben was right—after everything that had happened the past hour, why not?

Briar spun into Phillip's arms and looked up at him. She was smiling widely, and she couldn't remember the last time she had done so with such sincerity.

Phillip beamed down at her, eyes darting over her face, absorbing the sight. "Ah. Finally."

She cocked her head. "Finally?"

"I told you, I'm incredibly selfish. All I've wanted is to see you smile like that again."

Her chest filled with joy, unrepentant and wild, and she pushed up onto her toes to rest her lips on his.

"You came for me," she said against his mouth. It was a question and a statement.

He tightened his hold on her. "Always."

“And you faced her.” Briar arched back to look into his eyes. Still clear, still steady on hers, brightened by his smile.

“I did.”

It was the way his smile didn’t waver that let her grin stretch. “The Pain from Lorraine’s greatest victory yet. How can I make it up to you? As your empress, or queen, or wife?”

What a great many titles she would have.

Once, that would have made her buckle.

Now, she laughed, because it was still so absurd, and impossible, and wonderful in that impossibility.

And she wouldn’t bear any of this weight alone.

Phillip put his lips on her neck, a feather-soft kiss now, and it turned the rapid flush of joy to syrupy sugar in her veins.

“As my wife,” he said into her skin. “Always that first.”

She pressed into his touch. “Together.” The word burst out of her.

Phillip glided his lips up to her ear. “Together,” he finished, that promise between the two of them now stretching out to encompass Frieda and Ben, united in this, the barest beginnings of a foundation that Briar had never dared to dream of.

Chapter Nineteen

Briar reread the first line of the letter she had received from her mother.

The body of it was filled with the grace and poise Queen Leah always displayed, praising what Briar had done in Frankfurt and promising to arrive in time for the coronation. Indeed, Briar had already heard that the Austrian party had gotten in late last night, so she knew Leah would be at the cathedral in only an hour now.

Also in attendance, a different letter had told her, would be Johann, overjoyed to be seeing her again. He had signed his letter *King Johann*, no mention of zauberer or magic at all.

It had been a time for significant names in letters, apparently. Briar held such a letter, the one from her mother, as she stood in her suite's front room by the window.

My dearest Briar Rose.

She read it twice more, each character filling up a hole inside her.

Briar.

Not Aurora.

Empress Briar Rose.

It was terrifying, still. It would never *not* be terrifying. But Briar didn't fear it as much as she had feared being Queen Aurora, or even Princess Aurora.

She lowered the letter. The dressing mirror was across the room, angled so she saw her reflection in the morning's pale light. A rosebud-pink gown hemmed in glinting gold, her hair curled in perfect waves, the Austrian crown already on her head, shortly to be removed and replaced by one of two crowns from the Holy Roman Empire's jewel vault.

One, the crown typically used in declaring the new emperor, inlaid with opulent stones and fine intricate goldwork.

Another, ancient in its design, said to have been formed at the start of the empire itself, a simpler gold band set around an iron circlet, with fewer gems and stones, but still lovely.

The fact that servants had uncovered two crowns in the treasury only sealed this twist of fate even more.

Briar Rose and Frieda would both be empress.

Briar refolded the letter and put it back in the box on her table, one overcrowded with missives and documents and maps, a clutter of proof that she had spent the past two weeks since that banquet room confrontation getting sucked into the tasks that would be her life now. But in this rare moment of quiet—and solitude—Briar couldn't help but absorb the enormity of what had happened, if only to see how it still felt, to test her own responses.

She would be crowned empress this morning.

She smiled, watching her reflection in the mirror, seeing a

glimmer of the peasant bard in the crook of her grin, but the composure of a princess, too, and the stature of a queen, for however short a time she had been each.

There was no looming shadow behind her, no waiting other self who might swoop out and consume her. Going forward, she knew she would be a balance of these pieces, somehow, some way.

She could be many things all at once.

There was a soft knock at the door, and when it opened, in came the woman who now called herself Brynhild. Anyone else would see a magical illusion of her aunts still. Brynhild had asked if Briar would like to see that as well, but it would have been more uncomfortable to know that her aunts were *different* now and pretend they weren't.

Brynhild had begun to lay the foundation for her aunts' departure, though. Mentioning here and there that they had other responsibilities now that Briar would need greater advisers.

Part of Briar wondered if Brynhild's impending leave was in response to realizing the mistakes that she had made when she had been split into the fairies and Maleficent.

But the other part of Briar knew there was little left for Brynhild to do. This had been her task, hadn't it? To prepare Briar—and Frieda—to be empress. She had done her duty, and whether Briar and Frieda were up to the challenge was only something they could determine now.

So when Brynhild gave her a kind smile, Briar smiled back, holding that smile against the battering of tangled sorrow and gratitude and grief.

"You have a visitor," Brynhild said, and stepped aside.

Behind her, coming into the room with her focus on her silk kirtle, was Frieda.

"I'm off to wrangle the rest of your party." Brynhild slipped back out.

"How long must we be stuffed into these infernal gowns?" Frieda tugged her skirt straighter with a huff.

Briar looped her arm through Frieda's and pulled her in front of the dressing mirror, her pink gown against Frieda's blue, her blond hair against Frieda's brown.

"It will never stop being ridiculous to see us like this." Frieda heaved a sigh, rigid against Briar's touch. She was coming around, slowly, almost the Frieda that Briar had known—but there was a level of hesitation in every interaction, no matter how open and effusive Briar was toward her, as though Frieda was punishing herself for what she had done.

"To see *you* like this, maybe." Briar stood up straighter. "I look incredible."

Frieda didn't respond to that at all but to snort.

"One bit of credit I must give my mother: She preferred and encouraged far more functional dress." Frieda seemed to realize she had mentioned Matilda in the half beat after she spoke. She stopped, lips flattening, eyes on Briar's in the mirror.

"Have you spoken with her?" Briar tried, keeping her arm linked with Frieda's.

"Yes." Frieda's gaze dropped. "She will be brought before a tribunal shortly. Whether it is here or back in Bavaria remains to be seen."

"Austria will recuse itself from any involvement. If it makes things seem less biased, you should hold the trial—"

"That isn't a concern. Austria *should* be involved. You are the ones we have hurt most."

"Not 'we.'" Briar squeezed Frieda's arm. "*Her.* Matilda. Not you."

Frieda finally met her eyes again in the mirror. Side by side, and Briar leaned her head on Frieda's shoulder.

She heard Frieda's quick intake of breath, the grate of what might have been a sniff, saw the way her eyes reddened.

"How can you do that?" Frieda whispered. "Pretend that I'm not at fault for so much. If I had realized sooner—if I had trusted you and Ben over *her*—"

Briar looked at Frieda. "Because I tried being angry with you, and it only damaged who I am. I'm tired of lingering on mistakes made by people I care about. You're here now, and yes, we have wrongs to be righted. But we'll do it together."

Frieda gave her a disbelieving look. "I don't for one second believe you've *lingered* on any of my mistakes. You never did. You've always been too forgiving—look at your aunts! You and Ben both are too sentimental to be sane. God help me, you're identical fools."

"Are you saying we shouldn't forgive you? Would you feel better if we—I don't know—demanded recompense of some kind?"

"Yes! Something. I hurt you."

"Fine then." Briar straightened and feigned tucking back a hair that wasn't out of place. "I want you to sing the song about river witches."

"The—what?"

"That song I wrote you for your twelfth birthday. The one you laughed at, when it was meant to be *serious*, and I was so cross with you that we didn't speak for a week. Sing it and *don't* laugh."

Frieda's blank confusion broke in exasperation. "Be serious, Briar."

"I'm quite serious. I won't forgive you otherwise. In fact, I shall endeavor to be positively wicked to you until you sing it. Does that make you feel better?" Briar flipped Frieda a puckered look, all scrunched nose and tight lips in mockery. "*You're* the fool. Ben and I forgive you! What more do you want? Accept it, you nitwit, and let's move on."

Frieda rolled her eyes, still bloodshot and wet, and when she looked at Briar again, Briar only smiled.

"You're so infuriating," Frieda said.

Briar laughed. "I'm glad to have you back, too."

It was as simple as that. Yes, Frieda had done things that had hurt Briar—but she was here now. They were friends again, or on their way toward it, and maybe Briar should have been more cautious, less trusting, or go it alone. But that had never been her, so why should it be part of this person she was becoming?

If people could be more than one thing, then relationships could be, too. They could be joyous and loving and careful and healing.

They were all multifaceted, and Briar was afloat in that future.

The door thudded into the wall with an unceremonious bang.

"—with a red-hot poker," Ben was saying, head twisted over his shoulder to talk to Phillip.

"The imagery, good Lord, Benedikt." Phillip shuddered.

"What imagery?" Briar asked.

Ben looked at her, but his eyes immediately shot to Frieda, and his whole face transformed. His usual steady level of joy went catastrophic, all lustrous smiles and bright eyes and wild giddiness, and as he dove across the room, Frieda could only get out a feeble shriek of "Don't make them redo my hair!" before Ben hefted her up, lifting her against him and spinning them in a tight circle.

"I'm glad he has someone else to manhandle now," Phillip said to Briar, putting a much more sedate hand around her hips.

"What was that about a red-hot poker?"

He smirked. "Ah. Ben was listing the other things he'd rather do than ride a horse in a joust."

Briar whirled on Ben. "You don't want to be a jouster?"

He set Frieda down, cupping her face in his hands, seeming only half-aware of Briar and Phillip even being in the room. "That was never my goal, Bri. I *watch* jousting, I'm a rabid fan, but Christ above, to actually *ride* as a jouster? No, that's far too close to dancing with death for my tastes."

Briar grinned up at Phillip. She nodded toward Ben, an unspoken *Do you want to tell him?*

Phillip shook his head and waved his hand. *You be the one.*

"But what else are knights to do?" Briar asked, too loudly. "If not joust, then I suppose all that remains is to . . . marry an empress?"

It was far more satisfying than it should have been to watch Ben's focus snap away from Frieda. He thrashed his head toward Briar so rapidly that he whipped the tie off his hair.

"I'm sorry, I—I didn't catch that," he stammered. "Knight? Empress? What?"

Frieda's eyes were narrow in amused consideration, dipping between Briar and Ben, her face still pinned in his hands.

"Oh." Briar put a hand on her chest in exaggerated sincerity. "Oh, this is awkward. Phillip, darling, dearest one, did you not tell him?"

"I must have forgotten, my love."

"So careless of you, sweetheart."

"Heartless, I know."

"Shameful—"

"I hate you both," Ben cut in. They had his full attention for the first time in two weeks, Briar noted with a grin. "What are you talking about?"

"You're to be a knight, Ben," Briar said, unable to stop her smile. "If you want."

Ben gave a laugh that was more of a startled cough. Then he released Frieda's face to drop his head into his hands for one beat.

"Why do you keep doing this to me?" he grumbled halfheartedly. His head jerked back up. "I haven't been a squire nearly long enough to warrant anything close to *knighthood.* You're toying with me."

"Dear me, you're quite right." Briar put a finger on her chin in mock thought. "If only someone in this room had the power to waive those sorts of bureaucratic requirements."

"There are three someones with power of that nature in this room, by my count," Phillip said.

"Should we fight to the death for the honor?" Briar asked.

"This is the fourteenth century, darling; we need not do anything so barbaric."

Ben gestured between them. "You two are not in the least funny, trust me."

"Good," Briar said. "Because we aren't joking, Ben. Well, about the death-fighting, perhaps."

"You—" He flashed a startled look at Phillip. "You're serious? You're going to make me a knight?"

Phillip nodded, smiling too.

Ben huffed, head cocked as if waiting for the joke to land.

Frieda came up behind him and took his hand. "Are you all right?"

His eyelids fluttered. He met Briar's gaze and held it for a moment too long, enough that she could see the unspoken weight in it, the gratitude and amazement.

"A knight." He exhaled and faced Frieda, breaking into a gleaming smile. "A knight is fit to marry an empress?"

Briar gave a defeated sigh. "Well, this empress is already married."

Phillip pinched her hip.

Frieda leaned her forehead against Ben's. "Only if you still believe I'm fit to marry you."

All of Ben's humor vanished, leaving only rawness, truth.

"Yes," he said with unshakable confidence.

Frieda beamed at him, her eyes tearing up.

"This is quite a lot of mushiness for a coronation day," Ben said. But he kissed her and kept on kissing her, until Briar cleared her throat as loudly as she could.

"I finally understand what you were always complaining about when you were with Phillip and me. I don't remember you two being nearly this annoying in Hausach."

Ben laughed. Cackled, more like.

"This is your doing!" Frieda shot her an offended look. "You cannot set up this gift and then be appalled by the reception."

"You're right," said Briar. "This was a spectacular mistake on my part. Ben, I rescind the offer. I'll make you an earl instead."

Ben laughed again, a deep, resonant laugh of pure happiness. "Don't tempt me with that much power, Bri, I'd be too likely to overthrow you. Both you and Frieda. We can take them, can't we, Phillip? King and earl, start ourselves a nice little war."

Phillip arched one eyebrow. "Most people give jewelry as a wedding gift, not a war."

"Do not joke about a *civil war*!" Frieda looked admittedly horrified, but at Ben's persistent smile, she relented with an exasperated headshake and hugged him, her chin on his shoulder so she could look at Briar. "This is how it will be, won't it? Us ruling with this jester at my side. At least yours is tame."

Phillip barked with a surprising amount of offense. *"Tame?"* He looked down at Briar piteously. "She thinks I'm tame, Briar."

Briar was smiling, smiling and she didn't know if she would ever stop.

She felt the weight of Phillip against her, the palpable joy from Frieda and Ben. "I know the truth, don't worry," she said as she threaded her fingers through his.

Footsteps in the hall told her that Brynhild was coming back with her vassals, the rest of her party gathered for the coronation. They would meet with Frieda's party, too, and make a procession to the cathedral, where the joint coronation would begin. And then she would rule an empire—with her friend at her side, and Phillip and Ben as well.

That was why the image wasn't frightening. That was why she looked up at Phillip and her smile was so wide.

Because the future that lay before her would indeed be one of unity and peace, starting here, with those she loved. Anything they built on this foundation could only be good and true and right.

It could only be the stuff of dreams.

ACKNOWLEDGMENTS

I am unendingly grateful to all the people who helped me become a Disney Princess (title claimed, I'm going to have it engraved on my tombstone):

Amy Stapp, diligent agent, relentless cheerleader, and someone I am forever thrilled to have in my corner.

Jocelyn Davies, who might be the only person who loves this book more than I do.

Emma Theriault, Belle incarnate and lovely friend.

The rest of the Queen's Council squad: Livia Blackburne and Alexandra Monir, who are so passionate about their princesses and this series.

My family, who continue to set the standards for enthusiasm and support.

Everyone throughout the Disney book-making process: Kieran Viola, Jessica Hernandez, Sara Liebling, Guy Cunningham, Meredith Jones, Marci Senders, Scott Altmann, Crystal McCoy, Ann D. Saperstein, Kaia Hilson, Holly Nagel, Matt Schweitzer, Vicki Korlishin, Monique Diman-Riley, Andrea Rosen, Augusta Harris, Holly Rice, and Lauren Burniac.

Briar's story deals with many dreams, but the best dream of all was getting to write this book. She is a beloved icon, a fearless ruler, and an imperfectly perfect girl, and I hope I've done her and all who love her proud.